"Jackie," Zane said, his voice soft.

I turned around to look back at him, curious. "Yes?"

He paused, his gaze roaming over me in a vulnerable moment. "I just want to know . . . do you trust me?"

He'd asked me that before, and it had gotten me into trouble. But we'd come so far that I felt confident in my answer. I smiled at him. "I do trust you, Zane."

"Good," he said, his eyes intense on me. "Hold on to that, okay?" His face changed from the serious look into a smile, then he put a cigarette between his lips. "I'm going to finish this, and then I'll head back."

I headed back out to the Hummer, propelled by the subtle compulsion in our conversation.

Remy leaned against the hood of the vehicle, looking utterly bored. She eyed me. "You sure he's okay with this trip?"

"Zane's fine with it," I said to her, my tone convinced if my body wasn't. "He knows I need his help right now. He wouldn't abandon me."

"Oh, sweetie," Remy said, her voice sad. "When will you learn not to trust vampires?"

"He's fine. I'll go get him and prove it to you."

I stomped back to the bathroom. What I didn't expect to find was his long leather trench coat discarded in a heap in the middle of the floor.

He'd left me. Flown away without even saying goodbye.

This title is also available as an eBook.

Gentlemen Prefer Succubi

Also by Jill Myles

Gentlemen Prefer Succubi

Available from Pocket Books

SUCCUBI
LIKE IT
HOT

THE SUCCUBUS DIARIES

JILL MYLES

Pocket **Star** Books

New York   London   Toronto   Sydney

Pocket Star Books
A Division of Simon & Schuster, Inc.
1230 Avenue of the Americas
New York, NY 10020

First Pocket Star Books paperback edition February 2010

POCKET STAR BOOKS and colophon are registered trademarks of Simon & Schuster, Inc.

For information about special discounts for bulk purchases, please contact Simon & Schuster Special Sales at 1-866-506-1949 or business@simonandschuster.com.

The Simon & Schuster Speakers Bureau can bring authors to your live event. For more information or to book an event contact the Simon & Schuster Speakers Bureau at 866-248-3049 or visit our website at www.simonspeakers.com.

Interior design by Julie Adams
Cover illustration by Shane Rebenschied

Manufactured in the United States of America

10 9 8 7 6 5 4 3 2 1

ISBN 978-1-4165-7283-1
ISBN 978-1-4165-8815-3 (ebook)

Acknowledgments

I thanked pretty much everyone and their brother at the beginning of the last book, so that kind of made me wonder . . . was there anyone left to thank for Book 2? I'm lucky enough to have some people in my life that are so awesome that they deserve another round of thanks, so here we go.

To my husband, thank you for being the world's best guy and the best supporter a writer could possibly have. I use a lot more of your ideas than I give you credit for.

To my terrific agent, my superlative editor, and my editor's amazing assistant—you guys are awesome beyond belief. I'm so lucky to get to work with you on two books now! An email from New York is just like Christmas in my Inbox.

To my copyeditor—I cussed your name a lot, but it was all in love. A thousand times thank you.

To my family, for driving me to the airport at oh-god-in-the-morning so I can go to writers' conferences, all without a word of complaint. And for shoving my bookmarks under everyone's noses (even at Bingo). A girl couldn't ask for a better support team.

To the Mean Girls, for talking me down off ledges and supporting me, and for not being afraid to tell me when my work needs an overhaul. I raise a Slim Jim in salute to you.

To Kent—this one's for you, too.

SUCCUBI
LIKE IT
HOT

CHAPTER ONE

During the fund-raiser luncheon's after-party, the Itch hit me. As I shook hands with one of the rich benefactors of New City University's archaeology department, I felt the full-body flush take over me. Without looking, I knew that my normally bleached-gray eyes had turned a blazing blue.

That meant just one thing: I needed sex, and I needed it now.

The Itch is what drives succubi, forcing us to hunt down men and have amazing, mind-blowing sex every forty-eight hours. As you get closer to your time, your eyes darken to blue, your skin becomes sensitive and flushed, and everything turns you on. *Everything*. The Itch makes it impossible to forget sex—you live, breathe, eat, and drink it. Crave it like you once craved oxygen and water.

I had a definite craving right now.

"Jackie Brighton, so good to see you again," a voice boomed, and a hand slid over my bare elbow, pulling me to the side.

Dr. Morgan was my new boss and the head of the

New City University archaeological team. Anyone who was anyone in Wyoming university archaeology worked for him, and I was thrilled to be included.

He smiled at me. "How are you enjoying the fund-raiser, my dear?"

I smiled in return, wondering if it would be offensive to yank my arm away. The slight touch was maddening to my overheated flesh. "I'm great, thank you, Dr. Morgan. I don't suppose you've seen—"

"You seem a little flushed. Is something wrong?"

Why, yes. I'm actually a succubus. Got turned into one a few weeks ago, back when I was just a dumpy docent at the local museum. Now I'm the hot babe you're ogling, and I need sex to survive—right now. That's why my eyes are turning blue, my skin is feverish, and I feel the urge to rip off my clothing and throw the nearest man down on the carpet and make hot love to him.

But I couldn't tell my new boss that—no one believed that succubi were real except, well, other succubi. And their masters. So I kept the bright smile on my face. "I'm just fine, Dr. Morgan. It's kind of you to ask, though."

Dr. Morgan's hand slid from my elbow and caressed the soft underside of my arm. "I'm just looking out for my favorite new team member."

If I'd been a normal gal, that sexual harassment move would have sent me right to a lawyer's office. But since I was a succubus, a ripple of desire pulsed through my blood. And Dr. Morgan noticed, judging by the posses-sive way he stared at my now-heaving breasts.

"Is it warm in here?" I pulled my arm out of his and fanned my face. Stepping a few feet away, I plucked a glass of champagne off a waiter's tray. Time for me to leave the party, and stat. "Have you seen my date, Noah Gideon?"

Six feet tall? Utterly gorgeous? Blond? Fallen angel? Tattoos on his wrist?

Noah was one of the two men who had turned me into a succubus. The other was Zane, a vampire. A few weeks ago, I'd been an invisible docent with mousy brown hair and an expanding waistline, toiling away at the New City Museum of Art for a boss who hated me. Everything had changed the night I was transformed by Zane and Noah. I'd gone from plump and dowdy to svelte and stunning. My hair had transformed into a fabulous red mane, my breasts had more Ds than a bad report card, and men lusted after me. A lot.

You'd think there was no downside, except for the whole "master" thing that tied me to Zane and Noah. Any command one of them issued, I had to obey like some oversexed I-Dream-of-Jeannie.

Noah was my date to this afternoon's shindig, and it was a good thing, too. Not only was Noah one of the archaeology department's benefactors, but his presence would keep Dr. Morgan and his overly grabby hands away before I did something that both of us would regret.

Like throw him down on the floor and ride him like a bronco.

Dr. Morgan backed off at the mention of Noah's

name. He might like boobs a lot, but he liked archaeology funding more, and his upcoming Mayan dig was in need of additional money. "Mr. Gideon? I believe I saw him over in the east wing not too long ago. Would you like me to—"

"Not necessary." I gave him a quick smile, downing my champagne. "I'll find him."

I hurried through the crowd, the pulsing in my veins growing more insistent with each moment. It concerned me that the Itch had appeared out of nowhere—most of the time it was a gradual change in my body chemistry. To have it flip on like a switch was disturbing.

And until I fixed my Itch, my body would grow steadily more sensitive, overheated, and needy. If I didn't? Well . . . I'd never resisted for longer than a few days, because that way lay madness, pain, and death. In that order.

Not too irksome a fate if you had a hot man at your beck and call, and I had two of them. But since I'd just had sex last night with the vampire, Zane, I wasn't due for another two days.

The east wing of the archaeology department was crowded, benefactors and their trophy wives circling around ancient vases and clay figurines, and commenting about them as if they knew what the heck they were looking at. I looked for Noah's tall blond head in the sea of silver hair and poofy, frosted helmet-hair, but there was no sign of him.

I found him down one gallery hall, wine glass in hand,

gazing at a large painting. Noah Gideon was breathtakingly gorgeous—not a surprise, given that he'd fallen from Heaven. His dark blond hair had been brushed into a haircut that looked perfect despite the intentional tousled style. His shoulders filled out his designer tuxedo, and I paused to admire him from behind. Because damn, the man had a nice behind. It made me quiver just to look at it.

Then I noticed what he was looking at and froze. It was a dark painting, full of shadow and light (chiaroscuro to the art nerds like me). A crumpled angel lay at the bottom in one corner, collapsed in a heap of feathers and rosy flesh. At the top, crimson heavens seared the dark canvas. *Fall from Grace*, the plaque read. It was a painting that one of the professors was restoring for the Smithsonian, brought out to display so all the wealthy patrons could see the good things we were doing.

And Noah was staring at it with an intense look that made me think that he hadn't forgotten that part of his past, not by a long shot. As a fallen angel, he didn't like to be reminded of Heaven. Originally angels like Uriel and the rest of Heaven's warriors the Serim were condemned to live among mortals for all eternity because they'd had the bad luck to fall in love with human females. Exiled to Earth, they were doomed to have sex and give orgasms to their partners.

As curses went, I had no complaints (being the recipient of said orgasms), but Noah seemed sad for his loss.

Crap. How had I forgotten about that painting? Noah never talked to me about his past and how he'd fallen. I didn't know how old he was (though I knew it was *old*) or if he kept in contact with the other angels that had fallen, or anything like that. Heaven was private, and I didn't ask. I figured he'd open up on his own at some point.

From the devastated look on his face as he stared up at the painting, that point would be a long time coming.

"Noah?" I said quietly, moving to his side and slipping my arm into his. "Can we go now?"

He turned to me, the melancholy leaving his face so quickly I wondered if I'd imagined it. "Leave? But I thought you wanted to—"

His voice died at the sight of my bright blue eyes and the moist flush on my skin.

I gave him a faint smile. "Bit of a problem seems to have cropped up." I slid my hand down his chest, a blatant invitation.

His eyes grew darker, the gray turning almost black, then a deep blue within a second or two as his own desire flared to match mine. "You're never a problem, Jackie," he said in a low voice, and the husky timbre caused my entire body to tremble.

I automatically moved toward him, pressing my body against his and tilting my face toward his.

"Not in here," he said, glancing down the hall.

Oh, pooh. I frowned at Mr. Propriety, even though he was right. I just didn't like being reminded of it. "Where, then? It had better be someplace close, or I'm going to make a spectacle of myself." I slid my gaze over him meaningfully. "And you."

He took my hand and led me through the crowd, murmuring excuses to the people who tried to stop us with a greeting.

When we finally cleared the wall-to-wall throng, Noah headed toward the double glass front doors. "Is the limo okay?"

The limo? All the way across the parking lot? "I have a better idea." I tugged him down toward the professors' row of offices.

"Is one of these yours?" he asked, his hands sliding to my hips despite his reserve, and I nearly lost my breath. My body began to tingle even harder with excitement. Sex *now*.

"No." Good things the halls were clear—everyone was at the fund-raiser. I cussed under my breath when I discovered the first door was locked. I moved down to the next one—success. Pushing Dr. Morgan's door open, I dragged Noah inside, then locked the door behind me.

"Jackie," Noah warned, "I'm not sure this is a good idea."

"Morgan won't care," I said, grabbing Noah's tie and ripping my fingers through the knot. "He already suspects I'm sleeping with you for the good of the archaeology department. He'll think I'm trying to do some extra fund-raising on the side." I pushed him up against the heavy wooden desk in the center of the small room, and nearly swooned with delight when my hips pressed against the hardness nestled between his. Oh, yum.

"I can't say that I approve of him having that impression of you," Noah said, his voice sounding stern as he ran his hands over my hips again, teasing me.

A moan escaped me and I pulled his mouth down to mine, biting at his lower lip in excitement. "Right now," I said between fierce kisses, "he could watch and I wouldn't care."

The Itch had me in its grasp, and all I could think about was the erection inside Noah's pants and getting its wonderful, delicious length into my body.

Our mouths locked in a deep, thrusting kiss, and fireworks began to dance behind my eyes. I kissed him back, my tongue sliding into his mouth to taste him. His hands flexed on my ass and then I felt him hike up my skirt, my overheated skin tingling with excitement as I felt the brush of his fingers higher and higher up on my body.

He gave a loud groan as his hands encountered my bare ass. "Where are your panties?"

"At home," I said, nipping at his mouth. "Didn't want panty lines." I arched, wiggling against his hand suggestively.

That brought my cool, in-control Noah over the edge. He gave a fierce growl against my mouth and picked me up by the hips, and I wrapped my legs around his waist eagerly. Within two seconds it was my ass plastered to the desk, and Noah's hardness pressing me down against the surface in the most amazing way. A stack of paperwork jabbed me on one side, but I didn't care. My fingers reached for his shirt and began to undo the tiny white buttons. I needed to feel his warm, hot flesh pressed against mine. I ripped the shirt out of his waistband and slid my hands underneath, trying to pull his body tighter against mine.

"I'm flattered that you waited for me for your needing," he said, his breath warm against my skin.

Oh, *uh oh*. He thought I'd waited two days to see him again, just so I could have sex with him? Nice thought . . . except I hadn't. Not the time to bring that up, though. My fingers slid to Noah's nipples and I brushed across them to distract him, but Noah wouldn't let it go. He pulled off of me slightly, a serious look on his face. "Are you and Zane having problems?"

I would have taken that as concern, except for the hint of smugness in his voice. Noah hated my vampire lover. Most of all, he hated sharing me.

Vampires and fallen angels got along about as well as . . . actually, they didn't get along at all. Both were forced onto the mortal plane when they fell from Heaven. But while the Serim strove to eventually work their way back to the good graces of Heaven, vampires had pretty much given up on that. Instead, they sold their loyalty to demons in exchange for wings and lived a life of selfish debauchery.

The vampire I was sleeping with was *great* at debauchery.

So, yeah. Serim and vampires did not get along. Add

in the fact that there was some sort of weird, tense undercurrent between Noah and Zane—some old rivalry that neither would discuss with me—and that left me stuck in the middle. Both wanted me to pick sides, but I refused.

Like right now. I lifted my chin, trying to angle my face so Noah would kiss me again. "Do we have to talk about Zane right now?"

Noah just gave me a long look. "Tell me the last time you saw Zane."

That was low of him. Noah had just given me a direct command, so I had to obey it. I sighed, sensing where this was going. "A few hours ago, asleep in bed."

That killed the conversation fast. Anger tightened Noah's face. "I see." He began to pull away.

"No, you *don't*. You never see. Why did you ask that, unless you wanted to know the truth?" Honestly, this silly tug of war between the two of them just ticked me off. They hated each other passionately, and sometimes it made me think that they didn't like me nearly as much as they liked fighting *over* me.

"I thought perhaps we were ready to commit to each other."

Yikes, the "C" word? I stared up at him in shock. "Noah, I'm a succubus—"

"And I'm a Serim," he interrupted. "It is in my nature to want you only for myself, that is who I am. And vampires are my enemies. So to think of you rushing from my bed straight to his . . ."

He didn't finish the sentence, and I didn't rush in to do so, either.

After all, what could I say? Noah's kind went into a deep sleep at the sight of the rising moon and didn't awaken for the next twelve hours or so. Vampires were the opposite; they slept through the daylight hours and prowled through the night.

I didn't sleep at all, being a creature of both worlds. So it seemed ideal to me to have one Serim lover and one vampire lover. Judging by the scowl on Noah's face, I was the only one thinking that way.

"I can't do this, Jackie," he said, shaking his golden head like an angry lion. "We are not going to keep playing these mind games. I'm not going to play along."

So I wouldn't be having sex with Noah unless there was some sort of commitment involved, like *I won't sleep with Zane ever again*? I couldn't keep that sort of vow.

Rats. I leaned up on my elbows as he pulled away from me, straightening his shirt. He wouldn't look at me, but he didn't move away. He was waiting for me to say something to make him change his mind. But I wasn't going to.

I sighed and gave Noah a gentle push on the shoulder. "If we're not going to do this, let me up. I think I'm lying on a stapler."

He moved back with a frustrated glance at me, and we fixed our clothing in silence. My body still throbbed with need, but Noah's movements were angry and jerky.

Easy for him to forget about sex—Serim only needed it monthly.

I tried to slide my hand into his once he had shrugged his jacket back on. "Noah, are we good?"

Normally Noah was my solid one, my rock. Normally he'd give me a faint smile, apologize for hurting my feelings, and we'd be friends again. Friends and lovers, the best kind of friends. He was always there for me.

He shrugged my hand off and shook his head. "I need time to think about all of this, Jackie. Maybe it's best if we keep things at a more professional level."

Professional—like master and succubus. Not lovers. Not friends.

He wanted to be strangers.

That hurt, but I forced a smile to my face. "Sure. Whatever you want."

He nodded and let himself out, leaving me alone, rubbing the stapler-shaped bruise on my butt.

CHAPTER TWO

Though Noah politely took me home after the party, he didn't come in. I stewed in my frustration for a while. Who was he to try and dictate my life? Then, after I calmed down a little, I tried calling him to talk things over. Or to yell at him.

But he hadn't picked up, so I left a message. That was hours ago.

Noah *always* returned my phone calls, and I started to worry that he was taking this far more seriously than me. It couldn't be over just like that . . . could it? I left him a few concerned voicemails as the hours passed. I even caved and told him that I'd *think* about his unhappiness with the situation. What he wanted was impossible, but I was willing to let him come over and try to convince me otherwise (hopefully with a lovely round of make-up sex).

But when dark hit and the moon rose, I knew he wouldn't call. Noah had gone into hibernation for the night or dumped me . . . or both.

I didn't like to think about that.

Zane was nowhere to be seen. My small apartment

showed signs of habitation—his dirty shirts were tossed in a corner of the bedroom, his favorite towel discarded on the corner of the bed. He'd been here recently, and judging by the fact that he'd left his favorite lighter on the kitchen counter, he'd be back. I settled in to wait. He was probably out looking for some hapless girl to feed on, and I hoped he wouldn't be long.

After two cold showers and endless twitching, I called Zane's phone. It was stupid and needy, and I hated myself for dialing him.

"This is Zane. Leave a message after the beep." *Beeeep*.

Drat, his phone was off. I hesitated, wanting to leave a voicemail that sounded sexy, not needy. But thinking of the desperate string of messages I'd left on Noah's phone, I hung up instead.

Even I had my standards.

Until Zane returned I was stuck with my own company, so I decided to settle in with a couple of pizzas— Suck metabolism required that I stuff myself like a pig—and a movie that neither guy would watch with me except on pain of death.

As I watched *The Notebook*, the doorbell rang. Nice. I hopped up from the couch with excitement. It was food or sex at the door, and either would make me a happy girl.

It turned out to be food. The delivery guy was your typical nerd-in-crisis sort: short, fat, a ponytail, and pushing forty. He stared at my boobs, but that was all I got anymore. I was starting to get used to it.

"Pizza for a Ms. Brighton?" He peered at me through his thick glasses, smiling and displaying a need for orthodontia. "A beautiful woman like you, alone tonight?"

"Save it, Casanova. Can I just have my pizza?" Once upon a time, I might have been flattered by the attention—any attention—from a stranger. But it had hit the saturation point weeks ago, and now the leering just pissed me off.

"Twenty bucks."

I slapped the money into his hand.

He collapsed like a ton of bricks, going down and taking my pizza with him.

Well, that was unexpected. I blinked for a moment, staring down at him. Was this a joke? But he didn't move, even after I nudged him with my sneaker.

I knelt beside him and tapped his cheek. "Are you okay? Hello?" Maybe he was having an epileptic fit or something. Maybe he was trying to scare me.

It wasn't a joke, though. His eyes were shut, his face slack and pale, and I jammed my fingers against his throat to try to find a pulse. Then I heard a faint snore come from his throat.

A snore?

Oh *crap*. I'd somehow used my Suck powers to put him to sleep.

Succubi can touch a person and shut off their mind just by using their powers. Some of the less ethical succubi used their powers to ferret out information and influence others. I avoided using them at all, since I was

still new to the whole succubus thing. I could put someone to sleep if I really concentrated, but I had to think
about it really hard to make it work.

Glancing down the hall to make sure my neighbors
didn't notice anything out of the ordinary, I gathered up
the pizza boxes and dragged the guy into my apartment
by his legs—not an easy trick, since the Mr. Cheese guy
wasn't any lightweight.

Once he was safely in my apartment, I shut the door
and stared at him. What now? I'd only done the mind-
control thing twice, and the first time had been a real
disaster when I couldn't figure out how to turn it back
off again.

At least the delivery guy was breathing normally. I
touched his forehead, letting my mind sink into his body.

As a succubus, I get a few nifty perks. One of them
happens to be the ability to read other people's minds if
I touch them. Whenever a succubus interacts with the
mind of another person, the absorbing of those memories throws in a lot of visual associations. I guess that was
our way of processing another person's thoughts without
overloading our own minds. My friend Remy, the porn
star, sees a lot of movie sets in people's heads. I mostly
see them in their cluttered bedrooms, usually something straight out of their high school years. From these
"rooms," we could pick up mental clues about what's
going on in the victim's mind.

Mr. Cheese had a typical mental room. A TV in the
corner—playing *Star Trek,* big surprise there—and a

bunch of fantasy posters on the wall. A beanbag chair sat in the corner and he had a twin bed with Yoda sheets. Yeesh. A stack of books—usually the best way to sift through the memories of the person I was "visiting"—sat beside the bed.

But I couldn't find Mr. Cheese anywhere. His brain was on, but no one was home. That never happened. Just to be sure, I even looked under the mental bed, and in the mental closet (just in case the jokes held true).

Nothing. He'd vanished.

I jerked out of his mind and tried pinching him, and when that failed I even kissed him to see if that would work, à la the frog prince.

No dice. You can't wake someone up if they're not there in the first place.

So I did what I always did in emergency situations—I called Remy.

Remy Summore wasn't what I'd call a . . . normal friend. For one, she was a porn star. For two, she was the only other succubus in New City. Several hundred years old, she'd seen and done a lot more than I had, and we'd fallen into a mentor-slash-friends relationship. She taught me the ropes, I argued with her a lot, and we went shopping and ate a lot of food court meals at the mall. It worked out well for the most part, even if I did occasionally want to choke her.

"No, Jackie," she teased as soon as she picked up the phone. "I won't let you borrow my bra with the tassels."

"Gross." I paused, digesting that mental image, then

shook myself back on track. "Remy, I have a big problem."

"Do tell." I could hear her flipping the channels on her TV. "Hey, did you see that my new movie, *Babes in Boyland,* is on the Spice channel?"

"That's nice," I said hurriedly. "So I kind of sort of stole the mind of the pizza boy. And I can't get him back."

"Mmm, what kind of pizza?"

I rubbed my forehead, trying not to get too annoyed with her. "Remy, I'm serious. I touched the pizza boy's hand and he went down like a light."

"Woohoo! He went down on you?"

I nearly choked. "Not like that—"

"You went down on him? You little minx, you—"

"No!" I yelled into the phone. "Listen to me! I made him go to sleep by accident. And when I went into his mind to wake him up, he wasn't *there.*"

"Really?" Her interest perked, and I heard the TV shut off. "What did Zane say when that happened?"

"He's not here—he's out feeding. Can we get back to my problem here? I'm having a really bad day—"

"Oh?" She yawned.

"I just broke up with Noah, and I've got some comatose nerd sprawled on my floor and I don't know what to do with him." My voice rose a shrill octave and I forced myself to calm down. *Breathe. Breathe. This is fixable.* I just didn't know how. Surely Remy would know.

Remy, however, was still fixated on my sex life. "You broke up with Noah—"

"Can we focus on the comatose nerd, please?" I was going to hyperventilate if she didn't help me soon.

"Okay, okay. Did you try to wake him up?"

Thank you, Captain Obvious. "Uh, yeah."

"Well, go into his brain and talk to him. See what the deal is." After a short pause, Remy whispered away from the phone. Of course, she wasn't alone. Her bed had a revolving door.

"He's not *in* his head, Remy. That's what I'm trying to tell you. I checked and he's not there. His mental furniture is there, but he's not."

"He's not?" She paused. "But . . . they're always there. Where else can he go?"

"I don't know!" I wailed. "You're the expert here. Help me!"

God, I really wished I could call Noah. He always knew what to do. But he wouldn't be up for several hours; I wasn't sure he'd want to talk to me, what with the "time off" our relationship was having.

Remy sighed. "All right, all right. I'll come over. Stay right there."

Like I was going somewhere, with an unconscious pizza boy at my feet?

"Hurry," I said, and then hung up the phone. Luckily, one of the pizzas had landed right side up, so I sat on the floor cross-legged and pulled it over to me. As I ate, I tried not to panic. There had to be a way to fix this. *Had* to.

If Remy didn't have any ideas about how to get him back in his head, I could call Zane, but I doubted he'd have any better ideas. Remy was the succubus expert and if she didn't know, then things were scary indeed. I squirmed uncomfortably and crammed another slice into my mouth.

What if I had to get outside help? Again—like in the form of angelic assistance? I shuddered, thinking of beautiful, calculating Uriel. He was the only true angel that I'd ever seen, and the memory was seared into my brain. Immortals called them dealers because they liked to bargain with you, and the bargain never turned out in your favor. Last time Uriel had "helped" me by giving me a blessing that would stop my Itch for a week, in exchange for the "easy" task of getting information from vampires.

There is nothing easy about dealing with vampires— nothing. *Or* angels. As a rule of thumb, I tried to avoid both.

Except for Noah and Zane, of course.

I polished off the pizza, but still no Remy. I picked up my BlackBerry, intending to call her and see where she was.

Instead, I dialed Zane.

It was a stupid thing to do. Zane valued his space— that was blatantly obvious as soon as he moved in and began to disappear for hours on end. I told myself I didn't mind, because he'd always kiss me (or more) before he left and we spent plenty of time before the sun came up. I really liked Zane. I might even be crazy over him, but we were still getting used to each other.

But tonight there was no note, or a flower like he normally left when he went out hunting. After the trouble with Noah, that hurt my feelings. Was I being set up for a double dumping?

To my relief, Zane picked up on the third ring. "Hey, Princess."

The low, sexy rasp of his voice sent a tingle straight through my starving body. "Hey, Zane," I said back to him, trying not to blush like a schoolgirl. "Where are you?"

His warm chuckle did wonderful things to my insides. "Missing me?" He sounded like he was about to say something else, but then he covered the mouthpiece, and I could hear a muffled conversation on the other end.

Which made me uneasy. "Who's there with you? What are you doing?"

A pause, then, "I'm out feeding. You know how it goes."

Yeah, I knew, because I wouldn't let him feed from me. Vampires had to feed on a daily basis—their need for blood was more powerful than my need for sex—and that caused a constant strain in our relationship. I didn't refuse to let him feed on me because it was disgusting or immoral—a vampire-feeding was a precursor to the best orgasm ever—but because it meant that I was giving my body over to him and putting it in his control. Vampire feedings induced a strange mind-meld on succubi—part out-of-body experience and part dream—with the vampire that had just fed. And the last time Zane had fed from me, he'd stolen my powers, left me tied to a bed, then kidnapped my friends.

There were a few trust issues.

Despite his wild side, there was something about Zane that . . . called to me. Maybe it was his roguish attitude, or his lust for pleasure, or the tender way he held me close when we made love, as if he was afraid I'd disappear and he'd never see me again. Or the fact that he'd turned his back on vampire-kind just to be with me. Heady stuff. Remy and Noah disapproved of him, but I kept coming back like a junkie needing a fix.

And even though I was completely goofy over him, I didn't trust him to feed from me again.

Zane knew it and hated it. Vampires *love* succubi. We're the blood equivalent of an aphrodisiac, so for me to withhold my blood from him, he considered that a grievous crime.

I considered it common sense.

Even if it did suck, a little.

For him to now point out to me that he was feeding—probably from another hot, turned-on female—was painful. My throat tightened. "So when will you be back home?"

"Not until late, I'm afraid." Zane's cheerful voice echoed through the phone. "Something has come up, and I'll need to be out for most of the night."

"But I need you here," I said, hating the whine in my voice. "I have a problem."

"Princess, I'd love to be there with you, helping you

with your problem." His low, sensual voice set my body on vibrate once more. God, I loved it when he said my nickname. "But I have a few things to take care of first, all right?"

"Fine," I said, feeling the low pulse start in my groin again. My voice dropped to a low whisper as well. "You promise?"

There was a pause on his end, and his voice grew even more strained, rough. "I promise. I'll see you soon, Jackie, and when I do, it'll be just me and you."

I was ready for that right now, and squirmed with anticipation. "Sounds great."

There was an uncomfortable pause at the moment where couples normally exchange "I love yous." We weren't quite at that stage, so we muttered a few platitudes, then hung up.

Now I was turned on, lonely, cranky, and I still needed help with my pizza boy.

The doorbell rang, scaring the heck out of me, and Remy came in.

"Hey, doll," she said, running a hand through her long fall of silken black hair. Her gaze settled to the man on the floor. "That your new friend?"

Count on Remy to make jeans and a T-shirt look über-sexy. Her darkly olive skin and gray eyes were striking, even in a tacky red shirt that proudly proclaimed PONY RIDE across her breasts. She looked completely put together despite the fact that it was late at night. I would have hated her if she wasn't my new best friend.

Her eyes were bleached silver, which told me what she'd been doing before she came over, and the fact that she'd abandoned her new plaything for me spoke volumes about our friendship.

Succubi have to stick together.

"Thanks for coming, Remy." I gestured at Mr. Cheese. "That's him."

She wrinkled her nose. "Ugh. I was kind of hoping he would be hot." She nudged the unconscious pizza boy with the toe of one strappy red pump. "He looks more like a lump of dough."

"Yeah, well, my lump of dough has nothing going on in the oven, if you catch my drift." Feeling a little hysterical again, I picked up his hand and then released it. It banged lifelessly to the floor. "See? He's not in there! I don't know where he is, but he's not in his body."

Remy waved a hand and crouched next to the body. "They're always in there. Maybe you just missed it." Extending one finger, she very gingerly touched his forehead and closed her eyes, searching his mind.

A moment later, she opened them and stared at me, wide-eyed. "What did you do?"

I threw up my hands in despair, ready to start wailing. "Nothing! I didn't do anything to him!"

"Okay, calm down. Don't get upset. Let's try and think this through." She sat next to me on the floor and sniffed the air. "You have any more pizza?"

I glared.

Remy sighed. "Fine. Let me think. There's got to be

a logical reason for how you managed to wipe out his brain."

I buried my face in my hands and moaned. "All I did was touch him with my finger, I swear. Just a tiny poke."

"He looks like the type to have a tiny poke," she quipped.

"Be *serious*, Remy. I just killed a man."

"He's not dead," she said, patting my shoulder. "Don't worry. He's got to be somewhere. I mean, he's not a ghost, right? That's always a plus."

"What do you mean, a ghost?"

"You know. Casper? Beetlejuice? If he were a ghost, you'd see him floating around here, sweetie. A ghost can't go back into his head, because the body is dead." Remy tapped her chin with a long fingernail. "Hmmm . . . he's *not* in his head." She twirled a lock of her hair, her brows scrunched together in thought. "I don't know what to make of it . . . unless . . ." Her eyes widened.

"What?" I leaned in, nervous. "What is it?"

"Unless you've been cursed."

I sat up straight. *Cursed?*

CHAPTER THREE

When someone as jaded as Remy stares at you with horror, it tends to ruin your day a little.

When she remained silent, I prompted her anxiously, "What do you mean, I'm cursed?"

She blinked at me. "You know, voodoo, a hex—"

I interrupted her, my hands on my hips. "I know what a curse is. How do you think I'm cursed if all I've done is blanked out the mind of a pizza guy?"

"It's not just him," she said, getting to her feet and dusting off the seat of her jeans. "It could be any number of things. The last curse I remember was on a succubus named Victoria. Happened about two hundred years ago."

"Victoria? I don't know who that is."

Remy's beautiful face was unnaturally solemn. "That's because she's dead."

"Dead?" Succubi rarely died. We regenerated bullet holes (I'd learned that the hard way), couldn't drown, didn't age. There were only two ways to kill a succubus. Kill both of her masters, (angelic and vampiric) and she would be instantly removed from the mortal plane and sent to Heaven or Hell. The other way to kill a succubus was sexual starvation. Not feeding the Itch would cause our bodies to break down in a matter of days, until there was nothing left but a dried-up husk.

"Victoria liked to play with power," Remy said, gazing down at the pizza boy with sympathy. "Got off on it, was drawn to it, and actively pursued men that had it. She was constantly hopping from the bed of one vampire to the next, one Serim to the next, always heading after the man with the most influence, money, and power. One of her ex-lovers was a warlock, and when he found out about her cheating on him with a vampire knight, he cursed her."

There were a lot of loaded questions in that simple statement. I wanted to ask what the heck a vampire knight was, and if warlocks really existed—but I kept going back to that "curse" thing. "So what happened to her?"

"Nothing, at first. But she began to notice when her powers began to increase." Her gaze strayed down to the comatose pizza boy. "She began to wipe the minds of humans around her and grew stronger, more powerful. More irresistible to mortals. More everything." Her gaze flicked back to me. "Her Itch was amplified, too."

This sounded frighteningly familiar. "Let me guess. She had to have sex more often?"

Remy nodded slowly. "It was hard to tell at first—Victoria wasn't exactly the most chaste of succubi, not like you or me."

Boy, if porn star Remy was an example of chastity, Victoria must have been a hard-core tramp.

"Her curse made the Itch reappear every few hours. Then every hour. Then, even less time than that."

Good lord. While I loved having sex with Noah and Zane regularly, the thought of the Itch being only an hour away was frightening. Even ice cream sundaes would get old if I had to have them every hour, on the hour. "So what did Victoria do?"

Remy shrugged. "She kept having sex, but it wasn't enough. Her skin became gray and washed-out, her hair fell out, and her body began to thin. She starved to death right in the middle of an orgy." Remy looked away from me.

"Oh my God." I wrapped my arms around my body and closed my eyes—my eyes that were vivid blue, despite having sex less than a full day ago. "Do you really think I'm cursed?"

"I don't know what else it could be," Remy said softly. "That's the only thing like this that I've seen in two hundred years. Victoria used to have the same problem with her powers and with touching mortals. She'd accidentally brush one with her hand, and their minds would just vanish. A few days later, their bodies would die of starvation. No one knew how she did it—it just happened. Suck powers out of control."

"But . . . ." I hesitated, thinking hard. "I touched Noah

earlier. How come I didn't suck his mind out?" A thought occurred to me, and I reached over and tapped Remy on the shoulder.

She slapped my hand away. "Hey! Quit that!"

I pulled back, remorseful. "Sorry, I wanted to see if it worked."

"By trying to eat my brains?" She scowled. "You're lucky that it doesn't work on immortals."

"It doesn't?"

"Not that I've ever seen."

I felt weak with relief. So I couldn't hurt Noah or Zane. Good to know. The room fell silent, except for the snores of Mr. Cheese. "Do you think it's reversible?" I looked down anxiously. What was I going to do if I couldn't find out how to get him back in his body?

Remy shrugged. "If we can figure out how his brain left, I suppose we can figure out how to put it back."

I focused on the positive. Good.

"But you need to get rid of your own curse first," Remy reminded me.

Not so good. I collapsed onto the sofa and stared at the wall. "Who would have cursed me? Who have I pissed off enough to want to get rid of me?"

"I don't know," Remy said, sitting at my side and putting her arm around my waist. "But I think I know who might have more information about this."

"Zane? Noah?"

She shook her head. "No." Her voice was very small. "You know who I'm talking about."

Aw, hell. I did.

Dealers.

If you ask anyone on the street what an angel is, they'll call forth an image of a sweet, spiritual being with big fluffy wings that will guide you and keep you safe.

While the wings aren't a crock, angels aren't nearly as sweetly innocent as society likes to portray them. My kind calls them dealers because angels like to bargain, and the currency they like to play with is your immortal soul.

Deep down inside, beneath the Playboy Barbie exterior, I still had a soul. It could still be affected by what I did here on earth. And if I asked the dealers for help with something, they'd be more than happy to help me.

For a small price.

At least, it was small to them. Though the deal might be as simple as "Get this book for me," they didn't tell you that getting the book might mean that you have to murder someone or steal it from a child dying of cancer. But once you'd agreed to do the task, you had to, because lying to angels was the worst kind of sin to go on an immortal soul. And they didn't forget a broken promise. Ever.

"Dealers? Do we have to? I'm still smarting from the hole that Uriel's goons blew into me after the last deal I made with them." Immortal or not, it's damn hard to regrow your abdomen when there's a hole the size of a dinner plate in it. I rubbed my stomach just thinking about it.

When I'd first become a succubus, Uriel tricked me into approaching the vampire queen Nitocris in her den. That had gotten me into serious trouble. Uriel had been chasing the halo of the first of the fallen—Joachim—and had pulled out all the stops to get it before the queen could. He'd even possessed a priest to try to get to me (and the halo). And given the fact that Remy had accidentally absorbed the halo and Joachim's powers . . . well, I wasn't in a rush to see Uriel again.

"I can't think of anyone else able to identify your curse," Remy said. "New City's pretty light on immortals. Unless you want to take it up with the flip side—they'd have the knowledge you need."

When she said the flip side, she meant the other end of the dealers: demons.

I shuddered. "No, thank you. At least Uriel's got some sort of honor, wacky though it may be."

After all, he believed he was doing something for the good of the Heavenly Host. The fact that giving him the halo would have wiped Noah and the rest of the Serim from the planet? Minor detail.

"'Kay. We don't have to go to Uriel," Remy offered. "If you go to a church, that's directly asking for assistance. You always get the big guns in a church."

"But angels can't leave hallowed ground," I pointed out. "Unless they possess someone. And I doubt they're wandering around New City in borrowed flesh, just looking for the chance to say hi to me."

"You're right," she said, crestfallen. "Angels hate possessing people. They think it's gross."

I didn't blame them. I'd seen a few of their choices, and it didn't look like much of a party.

Remy brightened. "But I know where we can find a few of the minor leaguers."

"Oh? Where?"

She raised her finger in the air to punctuate her brilliant idea. "A graveyard!"

If there was one thing that had changed since turning succubus a few weeks ago, it's that my Saturday nights were never dull. After all, when I wasn't having sex with a vampire or a fallen angel, I was trotting after the hottest immortal Ottoman woman this side of the Mississippi, on yet another one of her harebrained schemes.

As I watched, one of Remy's tall red heels sank into the moist earth as soon as she stepped off the sidewalk. She flung her hands up in the air, wobbling to one side with a horrified expression. "Oh ew! I think I just stabbed someone in the forehead."

I flipped on my flashlight, watching Remy struggle to shake the mud off her expensive shoe. "I sincerely doubt that they're burying people two inches deep nowadays."

She gave me a wary look and shook her pump again to dislodge the dirt.

"Speaking of, why couldn't you wear normal shoes?" I was wearing grubby sneakers, myself.

"I didn't bring any other shoes with me. When you called me, I didn't think we'd be spending Saturday night in a graveyard." Remy eyed our surroundings with distaste.

That made two of us. "You could have borrowed a pair of mine." I followed as she wobbled through the grassy turf.

She gave a haughty sniff. "Yours were ugly."

"You picked them out for me!"

"Well, they're perfect for you. Ugly for me." She gestured at the row of tombstones behind the tall iron fence. "Besides, we're almost there."

I shone my flashlight on the iron bars, ignoring the prickle on the back of my neck when an owl hooted nearby. The full moon was out and shining high, and the squeamish girl inside me was screaming in terror, even though I knew full well that there was nothing to be scared of. I mean, I regularly slept with the things that go bump in the night. I was immortal. Nothing could harm me in the middle of a creepy graveyard in the dead of night. Right?

Right?

Remy swore again as her heels sank into the ground, and she bent over to remove them. As she did, I noticed another flashlight bobbing along the walk, just a short distance from us.

"Crap." I grabbed Remy by the arm. "Someone's coming this way."

She glanced down the walkway. "So what?"

"We're going to get caught, is what." I clicked off my flashlight and stuffed it into the waistband of my jeans. "And I would really appreciate not going to jail for trespassing in a graveyard."

Remy snorted in a rather unladylike fashion. "No one's going to jail, you ninny." She stood, handed me her shoes, then headed down the path toward the flashlight, hips swiveling and her hair swooshing around her shoulders in a move perfected in Pantene commercials. I could hear her faintly humming a cheerful tune.

Shoes in hand, I followed warily.

I approached the two of them just in time to hear the guard say, "The grounds are closed after dark, ma'am. You'll have to come back some other time."

"My boyfriend left me here," Remy said, giving the fakest sob I'd ever heard. Porn stars weren't known for their *acting* skills, after all. "And it's dark and scary out here, and I twisted my ankle."

Corny or not, nothing with a dick could resist a succubus in need. The man had his arms about Remy's waist in the next moment and she collapsed against him, flinging her arms around his neck. He didn't look like he was complaining. Confused? Yes. Rapturous? Definitely.

"Just calm down, miss. I'll take care of you," he said over her theatrical sobbing, then glanced over at me.

"You have a friend here?" His soothing changed to confusion and suspicion.

"Oops," said Remy, frowning at me for ruining things. Would you believe it's a double date?"

At his skeptical look, she sighed. "No?"

"I can explain . . ." I began as the guard tried to untangle Remy's arms from around his neck.

Remy dragged the guard's face down to hers and plastered her mouth on his, locking him in a very long kiss. When it was done, he slid to the ground in a boneless heap.

Looking very pleased with herself, she glanced over at me. "Good kisser," she said, then bent over him. "The passcode is an easy one, too." Remy rummaged through his pockets for a moment, then emerged with his keys. "Just in case."

She brushed past me and headed for the gate, all decisive motion and swinging hair. I glanced down at the guard for a moment more and felt the stirring of lust. He was a good-looking man. Maybe thirty, thirty-five. No gut, nice eyes behind the glasses . . .

I cringed as my body pulsed in response. Normally when I'd skipped a "meal," the Itch pulsed in a constant whisper at the back of my mind. Today it felt like a sonic boom. Terrified, I trotted after Remy, trying not to think of Victoria and her starving to death in the middle of an orgy. Starving during *sex*. Nope, wasn't going to think about it. "Let's get this show on the road, can we?"

She reached for the keypad on the electronic gate. "I'm hurrying. Just give me a moment." Remy pursed her lips, then typed in the key code on the illuminated electronic pad.

8008135.

The gate clicked, the light on the keypad flicked from red to green, and the heavy iron gate began to open slowly.

Remy giggled. "Guess why he picked that code?"

I gave her an exasperated look. "Do I have to?"

She pointed at the digits. "When you type it in, it looks like the word *Boobies.*" She laughed as if it were the funniest thing she'd ever heard. "Just like the calculator joke."

Oh jeez.

When I didn't laugh, she said, "You're such a stick-in-the-mud, Jackie. Lighten up."

I followed her through the gate grumbling, "Easy for you to say. You're not the one who's sucking out the brains of random men."

"True," she said, her bare feet padding down the sidewalk. "I just have a half-demon Serim vampire thing inside me, thanks to your last adventure."

"You just *have* to keep throwing that in my face, don't you?" It was only partially my fault that she'd accompanied me to Egypt to retrieve the halo, and mostly her *own* fault that she'd absorbed it (we'd fought over it like a chicken bone and she'd won). Sheesh.

"Yeah, well, I don't let things like that ruin my day, and

neither should you," she said to me with a cheery smile. "Now, where do we want to do this?" She put her hands on her hips and surveyed the quiet graveyard.

It looked quite well kept, since this was the nice part of town. If we raised the dead, I'd rather have little old rich ladies than dead junkies and street rats. The tombstones here were pale white marble, with small bouquets of flowers placed on each marker. Some didn't even have gravestones, going for the more understated "plaque in the grass" look. In the distance stood a row of mausoleums for the truly rich.

Directly to our right? A nice, freshly dug open grave. No one was in it, but the sight made me clutch Remy's arm and stand a little closer to her. "Let's go wherever this will be done the quickest."

She thought for a moment, then snapped her fingers. "Let's find a Catholic grave. They're usually big on blessings and last rites."

"Um, call me crazy, but I don't think they designate what religion people are on their tombstone." The longer we stood here in the middle of the graveyard, the more this felt like a bad idea. "Maybe we should just go find a church—"

"No," Remy said firmly. "We're going to get you some real help, and we're going to avoid Uriel if at all possible." She clasped my hand and began to head into the graveyard. "Maybe we can find a nice Irish-sounding name, or an Italian one. Look for something that either starts with an O or ends with one."

Ethnic profiling? Nice. I let her drag me after her, my sneakers squeaking on the wet grass. "I'm not sure—"

My voice died when a horrible, smoky smell touched my nostrils. I pinched my nose and looked around the quiet graveyard as my insides quivered uncomfortably.

A woman with red eyes leaned against a nearby tombstone, the marble angel above looking ready to attack her. Her tweed suit looked more suited to an office than a graveyard in the middle of the night. The woman's long, lean frame shifted. "Hello, ladies," she said in a cool tone, tilting her head down to look at us over the rims of her glasses. "Enjoying the night?"

At my side, Remy swore. "Of all the luck. A friggin' demon."

I stared at the woman, unable to take my eyes off her. "How do you know she's a demon?" I whispered to Remy.

"She's female. Other than demons, succubi are the only female immortals."

Another tidbit of knowledge no one had bothered to share with me. I'd only seen males so far (other than Remy), but I hadn't known that was a hard-and-fast rule. She wasn't a succubus, that was for sure. Being a succubus, I recognized the faint internal vibe that Remy gave off, kind of like spiritual tuning chords. Remy's chords resonated like mine, just like my innards resonated differently than Zane's or Noah's.

This woman's tuning chords were scaring the hell out of me.

The woman smiled, revealing razor-sharp teeth beneath the demure exterior. "Hello, darling. So nice to see you again."

Remy snorted and took a step backward. "Which one are you?"

The woman waved her hand with an airy gesture. "Very small-time demon, I assure you. The big leaguers are too busy to hang out in graveyards tonight, no matter who may show." Her red eyes flashed in the darkness. "You may call me Mae."

I leaned over to whisper to Remy, "I thought we were here looking for an angel?"

"Not all the ground in a graveyard is consecrated by above," Mae said, arching an eyebrow at me. "And I can hear everything you say." The unnerving teeth closed and Mae gave me a tight, small-lipped smile, seemingly human again. "So what brings you ladies in search of angels tonight?"

"None of your damn business," Remy said, squeezing my hand to keep me silent.

"Damned business is my specialty," Mae purred. "I can offer the same kind of assistance as any angel, and I won't cloak my meanings with fake platitudes and prayers." She leaned back against the marble angel perched on the head of the tombstone and touched the cheek of the cherub in an almost obscene fashion. "So how about it, ladies?"

I looked over at Remy. "What do you think?"

She glanced at Mae, hesitating. "It's not ideal. Not

ideal at all." Before I could ask her what that meant, she gave a small sigh. "But I think it's just as safe as making a deal with an angel, provided you're extremely specific about everything."

Well, there's a ringing endorsement.

"Should we wait for an angel to show?" I asked. If angels showed up, would it be some sort of celestial showdown? An immortal duke-out?

Remy shook her head, disappointed. "Won't happen now. Not with a demon nearby."

Mae smiled. "I'm afraid it's me or nothing, sweet-cakes. Make up your mind."

I mulled that over, looking at Mae's attempting-to-be-harmless-and-failing form. I could decline her offer and leave the graveyard and try another night. Or I could try a church and take my licks with Uriel, such as they were.

One of the demon's hands reached up to caress the marble cheek of the angel again, and my body throbbed in response at the sight, reminding me that I didn't have a lot of time if I was truly cursed.

"I need your help," I blurted. Remy patted me on the shoulder, either approving my decision or sympathizing that I had to make one. "I might be cursed, and I need to know for sure."

"You've come to the right demoness." Mae stepped forward, her red eyes lighting with interest. "I can help you with that."

"You can remove it?"

She shook her head. "Removing the curse is an entirely different matter. But I can help you identify it." She smiled again, the demure, closemouthed smile. "For a small favor, of course."

My spirits plummeted. "Of course," I replied, losing what little enthusiasm I had. I hated favors, especially favors for the Infernal Host.

"'Kay, but name your favor first," Remy said. "Then she'll decide whether she will agree to do business with you."

Smart Remy—I could have kissed her.

Mae's tiny smile remained undimmed. "I just need you to carry a message for me."

I eyed the demoness. "What sort of message?"

"A simple greeting, that's all. A tiny reminder for an old friend to invite me over sometime." Mae took another step forward. The air around her flashed, and the smell of sulfur rode thick in the air again. She froze in place. "As you can see, I am bound by this small piece of earth." She gestured to the edges of the particular grave she was standing on. "I can't leave these boundaries, except to return to Hell."

Well, thank goodness for that. "A message? And that's it?"

She spread her hands. "That's all. I assure you that you will not be in the slightest bit of danger."

Yeah, sure. I gave her a skeptical look. "Who is this message going to?"

"A woman who currently resides in New Orleans."

Again, that tiny demure smile hiding the wicked dagger teeth. "Just tell her that Mae can come over. She'll know what that means."

Some sort of unholy RSVP? It didn't sound like a trick to me. I tried to puzzle it out, knowing that she was trying to catch me. There had to be a secret meaning to the message—I just couldn't figure out what it was. Sure that I was missing something obvious, I glanced at Remy.

She shrugged at me.

"All right," I said, even though it felt like a bad idea. I crossed my arms over my chest and gave her a brief nod. "I accept the offer. I'll go to New Orleans and tell this woman that you're coming to her party, and you'll help me out?"

Mae inclined her head in a gesture of acquiescence. The smell of sulfur grew thicker. "That is correct. But you must deliver the message in person."

"All right," I said grudgingly. It didn't sound so terrible, though I was sure I was going to regret the agreement later. "Now, can you help me with my curse?"

"The agreement," Mae said, her voice suddenly all business, "was for me to tell you if you were, in fact, cursed."

Yeah, I remembered. "So? Am I cursed or not?" My heart began to pound.

"Come forward," she said, beckoning me. "I have to touch your skin to be able to tell."

Ugh. Swallowing, I took a few steps forward, standing just outside her reach.

"Just a bit closer," Mae said, the smile still in her voice. "I assure you, I don't bite."

She reminded me a little too much of the vampire queen for me to take that comment at face value. Probably because Queen Nitocris wasn't really a vampire at all, but a human who had willingly joined her body with a demon's soul, rendering her immortal and fucking scary. The vampires worshiped her and let her rule over them as some sort of goddess. Unfortunately, she hated my guts. Not only did I stop her from getting Joachim's spirit (and certain world Armageddon) but I'd also replaced her in Zane's heart, and she was possessive.

To see Mae's sharklike smile curve just like Nitocris's was a little unnerving and brought back bad memories. But I stepped forward again, burning to know if I was cursed.

She placed her hands on my arms, her flesh scalding hot. Before I could ask her to remove her hands, she leaned in and brushed her mouth against mine.

An instant tingle shot through my body, and the Itch exploded in my head. My body felt like it was on fire, a volcano of intense longing and desire coursing through me. My hands wrapped around Mae's head of their own accord, and I pulled her mouth to mine again, seeking that warm tongue and the lick of heat that it brought. I needed more of her, more of that delicious burning flame deep down inside of me—

Rough hands jerked me backward, and I slammed into the wet, cold earth, and back to reality.

My head spun for a minute, and the air sucked back into my lungs, and I panted, coughing brimstone. I struggled to refocus on the too-sharp world around me, the Itch blazing through my body. My face scalded and I touched it, feeling the blisters on my skin where I'd made contact with Mae's flesh. I glanced back up at her with shock.

The demon stood there, her red eyes burning bright as she looked down at me. Longing filled my body at the sight of her. I needed sex. Had to have sex. Would not be able to function until I had sex. I yearned to be back in her arms, that wonderful touch, like caressing a living inferno. I whimpered.

"Snap out of it!" Remy's hard voice broke through my daze, and her hand cracked across my sore face.

"Ow." That woke me up. I shook awake, then stared in horror at Mae. "That wasn't part of our agreement." I rubbed my face again, feeling the blisters. Already they disappeared under my fingertips—Sucks heal fast—but the memory repelled me as much as it made the Itch run wild under my skin.

"I don't know why you're so upset." The demoness gave me an innocent look. "You did agree to let me touch you."

"I thought you meant on the arm!"

Mae's lips curled into a smug smile. "You know what they say about assuming."

The more time I spent around Mae, the less I liked her. "So just tell me, am I cursed or not?"

Her teasing look slid away, and she was all business once more. "It's interesting. When you two entered the graveyard, your power signatures were off the charts. Much stronger than any normal succubus. It's what drew me here tonight." She glanced over at Remy, who still hovered protectively over me. "But after kissing the red-haired one, I've determined that the power isn't coming from *her* body after all." Blatant interest showed in Mae's face as she watched Remy. "Care to tell me your little secret?"

A month or so ago—in my first disastrous run-in with the Infernal Host—Remy had become possessed by the spirit of Joachim, one of the first and strongest (and craziest) Serim to fall from Heaven. I thought she was overcoming her problem, but when her eyes flashed bright red to match Mae's at the question, I knew that wasn't the case.

Remy looked furious. Mae simply looked fascinated.

I cleared my throat before things got out of hand. "Hello? Remember me? The girl with the curse?"

"What? Oh, yes." Mae turned back to me, reluctantly drawing her eyes away from Remy. "You asked if you were cursed. My answer would have to be not directly."

I pulled myself to my feet with Remy's help, making sure to keep us away from the edges of Mae's circle of unhallowed ground. "What do you mean, 'not directly'?"

"Curses can work in many different ways," she said. "You can force someone to ingest a cursed item or trick them into accepting the curse. Or you can imbue an object that the owner will use on a regular basis. Another way is to curse someone else directly, and they in turn pass it on to the true recipient."

I frowned. "So which one is it?"

Mae grinned. "That would be another question, and that would require another deal, obviously. I'm game if you are." She pursed her lips in a kiss and winked at me.

"No, thanks," I blurted, taking an involuntary step backward. "So you can't tell me anything more than that?"

"I could, in exchange for a teeny tiny favor."

Remy shook her head and pulled at my arm. "Forget it. She's not going to play fair." Her eyes had returned to their normal bluish-gray hue, no traces of red remaining. Remy was back in control. "This was a bad idea, and I'm sorry I suggested it. But the good news is that I have a new idea."

I stared at her. "You couldn't have had this wonderful new idea a few hours ago, before we came here?"

"I didn't think of it until she mentioned New Orleans," Remy said, turning me away so I didn't face Mae any longer. She leaned in and said, "I think we should visit Delilah. She'll know the answer to your questions."

"So who exactly is Delilah?"

"Delilah's the oldest succubus in America," Remy said, squeezing my arm in encouragement. "She came over to escape the French Revolution and settled in New Orleans. If there's anything that a succubus has run across, Delilah's bound to know about it." She smiled at

---

my dubious look. "She's also a part-time voodoo priestess, so that should help."

"Oh sure," I said, trying to disentangle myself from Remy's grasp. There was something almost desperate about her clingy touch, and it was bothering me. Especially after the demon's touch. "I was just thinking that we needed a big helping of voodoo to go with our curses and demons tonight."

"What a coincidence," came Mae's smooth voice. "Delilah is just the person that you need to take my message to."

CHAPTER FOUR

I poked at my stack of Rooty-Tooty-Fresh-'N-Fruity pancakes, unable to muster the enthusiasm to eat more than three of them. "So I guess we're flying out to New Orleans, huh?"

Across the table from me, Remy gave me a puzzled look and shoved another forkful of strawberry blintz into her perfect mouth. "Why the hell would we fly there?"

"Uh, hello? Did you forget that little interlude with the demoness tonight? The one that was your bright idea? You know, where I agreed to bring a message to her friend in person?" The fact that Delilah was the demoness's friend as well as Remy's bugged me, but I didn't say it aloud.

I trusted Remy. We bickered like siblings, but she was one of the best things in my Afterlife—sister, mentor, and buddy rolled into one. We might not always see eye to eye on things (like whom one should sleep with and how many), but she had never let me down.

Remy wrinkled her nose and shrugged, forking up another mouthful of blintz. "Yeah, but why do we have to fly? Let's go on a road trip!"

I flicked one of the blueberries off my pancakes and shoved it to the edge of the plate. "What do you mean, a road trip?"

"Like Thelma and Louise."

"They died in that movie, Remy."

She grinned. "Yeah, but we're immortal, baby. We can drive off as many cliffs as we want."

True. "I don't get it, though. Why a road trip?"

"I need to publicize my new movie." Remy's eyes were practically lit up with enthusiasm. "So I figure we can go in my Beemer and hit a few stops along the way, I can sign some copies of *Babes in Boyland,* meet the fans, and do a few photo ops." She winked at me. "Besides, do you really want to go to work in the state that you're in?"

My job. A bolt of longing shot through me. Just when I was getting somewhere with my career, the supernatural had to go and make my life hell again. She did have a point about working in my current state, though. I'd probably get horny as soon as I saw a naked statue. Still . . . "I think I'm going to say no."

She frowned. "Oh?"

"I'm gonna take a pass. All that porn stuff weirds me out." And turned me on a little too much in my present state. Just thinking about it made a tremor shoot through my body again. I took a sip of cold water to refocus.

"Prude." Remy picked up her coffee cup. "Be that way. I just won't help you, then."

"Wait. Help me how?"

"Who's gonna show you where Delilah lives, smarty pants?"

I scowled. "I need Delilah's help, Remy."

"And I need an assistant on my tour," she said. "I'll look important with an assistant."

I rubbed my forehead. "Do we *have* to do a porn tour?"

Remy dabbed at the corners of her mouth daintily. "It'll be fun."

Yeah, as fun as a pap smear, and involving more vaginas.

I tried to think of a way around this mess. "But if I've got to have sex every day now, I'm going to need to bring along someone for the ride."

"Bring Noah," she said. "I love him."

I stabbed my pancake down the middle. "We're taking a time-out on our relationship."

"Problems with the other Serim, I guess?" Her voice was understanding.

My head shot up. This was the first I'd heard of it. "What do you mean, 'problems'?"

Her eyes grew wide. "Nothing. You going to eat that?" She reached over and snatched a pancake from my plate.

"Remy . . ."

"Nothing I can talk about," she amended. "Or Noah would kill me. And I'm pretty sure I'm wrong, because he would have said something to you."

I frowned, wondering what she knew. But she did have a point. Noah would have said something. "It's just one of those commitment things. We don't see eye to eye."

"Oh." She sighed. "What a shame. Bring Zane with us, then." It was a generous offer. Remy wasn't exactly his biggest fan ever since he'd held a gun to her head. "I'll bring someone, too, so we don't have to share."

Probably a good idea. Much as I liked Remy, I didn't think a threesome would do wonders for our friendship.

"I do have to go to New Orleans," I said, mulling over the idea. "But the Mayan dig is in two weeks. I can't take a long trip." No way was I missing my chance-of-a-lifetime job for an extra autograph stop at a porn store.

Could I even still go on the Mayan dig? A vision of me atop a pyramid, writhing in sexual need, shot through my mind. Would I be forced to drag members of the archaeology team to my tent and have them service me? Hourly? How would I get anything done?

Or would I even live long enough for the dig? I rubbed my arms, suddenly cold.

"No long trip. Got it." Remy beamed, like this had been her plan all along. "I've only got a few stops anyhow. I'll call my publicist and let him know we're confirmed." She shoved the last bite into her mouth and grabbed the tab for our massive late-night breakfast. "The sun rises in a few hours—just enough time to pack."

And just enough time for me to track down my vampire lover and screw his brains out. I was Itching like crazy and I needed him bad.

Yet again, I cursed Mae and her damned burning kiss.

○ ○ ○

By the time Zane got home, the sun was just cresting on the horizon and I'd set my washing machine on spin cycle again in the hopes that the low rotation would ease me toward an orgasm and relieve the Itching that threatened to drive me insane.

I'd been cussing Mae for hours for leaving me with this endless heat in my blood and no outlet. Succubi needed a partner to feed their curse, and a washing machine wasn't cutting it. Masturbation didn't work, either—the magic was in being the recipient of an orgasm, not the orgasm itself (though that was usually pretty magical, too).

I heard the front door slam and leapt up, intending to rip into Zane. I was cranky, horny, and the sun was almost up. I'd only have a few minutes before he'd pass out for his daylight hibernation.

"Where have you been?" I stalked into the living room and scowled, intending on blasting Zane with a few scathing comments before I allowed him to grovel and we could have blistering hot make-up sex.

The sight of him stopped me dead in my tracks. It wasn't the angry snarl on his face or the unheard retort that he bit out. It wasn't the sexy leather trench coat or the messy fall of black hair over his forehead that made my burning body turn from a 6.5 on the Richter scale to an 11.

It was the burning red in his eyes as they met mine.

He was in need, just as badly as me.

"Oh . . . hey," I breathed, all the argument whooshing out of my lungs as the flesh between my legs grew instantly wet. I took a step forward, toward him. "I'm pissed at you."

It didn't sound like I was pissed. It sounded more like *Take me now, baby*.

He threw his car keys down on the table and glared at me. "I'm not in the mood, Jackie. I've had a shit night, and all I want to do is lie down and sleep until tomorrow."

Liar. He might not be in the mood for sex, but his eyes told me what he needed.

And I didn't care if he was in the mood or not. I was.

I grabbed him by the jacket collar, noticing that he smelled heavily of alcohol and cigarettes. He'd been to a club, but at least there was no lipstick on his collar. He hadn't fed. I tugged him toward me, his mouth angling toward mine reluctantly. I could see the barest hint of his fangs brushing against his full mouth, and lord, I liked the look of that.

I bit down on his lower lip, hard. The taste of cigarettes and rum touched my lips, and I swirled my tongue against his mouth, pulling him closer.

He groaned like a dying man. "Jackie, no. I can't do this." His breath was ragged and he feebly tried to push me away. "Not tonight, not right now—unless you want me to feed from you."

Heck no, I wouldn't let him feed from me since our last disastrous episode, when he'd betrayed my trust. He knew it, I knew it, and yet I couldn't resist. My hands slid to the waistband of his pants and I flicked open the button. "I have to have sex tonight, Zane. I can't wait."

Zane stared down into my intensely blue eyes, his hands sliding over my back and ass as if he couldn't help himself. "You're in a bad way."

"Very bad," I agreed, my voice sounding like a sultry purr as his hands slid over me.

A slow, devilish smile spread over his mouth and he raised one hand to cup my cheek, grazing his thumb across my mouth. His eyes were locked into mine, fascinated by the intensity of color. "Been thinking of me all night? So much for Prince Charming, eh?"

A subtle dig at Noah. I nipped Zane's thumb, distracting him. "Let's not talk about Noah."

He stilled, his attention focusing. "Did you guys have a fight?" His voice had a gloating touch to it that irritated me.

Why was everyone so fascinated with whether Noah and I were sleeping together? I moved my hands down the front of his pants, sliding against the hard length waiting there.

"Jackie," he warned, but his hands dug into my hips, dragging me closer to him. Not much of a protest, and I knew I'd won.

Pushing backward, I edged him to the corner of the bed and knocked him onto it. Hooray for a bed. Most of the time we never made it to the bed before we had wild monkey sex.

We fell and I felt Zane adjust under me, shifting to take the pressure off the long black sweep of vampire wings under his leather trench. I grabbed the front of his button-up shirt and ripped it apart. He wasn't protesting any longer, and I straddled him, rotating my hips on top of his as I leaned over him to give him a long kiss.

Our lovemaking was a mutual takeover. His hands jerked at the waistband of my jeans, and I helped him rip them off my body.

Even as I slid my naked flesh over his body, he strained. I could feel the wings ripple under him, trapped by layers of half-discarded clothing and his own body weight. "Need blood," he said, his red eyes flaring as he guided my hips over his thick length and settled me over it.

My entire body quivered with anticipation at the long-sought relief, so damn close. "No blood," I said, rotating my hips and digging his cock deeper into me. "Just sex."

He groaned again, throwing his head back as I squeezed my internal muscles around him and lifted, then lowered again. "Jackie," he warned.

I was past warnings. I didn't care. All I knew was that I had what I needed, and I was taking it.

My body clenched around his cock, fueling my rocking hips faster and faster toward the orgasm that spelled relief. His fingers dug into my hips as I rolled them over him, hard and fast.

It didn't take long. One moment I was shivering and tensing up as my body sped toward the orgasm, my breath catching in my throat as he slammed my hips down over his. Then lights exploded behind my eyes and my body quaked into a rough, ecstatic orgasm.

I breathed a long, low sigh of relief, wiggling my toes.

"I'm glad one of us got what we needed out of this," Zane growled under me, his fingers clenching the soft roundness of my buttocks. He rammed into me again, his eyes piercing red and angry as he thrust upward into my slick flesh.

Okay, so I felt a little guilty at that and rocked my hips against his as he continued to pump inside me, leading me toward another slow, delicious orgasm. Damn, I loved his body against mine. I was even feeling a little generous, now that all the urgent need had seeped out of my body. I reached out and twirled one of his nipples with my finger. "Problem?"

I gasped when he thrust hard and deep inside me, growling again. His fangs glinted against his full lower lip, and he stared at my throat. "You know what I need," he rasped.

Blood—he needed to drink from me. Vampire eyes turned red like mine turned blue—a meter of how badly we needed to feed our urges—and his eyes were a stark, vivid red. But letting Zane drink from me meant putting my body in his control totally and completely. It meant giving him a taste of my powers, and succumbing to the mind-blanking numbness of sleep. A scary thing for one of my kind, seeing as how we didn't sleep. Normally I would have said hell no, and slid off of him like yesterday's pony ride. But I was feeling unsettled and still a bit guilty.

I needed him for more than just sex—with Noah gone, I had no choice but to ask Zane to come on the road trip with me.

A compromise occurred to me, and I leaned back over Zane, letting my breasts brush against his chest as I reached down to kiss those pearly fangs. My carefully thought-out words died into an kittenish whimper of delight when he ground into me with one long, delicious stroke. Oh, yesss . . . I loved Zane's body.

I forced myself to concentrate and kissed his mouth. "I need something from you, too, Zane. Will you do me a small favor?"

His lips caught mine and I felt the scrape of fangs against my lip, biting into me. The mixture of pleasure and pain—and the taste of my own blood in my mouth—left me coiling with excitement once more. "Ask," he rasped, his lips trailing across my chin and down my jawline, hinting at my throat.

"I need a vacation," I said. "A little road trip. And I need you to come with me. Please?" I slid my fingers behind his neck and pressed his mouth against the soft skin of my collarbone. If he bit, I knew I had him—and my trip.

"Whatever you want," he growled against my throat, and I felt his fangs puncture my flesh. The sharp sting was followed by the most delicious feeling of warmth as he began to feed from my throat. Heat rolled through my body and coaxed me into another orgasm, hard and fast. His came moments after mine.

Just like the last time Zane had fed from me, he clasped me to him, stroking my body until the aftershocks left me, his thrusts slowing. My eyelids began to flutter closed, my body drifting into the feeding-induced sleep brought on by a vampire's bite. I wrapped my arms around my lover and held him close, even as I began to drift away, and I felt his tongue rasp against my skin, closing the bite marks with tender care.

"It's not like you to make deals, Princess," he said, his voice sleepy in my ear. "Next thing you know, you'll be working for the queen."

Ouch. I was *nothing* like the queen, or any of the other deal makers who used people to get their way. But the thought disturbed me long after I drifted away.

Succubi don't dream like normal people. Our bodies don't have a "sleep" mode like vampires or Serim, so the only time we get to shut down is after a vampire feeding, since it's magically altered to put the victim to sleep. Which doesn't really bother me for the most part, but there's times that being wired at four in the morning can get to you.

Still, sinking into the bite-induced sleep was not a comfortable feeling, either. I'd grown used to the control I had over my body, and to slide into unconsciousness was disturbing. My pulse pounded with worry even as everything in my body went limp with sleep. I didn't have my own dreams, though. That part of my brain was turned off for good. Instead, I hovered on the edge of Zane's conscious mind, leeching off of his thoughts. My physical form had been turned off, and my mind transferred to his.

The landscape around me was the same, the small, slightly messy room of my apartment. Clothes were scattered on the floor, and one of my legs hung off the bed. I even snored—much to my dream-embarrassment. Zane slept peacefully next to me, his arm locked around my waist.

He lay on his stomach, nude, and the black sweep of his glossy wings flexed over my body. Even in my sleep he sought to protect me.

A warm, squishy feeling took over me and I relaxed. Zane had gone into day hibernation, and his dreams were calm and normal. There would be no betrayal this time. The bad times were in the past, and we were moving on to a bright new future.

Happy, I settled into his mind and made sure that he dreamed about me.

At some point later, I awoke and realized I'd slid back into my own body. Zane still slept next to me and the sun was high in the sky, which meant that he'd sleep for a while longer. That was fine, because I had a lot to do before he woke up.

No messages from Noah on my cell phone. I contemplated sending him a text but I didn't like the idea of him "punishing" me by depriving me of his presence. Plus I was still fixed on Remy's slip of the tongue last night. What had she meant by "the Serim wouldn't allow it"?

After a gratifying lunch of four sandwiches, a full bag of Doritos, and two beers, I packed for the trip. According to the internet, 1600 miles lay between here and New Orleans. Twenty-six hours in the car. Even with Remy's few stops, we could be done with this whole ridiculous curse thing within a matter of days since we didn't have to sleep.

That thought cheered me immensely, and I even ate a couple of Twinkies to celebrate.

Getting the time off work to go on the road trip was stunningly easy. All I had to do was call Dr. Morgan, turn on the waterworks, and explain that I was having some personal issues because I'd just broken up with my boyfriend.

"Mr. Gideon is still going to fund the Mayan expedition, isn't he?" Fear edged his voice. "We leave in two weeks!"

So glad he was worried about me. "I'm sure Mr. Gideon won't change his mind about the expedition—"

"You're sure?" He sounded relieved, then his voice turned suave again. "You're still going to be coming on the dig, aren't you? I hope that your troubles with Mr. Gideon won't affect your work. You know I'll need someone I can lean on."

And someone whose shirt he could look down. "Oh, I'll be there, Dr. Morgan," I told him. "This is my first archaeological dig, and I'm not going to miss it just because Noah's being a control freak. I'll avoid him."

"Hmmm." Dr. Morgan didn't sound convinced. "It's vital that Mr. Gideon remain interested and active in the dig. Perhaps you should apologize to him."

Apologize? I could feel my face purple at the thought and bit back the retort that bubbled up. If I protested any more he'd kick me off the trip, and that was the last thing I wanted. I'd been looking forward to this dig for weeks. "I'll talk to Noah. By the time of the dig, I'm sure we'll be back together." I couldn't imagine him staying mad at me for that long.

"You're a good girl, Jackie. Just think of what's best for the department. I know you'll make the right decision."

In other words, he wanted me to swallow my pride and whore myself out, as long as he got to go on his precious dig. I hung up. Everything was in place now.

I was struggling with the suitcase zipper when a gentle snore made me pause. I glanced over at the bedroom, but Zane wasn't in the bed any longer. The sun had gone down, and rumpled sheets were the only thing left on the mattress. He whistled in the distance, and the shower turned on, drowning out any noise he made.

The snore came again, from the other side of the couch. With dread, I slid over to the side and peeked over.

And groaned.

My pizza boy from the night before was still there, still unconscious.

How could I possibly have forgotten that? I was the world's worst person ever.

I was still staring at his sleeping body when Zane wandered into the living room, half-dressed. "What's wrong, Princess?"

I gestured at the comatose man on the floor. "This. I don't know what I'm supposed to do with him." I tugged on the ends of my hair, trying to think. "I can't just leave him here."

Zane scratched his hard stomach and leaned over the pizza boy, looking as if it wasn't any dire problem. "Want me to get rid of the body for you?"

I gasped. "He's not dead!"

The vampire grinned, the look on his face sly. "Want me to kill him and *then* get rid of the body?" His eyes flicked red.

I threw a couch cushion at him. "That is *not* funny." I ignored his chuckle and looked down at the pizza boy again. "I need to get him out of my apartment—alive—and somehow not get caught by the police."

He gave me a skeptical look. "You won't get caught by the police if he's buried in a fiel—"

"No!" I buried my face in my hands. "Can you please just help me with this and not make it worse?"

"Whatever you want," Zane said. His casual, easy look turned shuttered. "This road trip . . . is Noah going?" The jealousy had returned to his face, turning its beautiful planes hard.

That was a rapid topic change. "No," I assured him. "We're taking a little time off from each other."

Silence.

The smile returned to his mouth, and he moved over to my side. "That," he said, stroking my cheek tenderly, "is very good news. So you've finally made up your mind?" He dipped to press a light kiss on my mouth, his tongue whispering against my lips. "Glad you've come to your senses about that self-righteous asshole."

I pulled away, frowning up at him. "Noah broke up with *me*."

He shrugged, his grin displaying gleaming white fangs. "I don't care, as long as this means you and I are exclusive. No more seeking him out for sex, and I won't have to go hunting in bars for blood—"

"Whoa, there." I pulled away from him, my eyes wide. "I'm not going to be your one and only blood supply." That would mean dooming myself to only half the day again, and if my schedule was going to match Zane's, that meant no daylight, no regular shopping hours . . . and no Noah. Ever. The Serim slept through the nighttime.

His mouth tightened slightly. "You just fed me and things were fine. Don't tell me we're going back to this."

I thought hard, trying to come up with something that would appease him and still give me my freedom. "How about a test run? We stay exclusive for the next few weeks, I let you drink from me, and we'll see how this road trip works out. I really need you for this."

Looking mollified, he nudged the comatose guy with his foot. "Well, then, what are we going to do with this?"

"We'll figure something out." I decided to call Remy, who had the answer, even if it was an odd one.

"Bring him to my house," she said. "Ethel is here and she'll watch him for us."

My brows furrowed as I tried to picture that. Her little old housekeeper would probably just dust around him. "You don't think he needs medical attention? Won't his body waste away and die in a few days if he doesn't get anything to eat or drink?"

"If it gets to that point, I'll have Ethel stage a break-in. She can hit him on the head with a vase and say he's never regained consciousness. The hospital will take him from there. It'll work. You'll see."

Was I the only one concerned about the fact he was in a coma?

Still, Remy's idea was the most plausible plan we had. Zane and I took the pizza boy's arms and tried to make it look like we were supporting a very drunk friend as we staggered down the halls of my apartment building and out to the parking garage nearby. A few of the neighbors gave us disapproving looks, but no one stopped us.

I drove the Ford Explorer—which I'd borrowed from Noah earlier this summer and had conveniently forgotten to give back—to Remy's mansion across town. Our luggage and Coma Guy were stashed in the back, and

Zane sat in front. He was unusually silent—no sharp observations or witty comebacks; the only sound was the faint sizzle of burning paper as he sucked on cigarette after cigarette.

I concentrated on driving, ignoring the fact that he seemed unusually pensive. The sooner we got to Remy's house, the sooner we could get this show on the road. At the end of Remy's winding driveway, I parked behind a gleaming new car: a gigantic, candy-red Hummer.

Remy came down the driveway as soon as she saw my headlights, and was at my window as soon as I put the car in park. "Hey! Do you like my new wheels?"

The monster vehicle was taller than I was; we'd need a stepladder to get into the thing. The tires looked like they could roll over small third-world countries. "It's . . . nice. We could have gone in your BMW, though. Don't these things guzzle gas?"

"Oh, pooh." She waved a hand, dismissing my concerns. "We need something that screams 'money', and I didn't want a limo dragging us around the country. You don't think this says 'road trip' to you?"

Oh, it was saying something all right. Something like *Please rob the overprivileged occupants of their wallets.*

"So, is Zane coming?" She looked over and made a little pout when she saw him emerge from the Explorer, a new cigarette in his mouth. "I see he is."

Zane slid around the front of the car and put an arm around my waist, giving Remy a casual smirk. "Anything Jackie wants, Jackie gets."

Really? Jackie sure didn't feel like that sometimes. If I got whatever I wanted, why did I feel like my life was out of control?

"Well," Remy said with a drawl, "I invited a friend, too." She linked her arm with mine and began pulling me toward her house.

"Who is this friend? Does he know about our problem with the pizza boy? Or the Itch?" Who was Remy trusting with our secrets?

"No, no, and you'll see." Remy beamed at me and strode through her massive front door. "Drake's harmless and perfect for this trip."

"Drake?" I raised an eyebrow at her. "That sounds like a porn star name."

I should have guessed by the way she grinned. Sitting in Remy's living room, pants unbuttoned, sat a greasy man of indeterminate age. A five-o'clock shadow covered his jaw, and a beer bottle hung from his hand. The hair on his head was slicked back—either from hair gel or the fact that he hadn't washed it in several days—and curled against the collar of his open shirt. Multiple gold chains looped his neck.

"Hey." He glanced over at me, and gave me a quick up-and-down look, his eyes settling at breast level. "You in the business, darlin'?"

"Uh, no." I jerked Remy to one side. "Can we talk?"

She wiggled her fingers at Drake and pulled me into the kitchen. "Something wrong?"

"Yeah. Who is that creep on your sofa?"

· Remy grinned. "He's my costar in the movie we'll be publicizing."

I groaned and peeked into the living room, watching Zane drag the pizza guy in and dump him on the couch opposite Drake. To his credit, Drake didn't freak out at the sight of my rather angry-looking boyfriend or the fact that he was dumping some unconscious guy there. He just took another swig of his beer and continued to flip the TV channel.

"You sure that you want to bring him along?" I asked.

Remy tucked a long strand of black hair behind her ear and shrugged. "He's harmless. I think he fried his brains on X in the eighties. He's got an enormous dick and he's usually good to go several rounds, so if you and Zane are fighting, I'm sure he'd be more than happy to help you out."

"Bite your tongue!"

Two porn stars, a sulking vampire, and me, crammed in a Hummer for the next week?

Fun.

CHAPTER FIVE

We weren't on the road for more than a few minutes when Zane frowned at me. "We need to talk."

I glanced up front. Remy had both of her hands on the steering wheel and was rocking her head to Green Day's "American Idiot." In the passenger seat, Drake leaned against his seat belt and snored, comatose at 3:00 a.m.

Zane and I shared the backseat, and it was just dark enough to allow us a tiny bit of privacy. Not enough for a quiet conversation, though, since I suspected Remy would listen in on anything we said, radio or no radio. That irritated me. Actually, a lot of stuff irritated me at the moment.

I leaned over to whisper in his ear. "Do we have to do this right now?" Damn, he smelled nice. A lock of his hair hung over his ear, and I reached up to touch it. Soft. I got all tingly just thinking about that brushing over my skin.

He slid down the seat—no safety belt for Zane—and moved against me. Desire shot through my nerve endings and I gave him a wary look, trying to scoot away from him. I didn't need him to turn me on in the car, not when we were just starting our trip. Nor did I trust the look in his eyes, which were quickly turning red with need.

"We need to talk about this road trip, Jackie." Zane put his hand on my leg, and my senses immediately flared to life. "A road trip with two porn stars? Where the hell are we going?"

I had omitted a few of the details of our trip. No wonder he was so irritated at me. I flushed in the darkness and shifted in my seat, trying to resist the urge to put my hand over his where it rested on my knee, and then move it farther up my leg. Nope, wasn't going to do that.

"To New Orleans," I said. The moonlight hit the hard angles of his face just right, illuminating his unworldly beauty . . . and the gleam of red in his eyes. "I need to visit a succubus named Delilah."

"New Orleans!" His voice rose. "Do you know how long it will take to get to New Orleans by taking the highway?"

"Twenty-six hours?" I said helpfully.

Zane swore, leaning away from me.

I felt his hand twitch against my leg, and against my will, I pried it off my leg. "Zane," I said quietly. "Don't touch me right now."

Don't touch me because I'm cursed. Don't touch me or we'll be making out in front of Remy and Drake, and I've no desire to have public sex.

Especially when the other two occupants of the car were porn stars.

It was the wrong thing to say to him. I knew it as soon as it slipped out of my mouth. Zane gave a low, ugly laugh and put his hand back on my knee, sliding it farther up my thigh. I sucked in a breath and just like that, the Itch flared into existence once more.

"Don't touch you?" Zane leaned back in, whispering low against my ear. "Isn't that what you wanted me for on this trip? To service you while you run off with your little friend?" There was a hard note to his voice.

"You don't understand," I said, squirming in my seat and trying to pull his hand away. Oh God, but I wished he'd move it higher even as I tried to pry it off me.

It was like he could read my mind. He ignored my feeble efforts to remove his hand and slid it all the way up to the apex of my thighs, rubbing his fingers against my throbbing cleft. "Don't touch you like this?"

I could feel the heat of his skin even through my clothing. A small moan escaped me and my legs clamped around his hand. "Zane."

"Isn't this what you wanted, Princess?"

Bastard.

A rest stop sign whizzed past on the empty highway. "Stop the car, Remy," I gritted out.

She turned down the radio, pretending to not be aware of what was happening in the backseat. "Do what?"

"I said, stop the car at the rest stop." My voice had risen a strangled octave.

"You got it, chief," she said, her playful words falling like rocks in the silent car.

Zane released me and leaned back, lighting up a cigarette.

I thought it would take forever for the Hummer to
reach the rest stop, but we finally pulled in and parked
at the curb. There was a public restroom with a side
for men and a side for women. Picnic tables littered
the empty grounds, and the only light came from the
nearby snack machine, the glass covered with moths
that swirled around it in the darkness. A half dozen
truck rigs were parked in the lot, the drivers asleep
inside.

Drake's sleepy question rose above the low, heavy
hum of an idling semi. "Where are we?"

"Restroom break," Remy murmured. "Go back to
sleep." She looked in the rearview mirror at me. "You
okay?"

"I'll be fine in a minute," I grabbed Zane's hand and
flung my door open. "Come on."

I expected him to retort something at my strident
tone, or at least to make some sort of sarcastic remark.
But he simply followed as I headed for the women's restroom, never letting go of his hand.

The bathroom was dingy, the counters coated with a
layer of grime that only neglect could foster. Toilet paper
streamed on the floor from under one of the stalls, but
all the bathroom doors were ajar, which meant that we
were alone.

Finally.

"What's the meaning of this, Jackie?" Zane said, pulling his hand out of mine as I strode into the bathroom. A fleet of moths fluttered overhead by the fluorescent light.

I turned back to Zane and put my hands around his neck, dragging his face down to mine for a long kiss that I hoped communicated my urgency. "I need you," I said softly.

His eyes darkened to a deep red and he stared down at me in surprise. "Your eyes. They're blue—"

I put my hands on his hips and pulled him toward the counter, not caring anymore how dirty the bathroom was. My body was a tight, tingling mess of nerves, and only one thing could help me. My fingers went to the buttons on his shirt and began to undo them. "I have a bit of a problem, Zane."

He chuckled, needing no encouragement to bend over me and nuzzle my earlobe. His weight pressed me against the bathroom counter. His hand reached between us, brushing against my erect nipples through my cotton T-shirt. "Doesn't seem like much of a problem to me. I thought we were coming in here so we could solve both of our problems."

"I'm cursed," I said.

He paused, his hands falling from my skin. "Cursed? What do you mean, you're cursed?"

I thought it was pretty obvious, but maybe it was just me. "My powers are out of control, and I need more sex, more often. If I don't find a way to fix it, I'll eventually die."

"How long have you known?" Zane dragged his hand through his hair, moving away from me and pacing in front of the mirrors. They showed nothing but my unhappy face; Zane had no reflection.

"Since last night," I said. "A demon told me I was cursed, but not directly."

"How did the demon tell you?" He sounded puzzled.

I didn't follow him. "Beg pardon?"

"You said that a demon indirectly told you that you were cursed. What did she do? Pass you a note after class?"

Jerk. "That's *not* what I said. A demon told me that I was cursed. The *curse* is an indirect one." Did he want it spelled out in crayon?

He looked at me with horror. "You've known since last night and you let me drink from you?" His shout was enough to blow my hair back off my forehead.

"Like I had a choice?" My own voice rose and I crossed my arms over my chest. "Noah is gone. You're pushing me, and I don't have any other options—"

His face grew cold. "So that's what this is about?"

I could have kicked myself. "That's not what I meant—"

"So it's not that you wanted me? You're just cursed and don't have any other options?" A flicker of raw pain showed on his face, quickly masked again. "Were you ever planning on giving up Noah? Or on being my blood partner? Or was that just desperation talking?"

I had no answers for him, and the conversation was getting into too-sensitive territory. "You know what?" I willed my lower lip not to tremble, but it didn't work. "Screw you. Not everything is about you, you know." I jabbed my finger into my own chest, glaring at him through tears. "I am *dying* here. This curse is going to kill me unless I do something about it. So no, I can't think about someone else right now. I have to think about me, and how I'm going to get through this. And if you can't wait for me to come out the other side and get better, maybe it's best that I find that out now."

Zane raked a hand through his hair, staring at the ground. He looked up at me and took a step forward, back to my side. The pain in his face was gone, all smooth, self-possessed vampire once more. "I'm sorry, Princess," he said huskily, running a hand up and down my arm to soothe me before reaching up to cup my face. He kissed my forehead, trying to comfort me. "We'll figure everything out later. It'll be okay. Do you know who did this to you?"

"No," I said. "I haven't done anything— or anyone— out of the ordinary." His hands felt good on my arms, soothing. I leaned into his touch. "Maybe I ate a cursed Taco Bell burrito or something."

He chuckled at my joke, some of the tension leaving his face. "I sincerely doubt warlocks are working at Taco Bell, waiting to strike down any succubi that go through the drive-thru."

"You don't know how often I go through the drive-thru. So it was a warlock who did this to me?"

His face became shuttered, and distant. "I don't know, Jackie. I don't know anything about curses." His gaze held me pinned in place as he stared down at me. "Are you telling me the truth? About the curse?"

"I am," I said, somewhat mollified by the contrition in his voice. "Don't look at me like that."

A hint of a smile touched his face again. "Like what?"

"Like I'm dirty."

"Baby," he said tenderly, his hand brushing my hair off my cheek. "You're not dirty. It's just a little . . . overwhelming."

"How do you think I feel? I'm the one that has to have sex every . . ." I checked my watch. "Twenty-three hours now, and it's getting worse. I stole the pizza boy's mind, too. My powers are going out of control and I don't know how to stop it."

"Is that why we're on a road trip with the porn stars?" Zane continued to stroke my jaw, speaking in that soothing voice that made me weak in the knees.

"Remy needs to promote her movie, and I figured it'd be a distraction. Besides, she said she knows this Delilah chick, and I need her help."

He sighed, pressing his forehead against mine. "What a mess."

"That's why I need you to come with me," I said, touching his cheeks and pulling his mouth back down to mine again. He pulled away, instead pressing his mouth against my jaw and nuzzling my ear. Distracted by the sensation of his teeth nipping at my earlobe, I wrapped my arms around him. "I'll go nuts if it's just me and Remy on this trip."

"Don't forget Drake," Zane said.

Ugh. I'd have preferred to forget about him altogether. "We could leave Drake by the side of the road," I said. "Remy could always find someone new. *Anyone* new."

"Don't want to share?" His hands settled underneath my behind and lifted me up on the edge of the sink, cradling me against his erection. "Because I'm sure I could handle both you and Remy at once, if I had to."

I smacked him on the arm, but it was obvious from the laugh on his face that he was teasing me. "You're a jerk. I don't know why I stay with you."

"Because you need me, Princess." The low, husky statement held a wealth of emotion. He put my arms around his neck and reached between us, unfastening my shorts. His fingers delved against my panties, and slid down to the wet, hot flesh underneath.

"Oh, yeah?" I meant for it to be playful, but when his fingers found just that right spot, it changed from a tease to a breathy "Oh, *yeah*."

"You know the best thing about being a succubus?" His hand splayed across my back as he leaned me farther back. The back of my head rested against one of the mirrors and I was pretty sure there was a faucet digging into my back, just like I was pretty sure that I didn't care. His fingers shifted again, touching my cleft and seeking the perfect spot within to stroke and tease. "They don't have to give pleasure—they can take it."

With that he slid a thick finger inside me, and I was lost. My cry of delight echoed in the bathroom, repeated again when Zane's seeking mouth latched on to my breast and teased my nipple through the fabric. His fingers pumped inside me, his thumb flicking against my clit as he made love to me with his hand, and I spiraled out of control, my hips bucking against him as the crashing orgasm overtook me.

When my hips slowed their undulations, Zane helped me down. He kissed my cheek gently, then helped me pull my panties and shorts back around my waist like a solicitous lover.

"Zane," I breathed, still feeling googly and panting from the hot petting. "What about you?" My hand slid down the front of his pants, molding the thick erection outlined there.

He pulled my hand away and deflected me with a quick kiss to my palm, his eyes bright red as he smiled at me. "Remy will be wondering where you are, Princess. My needs can wait for another day." He swatted me on the bottom. "Go on back and I'll catch up in a minute." He leaned heavily against the sink, but the smile on his face was the same old teasing Zane.

Concern furrowed my brow, but I didn't want to pester him. "All right." I turned to head back out of the bathroom.

"Jackie," Zane said, his voice soft.

I turned around to look back at him, curious. "Yes?"

"You're sure you don't know who did this?"

I straightened my clothes and pushed my hair out of my face, thinking that everyone could probably tell what we'd been doing. Lord. "I can't think of anyone, no. I mean, who hates me enough to kill me? Other than the queen, but I haven't seen her."

He shrugged. "We'll figure it out." His gaze roamed over me, looking vulnerable for a moment. Then he pulled out his cigarettes and tapped one against the box. "I just want to know, though . . . do you trust me?"

That was an odd segue. He'd asked me that before, and it had gotten me into trouble. But we'd come so far from the halo-hunting expedition that I felt confident in my answer. "I do trust you, Zane."

"Good," he said, his eyes intense on me. His serious look changed into a smile, and he put the cigarette between his lips. "I'm going to finish this and then I'll head back."

"All right." A bit bewildered by his abrupt changes in mood, I headed out to the Hummer, propelled by the subtle compulsion in our conversation. First item of business—new shorts and panties, since mine were damp and uncomfortable.

Across the parking lot, Remy leaned against the hood of the vehicle, looking utterly bored. She perked at the sight of me and approached with a bottle of hand sanitizer. "Did you touch anything in there?"

I obligingly allowed her to squirt me with copious amounts of the sanitizer and rubbed my hands with

it. I was still feeling a little boneless, but a lot better. Things were starting to look up. Even my appetite
returned.

"So are we about ready to go?"

I nodded. "I think so. Zane just needs a moment and
he'll be back." I gave her a bright smile. "Everything is
cool. Do we have anything to eat?"

She eyed me. "You *sure* he's okay with this trip? It
doesn't seem like Zane's kind of thing, if you ask me.
Vampires hate being dragged out of their territory."

"He's fine," I assured her, thinking back to his reaction to the whole Noah situation. How troubled he'd
been, and how hurt. I hadn't expected that. "I think the
curse took him aback. He didn't seem too pleased when
I told him." Opening the back door, I climbed over the
seat and dug into the luggage piled in the far end of the
Hummer. At the front of the vehicle, Drake still snored,
oblivious to his surroundings.

"I wouldn't imagine so," Remy said. "Considering that
they can be passed by exchanging bodily fluids."

I paused from my fishing around in the luggage.
"Really?" As my fingers latched around a pair of khaki
shorts, I felt an uncomfortable quiver. Our little scene
in the bathroom was the first time that Zane hadn't
gone all the way with me. Sure, we'd gotten each other
off before, but this it was the first time that our romps
hadn't ended with a major throw-down. Eyeing the
snoring Drake, I shimmied out of my damp clothes and
wadded them into a plastic bag, then stuffed it at the

bottom of my luggage. "Zane's fine with it," I told her, my tone convinced if my body wasn't. "He knows I need his help right now. He wouldn't abandon me."

"Oh, sweetie," Remy said, her voice weary. "When will you learn not to trust vampires?"

Irritated, I slid back out of the car and slammed the door shut behind me. "He's fine. I'll go get him and prove it to you."

Remy just gave me a pitying look. "I'll be here."

I stomped back to the bathroom, expecting to find anything. Zane feeding from another woman's neck. Zane jerking off in front of the mirror. Zane smashing something because he was trying to get control of his body.

What I didn't expect to find was his trench coat—the staple of his wardrobe, which concealed his beautiful wings from the rest of the world—in a heap in the middle of the floor.

And a note on top of it, written on a flyer for a nearby cavern.

Sorry, Princess. There's a few things I need to take care of first. We'll meet again soon. Promise.

He'd left me.

Flown away without even saying good-bye.

Dumped. Again.

I didn't know whether to feel sorry for myself or angry. With slow-moving hands, I picked up his jacket, brushed it off, and crumpled the note into my pocket.

So much for all that talk about trust and how far we'd come. I should have known I couldn't count on Zane when the chips were down. And with Noah out of my life, who did I have to turn to now?

Tucking the trench coat under my arm, I went out to tell Remy that she'd been right after all.

CHAPTER SIX

"Snap out of it, girlfriend," Remy said, patting my knee. "You knew he was untrustworthy when you took him in. Remember? That whole kidnapping-in-Egypt thing?"

In the front passenger seat, I leaned against the window and stared out at the flat, flat farmlands around us, an empty can of Pringles cradled in my arms. God, Wyoming sucked. Even the beautiful sunrise couldn't lift my spirits. "I thought he'd changed, Remy. I thought he loved me."

"Well, do you love him?"

I gave her a dirty look and reached for a new can. If I loved Zane or not, it wasn't anyone's business but mine.

She just grinned at me. "That's what I thought. So why's it matter if he loves you? He's probably all freaked out about the curse, darling. We'll get rid of it and he'll come crawling back to you in no time."

"But that's not the point," I wailed, cramming chips into my mouth. "I need him now, and he's abandoned me!"

A big, hairy-knuckled hand clamped down on my shoulder from behind, the thumb stroking my arm through my sleeve in a rather repulsive fashion. "I'm here for you, sugar," Drake said, his voice oozing sympathy. "If you need a shoulder to cry on, you just come sit here." He patted his lap.

"Thanks, Drake, but I think I'm okay." I shrugged his hand off my shoulder (damn curse—his touch actually felt pretty good). The last thing I needed was some porn guy thinking he could get an easy lay out of things.

He gave me a long, slow pat, his eyes knowing. "Of course."

Remy shot Drake a warning look and turned to smile back at me, all cheerfulness. "Look, Jackie, it'll be all right. Maybe he just had to leave for a bit. He could be coming back later tonight, when the sun sets."

I gave her a dark look. "We both know he's not coming back."

She checked her lipstick in the rearview mirror, then shrugged at me. "Well, how long until the next time the Itch hits?"

I wrapped my arms around my waist and hugged myself. "About a day. Maybe less."

Remy brightened. "That's not so bad. We're about to cross over the Colorado state line and we should be in Denver in a few hours. I have my first appearance at the Big Porn Barn there, and that should take your mind off things."

Ugh—that's right. I had to go on the porn tour with her as her assistant. "Do I *have* to go?"

She gave me a wounded look. "All the big stars have assistants."

"All right, all right," I said, feeling guilty for not sharing her enthusiasm. "But I'm going to be a very low-key assistant. Don't boss me around, and I'll try and look busy the whole time." I had a baseball cap and sunglasses in my bag. I could wear those, hide my hair, and let Remy have all the attention. *I* sure as heck didn't want any.

"That's great!" She glanced back at Drake and smiled. "Show her the T-shirt we got for her!"

"T-shirt?" The words were barely out of my mouth before a bright pink baby tee was pressed into my hands by Drake's sweaty ones. I shook it out, then stared at Remy with horror. PORN STAR'S ASSISTANT blazed across the chest in bright green lettering. "I have to wear this?"

"It makes it seem like a bigger deal if I show up with an assistant," Remy said, giving me a sheepish look. "This was all sort of last minute, so the budget wasn't that hot."

"Show her the matching hot pants," Drake said, a bit too close to my ear. "They say PORN STAR'S ASS on them. Get it? Assistant? Ass?"

"No," I said firmly. "No hot pants. I'll wear the T-shirt, but I will die before you get me in porn star hot pants."

"You're no fun," Remy sulked.

"That's what I've been told," I agreed, pulling out my

BlackBerry and checking my messages for the ninth time in the past fifteen minutes. Still nothing from Zane. And since the sun was high in the sky, I wouldn't get anything for the next several hours. I sighed, my spirits plummeting. He'd really gone and abandoned me after all.

"Why don't you call Noah?" Remy's voice cut into my thoughts.

Not such a good idea, even though I'd been thinking the same thing. "And what should I say to him? 'Hey, miss you lots. Zane dumped me, so we can be solo now. Oh, and I'm cursed, and a demon needs me to go and visit Delilah in New Orleans. How are you?'" I shook my head, rubbing my thumb along the side of my BlackBerry. "Somehow I don't think that would go over so well."

"Noah's an understanding sort," Remy said. "Maybe you should give him a chance."

Maybe she was right. I hesitated for a moment, then hit the speed-dial button for Noah's number. The phone rang seven times, and just when I was convinced that he was ignoring my call and I'd have to leave a message, the line clicked and picked up.

"Yes?" Noah's deep voice caressed my ear, turning my insides to liquid.

"Hey," I said, eloquent as always. I felt suddenly shy, realizing the others could hear everything we said. I turned toward my window, trying for any privacy I could get.

"Where are you?" he asked.

"Road trip. With Remy." I left out the fact that there was a greasy porn dude hanging over my shoulder, listening in to my conversation. "We've got something we need to take care of in New Orleans." I couldn't bring myself to tell Noah I was cursed. My pride still stung from the look of disgust that Zane had given me.

"I see." A pause, then, a low question. "You're not in any trouble, are you, Jackie?"

Me? Trouble? I laughed—perhaps a bit too gaily—to show him that I had no cares in the world. "Nah, just a road trip for the girls. Just fun."

"Ah."

Man, he sure wasn't very talkative. "You still mad at me?"

His tone grew decidedly colder. "That depends. Have you decided?"

"Decided on what?"

"On which one of us you choose. You can't have it both ways, Jackie. You can't have both a vampire and a Serim at your beck and call. I can't stand to be around that bastard, much less know that you're running from my arms to his." Vehemence filled his voice, surprising in its intensity. He'd never said anything like this to me before. "I'm tired of fighting for your attention, so you have to choose."

"Choose!" I sputtered into the phone. "Not this again. Why—"

I found myself talking to the dial tone. He'd hung up on me.

"Jerk!" I tossed the phone into my purse, resisting the urge to stomp on my handbag for good measure. "Who does he think he is?"

Remy shrugged, staring ahead at the open road. "When you live for a couple of thousand years, you tend to get cranky when someone else plays with your toys."

The Big Porn Barn was a converted barn on the highway just outside of Denver, sandwiched between a liquor store and a feed barn. I perked up at the fact that it was pretty much in the middle of nowhere. Maybe it wouldn't be too busy. Maybe no one would be around to see me in my tight, neon "Porn Star's Assistant" T-shirt. Maybe we could get this over with relatively quickly.

But as soon as we pulled into the parking lot, I knew this would be bad. Every space was full, and there were cars parked along the fire lane as well. A big banner hung from the door. TODAY ONLY—REMY SUMMORE & DRAKE LE SERPENT SIGNING AUTOGRAPHS!

Drake the Snake? I should have guessed.

Remy pulled up in the middle of the parking lot and looked in the mirror, smoothing her hair. She wore a white sundress that consisted of spaghetti straps, a few frills, and not much else. It showed off her lovely dark olive skin and the dark jet sweep of her hair admirably. "Isn't this exciting?"

I jammed a baseball cap over my bright red hair and put on a pair of sunglasses. "Not really."

She refused to be brought down by my sour mood. Giving me a cheeky grin, she slid out of the car and started for the store. Then, she paused and looked back at me. "Can you walk behind me?"

"Are you kidding me?"

"Like a real assistant? You can hold my bottle of water." She stuck her lip out, begging. "*Please*, Jackie? Pretty please please please?" She punctuated each please with a little hop.

"Okay, okay," I said, taking the water from her and eyeing the hopping. "Just don't ever do that again."

Remy beamed at me and headed for the store, and I reluctantly followed a few steps behind, trying to look as inconspicuous as possible.

The store was an absolute crush of men. As soon as Remy walked through the doors, a cheer went up and cameras began to flash. Drake seemed unsurprised, his expression unchanging as he held the door open for me. I quickly followed behind.

From there, the place turned into a madhouse. For hours, Remy posed with people for photographs, winked, vamped, and generally made every single horny, middle-aged man there fall in love with her. Her eyes were a sparkling blue, which told me that she was just as turned on as the crowd was. I did my best to slink around the back of the throng, nursing a water bottle and scowling at any man that got within ten feet of me.

Drake wasn't nearly as popular as Remy. He had his own table for autographs and photos, but there were no women in the store. A few men came up for an auto-graph, which made me eye him in a new light. Mean-while, Remy continued to sign a stack of calendars as high as my arm, and flirted and kissed every single man that came to her table.

I checked my watch for the ninth time in as many minutes. Four hours, and it didn't look like the crowd was dying down yet. I was hungry, but the only thing in the store were edible underwear, and I wasn't about to eat that in front of this mob. A few of the men had given me interested looks, but I shooed them toward Remy's table. When I couldn't stand it any longer, I headed over to Remy and bent to whisper in her ear. "It's half past noon, Remy. When are we leaving here?"

She pouted at my weary face. "I promised I'd stay for a few more hours and sign. We're selling a small fortune here today, and just think of all the publicity."

I groaned. "You lick men's schlongs on camera, Remy. If you really wanted publicity, you'd make out with one right here on the sales floor."

Remy brightened. "Do you think that would work?"

"Forget. It."

She gave me sad eyes. "Please? Just a little longer?"

"Oh, all right." I could never win with her. "One more hour, and then we're leaving. Remember my curse? The one we're supposed to stop before I starve to death?"

"I remember." She waved her hand at me. "Go do something assistant-ish."

"Excuse me," said a man to my side, pushing ahead

with his calendar. "You need to wait in line, just like everyone else."

I pointed out the helpful job title emblazoned across my chest. "See this? It says Assistant. I'm busy right now *assisting* Miss Summore."

Remy put a hand on my arm and smiled brightly to the man. "Ignore her. It's her time of the month."

Irritated, I retreated to the far side of the room and planted myself in the metal chair between the bondage videos and gay porn. I watched the proceedings with bored detachment, trying not to think about how much time was slipping through our fingers . . . or how much it hurt that Zane had abandoned me.

Somewhere in the middle of this misery, I noticed someone was watching me. The skin on the back of my neck shivered a bit, and I scanned the crowd. At first I didn't see anything—there was the usual set of college guys, balding men with spare tires, and a few random individuals that didn't stand out. But then I saw him at the back of the room.

Tall and well groomed with a mane of dark brown hair, he looked to be in his late twenties and well kept. And by well kept, I meant gorgeous. His lean face was something out of a Michelangelo sculpture, the dark, swarthy tan hinting at a mixed heritage as much as his neat clothing hinted at a real job.

He didn't seem like the type who would be inspired by a visit from a porn star. And given the fact that he was watching me and not Remy, it made my hackles rise a little. I flicked a quick look around to see if I was mistaken, but that didn't seem like the case.

When he saw me look over at him, he winked and sank back into the crowd.

Unnerved, I glanced over at Remy again. She had her arms around two military men and was posing between them as a third soldier snapped photos. She was doing her best sultry porn-star look and wasn't paying a bit of attention to me.

I looked back to the man in question, but he was gone. I hadn't noticed if he was wearing a long leather jacket, one of the trademarks of Zane's kind. Serim, maybe? Had Noah sent someone to follow me?

A hand tapped me on the shoulder. "Excuse me, miss."

I nearly jumped out of my skin.

The man standing next to me—balding with a ponytail—looked taken aback at my fright. He drew his hand back protectively, a business card tucked between meaty fingers. "Sorry, miss. Didn't mean to scare you."

I put a hand to my chest, feeling my heart flutter under my skin. "It's okay. I'm just a little edgy." And hormonal. And heading toward horny.

He eyed me strangely, then extended the business card again. "The guy over there asked me to give this to you."

Wary, I took the card from his fingers. "Which guy?" I looked back where the brown-haired stranger had been standing, but he was gone.

The man looked over at the exact same spot and made

a noise in his throat. "Huh. He must have left. It's a long line to see Miss Summore." As if remembering where he was, he eyed my figure thoughtfully, a hint of a leer in his eyes. "Did you say you're her assistant?"

No, my boobs did. I gave him a tight smile. "Thanks for the card." I tucked it into my pocket to end the conversation.

"That's odd. Can't seem to get the red-eye on this camera right."

From afar, my brain zoomed in on the red-eye comment and I glanced over at Remy's table. She was still there with the soldiers, her arm tight around one man's neck as she tucked his head under her chin, his eyes going automatically to her half-exposed bosom. The other soldier looked a little confused, but not nearly as confused as the one with the camera. He looked at the crowd. "Does anyone know how to work one of these? I can't seem to get it to fix the red-eye focus."

And that's when I noticed Remy was paying an unnatural amount of attention to the soldier's neck. She leaned over him, sniffed his skin, and I saw her tongue snake out. Tasting him.

I'd seen vampires do that move before, just before they were going to strike. Except Remy didn't need blood—but Joachim might. And that meant . . .

Oh, shit.

"Time to go!" I yelled abruptly, startling the crowd. "Miss Summore has other engagements she has to get to! Time to go!"

All eyes turned to me—including Remy's bright red ones.

Joachim had taken over her body again.

I rushed forward, shoving past the crowd of men and sweeping off my baseball cap. Elbowing between the soldiers, I put my arm around Remy's shoulders and stuck my baseball cap on her head, hiding her eyes. "No more pictures, please. It's time for us to leave."

A chorus of angry boos followed me as I shoved my way through the room with Remy, who was strangely compliant. Her skin felt scorching hot, and I knew it was the influence of the spirit inside her, rising to the surface.

Like we needed *more* trouble on this trip?

To my vast relief, Drake helped me push the crowd aside to get Remy out of there and stowed into the backseat of the Hummer. As soon as all the doors were shut, I tore out of the parking lot and zoomed down the highway, trying to put as much speed between us and the adult store as possible.

"What's wrong?" Drake gave me a wide-eyed look from the passenger seat across from me. "Why did we have to leave so fast?"

A low, inhuman chuckle came from the backseat, the deep sound tearing at Remy's vocal cords.

Drake glanced backward, then paled. "Oh my God," he said, his voice a couple of octaves higher than it should have been.

"Don't be scared," I said, trying to keep my voice level.

I glanced in the rearview mirror and saw Joachim's red eyes staring out from Remy's face, fixed unerringly on me. "It's just a little demonic possession. Nothing to worry about."

Well, not really a demon. More like a vampire that used to be an angel—or something. I didn't know *what* Joachim was anymore. All I knew was that he wasn't on our side.

"Demonic . . ." Drake's eyes bored into me. "You gotta be kidding me."

"Afraid not," I said grimly, then glanced in the mirror again. "Remy? You okay?" Could she even hear me?

I drove down the highway for a mile or two, glancing back in the rearview mirror, waiting for a response.

The hard chuckle erupted from Remy's throat again. "Remy's busy." Her hands slid over her body, sensually. "I need to feed."

Had Remy been feeding Joachim? If so, that was really, *really* bad news.

"Feed? Which one—sex or blood?" I put on the emergency blinkers, ready to pull over if she lunged for Drake.

"What are you talking about?" Drake sounded horrified.

"Sex and blood, sex and blood," Joachim sing-songed, sounding straight out of a horror film. "Does it matter which I crave?"

Oh yeah, it mattered. I pulled over to the side of the road with a jerk, ignoring the cars that honked at me.

The massive Hummer skidded along the gravel for a few seconds, then jerked to a stop. I threw on the emergency brake and leaned over my seat, looking right into Remy's red eyes. "Joachim," I said, my voice surprisingly calm. "I need to talk to Remy. Please let her have control of her body again."

He stared at me, and I wasn't sure if he didn't comprehend or just didn't want to comply. After a moment, a smile broke across Remy's face. "Why should I?"

What would cause Joachim to back down? What could I say that would make him realize that I needed Remy back? I crawled into the backseat, staring into her red eyes. I'd try guilt. "Remy's my friend, and I know she's unhappy when you do this. I care about her."

The evil glare focused on me, and a sneer cut across Remy's lovely face. "Friends." He laughed coldly. "What do I care for your friendship?"

He had a point. "Look, if you don't give her back right this instant, I'm going to turn this car around and drive you straight to the vampire queen. I bet she could find a way to suck you out of Remy and back into her body." It was a bluff—a big one—but it was all I had. I was starting to get scared for poor Remy, trapped inside there. Her skin was flushing an alarming shade of red.

That got his attention. A furious sneer broke across her face. "Fool," he said, the red flaring in his eyes. Her eyes. Whatever. She began to thrash, her body quaking as if covered with chills. A creepy laugh erupted from her throat.

"Here," Drake said, handing me her purse. His eyes were wide as he stared at Remy.

I was about to bite his head off for being dumb enough to think that I needed her purse right now, when something inside it sloshed. Maybe there was something . . .

Pinning Remy down with one arm, I rummaged through her purse with the other and found the sloshing object—a small white bottle with a cross drawn on the front.

Remy/Joachim hissed at the sight, all laughter disappearing.

Holy water.

Good enough for me. I flipped open the cap, eyed the squirt-lid for a moment, then squirted a long stream into Remy's mouth.

She gurgled for a moment, then began to cough.

"Remy! Are you okay?" I capped the bottle and stared into her face, searching for signs of possession. Her arm was burning hot, and a string of drool rolled down her cheek, her eyes closed. "Remy!"

"Try hitting her," Drake said, his voice a quivery warble from the front seat. "Maybe that will work."

I tapped her on the cheek, lightly at first, then harder a second time.

"Ow?" She cracked one eye open. One bleached gray eye. "That hurt."

Relieved, I obliged, sliding back to give her more room on the seat. She sat up, put a hand to her jaw and wiped the slobber away, then gave me a confused look. "Where are we?"

"Somewhere down the highway. I had to get you out of the store fast."

Her brows drew together. "Why?"

"Joachim made an appearance," I explained. "You don't remember anything?"

She shook her head. "The last thing I remember is some frat boy grabbing my ass for a photo." She sniffed. "He was cute, too."

"Yeah, well, when I looked over at you again, Joachim was giving the red-eye glare to everyone, and we had to get out of there fast."

Remy nodded, a bit pale. "Thanks." She turned toward Drake in the front seat. "Guess you found out my dirty little secret, huh?"

He was staring at her as if she'd turned into a nightmare. Heck, she had. I'd obviously have to deal with that later. There were more pressing things on my mind than whether or not Drake felt comfortable around us.

"So what did Joachim mean by saying that it was time for him to feed again? Have you been feeding him?"

She straightened in her seat, flinging her long hair off her shoulders. "What do you mean?" She didn't make eye contact, which was a bad sign.

If she was going to play stupid, there was nothing I could get out of her right now. Best to just settle down and let her handle it on her own. "Never mind. I have enough problems of my own to worry about. We'll talk later."

Remy shrugged, and her eyes focused on the bottle in my hands. "Is that my holy water?"

I handed it to her. "Seems to chase Joachim away."

She nodded as if that were no surprise and unscrewed the cap, taking a long swig and swishing it around in her mouth.

I watched her for a moment more, frowning. How long had this been going on? Was she alternately feeding Joachim and chugging holy water to get rid of him?

It hurt my brain to try to process all of it. First, Zane ditched me, and now Remy was unstable. I made my way back to the front seat. "Let's just get through Colorado before we have any more problems, all right? Because at the rate we're going, we'll hit New Orleans by the time I'm forty."

If I lived that long.

I started the Hummer again, pulling my seat belt across my lap. Something small jabbed me in the corner of my jeans pocket and I reached in, pulling out the business card. I'd forgotten all about it. It probably had some loser's phone number on it, trying to score a private one-on-one session with a porn star (or her lucky, lucky assistant).

Written on the back of the card was a scrawled message.

You and your companion are being followed.

Well, wasn't that heartwarming? I flipped the card over, ignoring the chill that washed over me, and stared at the front.

Luc Stone was all it said, with an email address underneath and a symbol that reminded me quite a bit of Noah's angelic alphabet tattoo on his wrist.

Another one of the Serim? If so, why was he warning me?

"Oh goodie." I pulled the Hummer back on the highway. "One more complication on this trip."

CHAPTER SEVEN

We made it through the rest of Colorado with no incidents. I remained tense and nervous, watching Remy in rearview mirror in case of any other mishaps, but nothing happened. We cut through Kansas and made it to the Oklahoma state line before the world collapsed on me again.

The sun had been setting in my eyes for the past half hour, annoying the crap out of me almost as much as the radio stations that Drake (who refused to talk) kept picking out. My stomach rumbled. Resolving to hand the wheel over to someone else in about five minutes, I shifted in my seat for the nine hundredth time, making my shorts rub against my crotch. My body nearly exploded, and the breath whooshed out of my lungs.

The Itch had returned.

My hands clenched on the steering wheel. A quick check of my eyes in the rearview mirror confirmed my fears. "Remy," I warned. "Big problem."

I heard her flip the pages of a magazine in the backseat. "What's that, hon?" I doubt she even looked up.

I glanced over at Drake. He was starting to look appetizing, which meant I had it bad. I could get him in a hotel room, wash that greasy shit out of his hair, put him in some real clothes . . . maybe . . .

He stared warily back at me. "What?"

"Nothing," I muttered. "I'm obviously delusional." I stared grimly out at the highway again. We were pulling into a small town called Ponca City.

Remy sat up. "Is it the Itch?"

I nodded, feeling miserable. "I need Zane, and he left me." I'd had lots of time to think about how pissed at him I was, and despair overwhelmed me. Here I was, hundreds of miles away from the familiar, and without either one of my boyfriends. Zane had abandoned me because I wanted him to commit to me and not to the vampire clan, and I'd driven Noah away because he wanted an exclusive relationship.

With a succubus. What a lark.

Yep, the Afterlife sucked pretty bad for me right now.

"I can help," said Drake.

We ignored him.

Just then my cell phone rang, and my heart leapt into my throat.

"Maybe that's him," Remy said, brightening. "It's nearing sunset, so he should be awake soon."

"I doubt it," I said but picked up the call anyhow, my heart hammering in my breast. "Hello?" Damn that breathless excitement in my voice.

"Jackie," Noah's voice said over the phone, a warning tone. "Let me talk to Zane."

My fingers tightened on the phone. I couldn't ignore a direct order from one of my masters, but this one was impossible to fill. "He's not here," I said between gritted teeth. "Is that all you called for?" Dake's hand had landed on my shoulder again and I swatted it away.

"Where is he, then? And where are you?" I could hear the frustration in his voice. "I've been waiting for you to get home all day, only to find out that you've already disappeared on your little trip."

"Really? You've been waiting for me?" My voice took on a husky note, and the pulsing between my legs began.

He paused, and the silence on the other end of the phone throbbed in my ear. "Jackie, is everything all right?"

I wanted to cry. "Define 'all right.'"

"Did Zane put you up to this?" The jealous anger was back in his voice. "Is that why you left? He wanted to get you away—"

My mirthless laugh interrupted his tirade. "Zane didn't put me up to this." If only it were that simple. No curses involved, no throbbing loins.

"What is it, then?" His voice dropped to a lower note. "Jackie, you know I could demand that you tell me, and you'd have to. But I don't want to do that to you."

"How kind of you," I said bitterly. There was no way I was telling him about the curse. I thought of seeing the same look on Noah's face and flinched. "I've got to go, all right?"

"Stop right there!"

A direct command from my master. I threw on the brakes, the car screeching to a halt.

"What the fuck?" Remy screamed in my ear, slamming into my seat. Next to me, Drake smacked into the dashboard.

My hand clenched on the steering wheel, frozen in place. I could hear cars honking on the highway behind me, but I was helpless to do anything about it. Noah had commanded, and I had to obey.

"What do you want?" My voice came between gritted teeth.

"Tell me the name of your town," he said calmly. Another direct order.

I glanced at the nearest motel. "Ponca City, Oklahoma."

"Tell me a landmark nearby."

I craned my head, staring down the highway. "I see a billboard for a casino," I said, feeling like a recalcitrant child.

"Excellent. The name?"

"Two Feathers Casino."

"Good." He heaved a big sigh of relief, and I felt a momentary twinge. Was Noah—strong, capable, never-worries Noah—actually concerned about me? Or was it about what he thought Zane and I might be doing together? "Now, Jackie, listen to me carefully."

"Like I have a choice in the matter?"

"Stay there until tomorrow. The sun's going down, so I won't make it to the airport tonight. Pick a nearby hotel, and stay there until I come into town the next morning. Do you understand me?"

"What? Noah, this is a bad idea—" Oh God, if he found out about my curse, what would he say?

"Stay in Ponca City." He hung up.

I threw the dead phone across the car. Drake stared at me with wide eyes.

Remy smirked from the backseat. "Put his foot down on you, didn't he? I knew he'd try to be all 'master' on you at some point. They all do."

I stared at the highway ahead of me, ignoring the cars that honked, flipped us off, and drove around us. My foot wouldn't move to the gas pedal on the car—it was like my muscles had seized up and refused to respond. "I can't leave town until tomorrow, when Noah comes to pick me up."

Remy chortled. "Oh, this should be good."

My blazingly blue eyes stared back at me in the rear-view mirror. Bad, bad news for me—I had to wait over twelve hours for Noah to get here.

Could I make it that long?

The exciting town of Ponca City, Oklahoma, didn't have a Ritz or Hilton, like Remy wanted. It did boast a nice Super 8 on the side of the highway, and we got three rooms there.

Drake muttered something about needing some time to himself and disappeared into his room. Worked for me, because he made me uncomfortable anyway. Not just because of his porn-star status, but because he now knew something really weird was going on with me and Remy, and I didn't have any answers for him.

Remy gave me a hopeful look when we ditched Drake, but I shook my head at her. "I'm not feeling so well. Maybe we should just call it a night."

"Excuse me? With a casino close by? Free drinks?"

But I felt sick. My legs were weak, my body hot and feverish. "Remy, I can't go out. Remember that whole 'curse' thing?" I put a hand to my forehead. "Noah won't be here until sometime tomorrow morning, so, the next twelve hours are going to be excruciating. I'd rather not spend them in a casino filled with other people."

Remy rolled her eyes. "You're *such* a martyr. So you have to have sex a little more often for the next few days. Why not spend a little time distracted, rather than watching reruns of *COPS* or *M*A*S*H*?" If you're going to spend the next twelve hours in desperate need for a man, you can at least be drunk."

She had a very, very good point.

CHAPTER EIGHT

"What do you mean, you don't serve alcohol?" Remy's gasp carried across the electronic beeping of the slot machines. "You're a casino! How can you not serve alcohol?"

The waiter gave her an embarrassed look. "Ma'am—"

"Miss!"

"Miss," he hastily corrected. "Two Feathers does not serve hard alcohol, but I'd be happy to bring you a beer or a wine cooler." He gave her a dazzled smile. "Anything you want, miss. You just tell me and I'll make all your dreams come true."

Well, *that* wasn't obvious. The look on Remy's face said that she was mollified and flattered by his attention, and she straightened on her stool, leaning back against the slot machine. "Then I'd like a Guinness. A big one."

"Of course." The tiny hint of a smile on his lips indicated that it wasn't the only big one he'd like to give her.

He looked over at me, his eyes suggestive. "And you?" The breathless tone of his voice proved that he wasn't just asking me for a drink order.

I avoided making eye contact and shoved my card

into the slot machine, punching buttons. "Coors Light. Whatever."

He lingered, and I finally looked up at him. "Is that all I can get for you?" His eyes dropped to my breasts, then back to my face.

Jeez, to think that once upon a time I'd been excited to be transformed into a hot babe. Now I'd trade it all away for an eternity of men that made eye contact with me. "Just the beer," I snapped. My machine beeped sadly at me. Two cherries and a lemon. Story of my life.

As he walked away, Remy nudged me. "You know, maybe you should try and get a little action here tonight. Feed your Itch ahead of time, so Noah doesn't have anything to hold against you when he gets here in the morning."

I shot her a quick look as my machine beeped again. Cherries, bar, lemon. It was getting worse. "You think he's going to hold something against me?"

Remy grinned and crossed her legs on the stool, an unfailingly elegant gesture. "Let's think about this one, shall we? You left Noah, the control freak, and didn't tell him where you were going. You left with his worst enemy—who also happens to be your other boyfriend—and he wants an apology. Oh, I think there'll be a little something held over your head, at the very least." She turned back to her machine and jammed her card in, then punched one button. Two bars and a cherry. Her machine whistled happily and made a crunching sound, spitting out a ticket. "Hey, look at that—I won!"

I jerked my card out of my machine. "I don't know why I'm bothering to gamble tonight. My curse probably extends to machines, as well."

"All I'm saying"—Remy punched one button on her machine again—"is that when he shows up in the morning, you're going to have to crawl back to him and beg forgiveness. For sex. And then tell him about your curse. Doesn't sound like a winning combination to me."

"Me, either," I muttered, picturing Noah's smug face. Then I pictured him kissing me. And then I pictured his heavy body on top of mine, filling me—

"Your drink, miss," came a voice at my ear.

I panted, blinking up at the waiter, who held a Coors Light longneck on a tray out to me. He had nice fingers, I noticed as I took the bottle from the tray. Really nice fingers. Long and smooth and well kept. I flicked my gaze back up to his face and studied him for a moment. Nice lips, even if his nose was a little big. His hair was terrible, but he was young and lean and looked good enough to eat.

Oh God, was I really even thinking about this? I still had a hard time wrapping my brain around the fact that I—who had been nearly celibate for most of my twenty-some years—was sleeping with two guys. Throw in a one-night stand, and my brain couldn't handle it.

"What time do you get off, sweetie?" Remy purred up

at the waiter as she took the massive mug of Guinness from him.

His eyes got dark in the way only a man in lust could look, and my body responded, my nerve endings tingling. "I get off at five a.m."

Rats. I sighed. "If I wait that long, I might as well wait for Noah."

"Uh huh," Remy said, barely glancing over at me. "If you don't want him, I'll take him." She gave the man in question a dazzling smile.

I waved a hand glumly. "You can have him." I sucked on my beer, feeling rather morose as Remy gave the waiter her room number and set up her date with him later. I wished desperately that I could be like Remy, with the morals of a cat and not a worry in my head. Getting pregnant wasn't a concern; Sucks don't breed. We didn't catch diseases, didn't die, didn't get a period. I sure didn't miss stuff like that.

But I had to have sex, and have it often, and since my normal partners weren't around, I had to pick a new one. Unfortunately, my subconscious was a Puritan nerd who couldn't grasp the idea that I needed to have a lot of sex to continue in the Afterlife.

Which was stupid, really.

"All right," I said impulsively, then swigged the last of my beer. I'd drunk it so fast that I had a bit of a buzz going (lucky for me, succubi could still get drunk). "Get me a few more beers and let's find me a date."

"'Kay," Remy said. She waved her drink boy over and

ordered a second round for us. "You sure you don't want him?" she asked, watching his ass as he walked back to the bar.

I watched it, too. It *was* a real nice ass. "Nah. You already gave him your number and stuff." To switch out on him now would be icky, like sleeping with your sister's boyfriend.

"Drake, then? I know he's got the hots for you." She chugged her Guinness, tipping back the glass to drain it. "He told me the other day that you had a great face for porn."

I flinched. What the heck did that mean? I didn't want to ask, considering all of Remy's close-ups involved other men's anatomy in the shot. "God, no. No Drake." Not in a million years.

"Yeah," she agreed. "Drake's kind of . . . well, Drake." Remy motioned for her cabana boy and held up two fingers, indicating that she needed refills. "Someone new, then?"

I scoped out the crowded room as I took the new longneck and gave it a swig. It was night, and the casino was in full swing. Nearly every machine was full, and the tables across the way were packed as well—with old people and men with mullets. Seriously, what was it with gamblers and mullets? "This isn't exactly what I had in mind, Remy."

Remy shrugged and licked the foam from her beer off her lip. "Beggars can't be choosers, my dear. And I'm afraid that you definitely fall into the realm of beggar.

So chug that beer, grab another, and let's go rustle us up some men," she said with a cowboy drawl.

I did as I was told, downing my beer and reaching for the next one brought to me. My head swam with the giddy buzz, and I let Remy grab my hand and drag me across the casino to get some chips.

Once we had our money exchanged, Remy sauntered over to the blackjack table and leaned over one of the men. He looked like a dirty trucker who'd stopped in for a beer, but Remy knew how to pick her prey. Letting her hair fall over his shoulder, she gave him a smile. "What are you playing?"

"Blackjack," snapped an older woman with over-bleached hair at the far end of the table. "Quit looking over his shoulder."

The man was all smiles for Remy. "You want to learn how to play, darlin'?"

"Oh, we'd love to learn how to play!" Remy cooed in his ear, and just like that, we had two seats at the table. The other women left in disgust.

Remy slid into the seat to her left and I took the other, sandwiched between two men. They both gave me appraising looks.

"What's your name, doll?" said one. He smiled and displayed a mouth full of bad teeth behind a leathery face. "I can show you how to play, if ya like."

I smiled brightly, determined to make the best of this. After all, I didn't have to sleep with him. There was bound to be a hot man in the casino somewhere; I just had to find him. "I'm Jackie." I smiled at the dealer—not bad looking. "And I already know how to play, thanks." Like it was that hard to figure out how to add up twenty-one. I fiddled with my chips. The two men sandwiching me were leaning awfully close, and the Itch was throbbing from my groin straight to a headache behind my eyes.

Farther on, a man smiled. He seemed nice enough and I smiled back. Youngish—maybe early thirties. Tanned but not icky. Maybe he was tanned all over. Nice eyes, with the sexiest damn crinkles around them—

I shook myself and concentrated on my chips.

Must concentrate on game. Must not think about sex. Must not think about being sandwiched between two men in any way except having to deal with poker. Two bodies pressing on mine, hot skin sliding over my body. Must not hit on the men next to me. The Itch would make them seem like princes, even if they were nasty. Must not let them hit on me. Must not—

"Miss?"

I looked up at the dealer, flushed and breathing hard. "What?"

"Hit, or stay?"

"What?" Had he heard my thoughts?

"Your cards?"

Oh. "Hit," I blurted automatically.

"On a twenty?" The younger man next to me chuckled, and that raspy sound made my insides quiver. I shifted on my seat, trying to will away the Itch. Like that had ever worked before.

I looked down at my cards, barely seeing the two jacks that stared at me through the haze. Blood rushed in my ears, the beer made my head spin, and all I heard was the roar of the casino around me.

"Thirty. Bust," the dealer said. I nodded, though to be honest, I couldn't tell what I was nodding about.

All I could think about was the liquid heat that swam through my body, desperate for release.

"Need another drink," I mumbled.

The younger man at my side pushed a drink my way. "Here. I ordered this for you, darlin'."

I knew I shouldn't take a drink from a stranger, but I was overheated and horny and it looked frosty and delicious. Screw it. I picked up the glass and sucked the soda down greedily, not caring that it was icy cold or that people were giving me odd looks. The drink helped alleviate some of the unnatural heat that radiated from my skin, though it didn't do much for my level of drunkenness. The room swam in front of my eyes. I glanced over at Remy, who had managed to plant herself in some big fat guy's lap and was enjoying the heck out of herself, but I couldn't bring myself to do the same. Young, old, ugly, poor—Remy loved them all, as long as they loved her.

Why couldn't I be like that?

A hand touched my arm and my nipples immediately hardened, and I had to bite back the moan of pleasure that rose in my throat.

"You okay, honey?" It was Young and Moderately Handsome, the one who'd given me the drink. He smiled at me, the look inviting.

I made up my mind as his finger grazed the bare flesh of my upper arm in an agonizingly slow motion. I winced, expecting him to fall flat at my feet, snoring and brainless like the others.

Nothing. He even smiled suggestively at me.

He'd do.

"I need air." I set down my empty glass and stood. "Wanna come with me?"

He rose so fast that my drunken head spun a little. Well, okay, it spun a lot. I must have wobbled, because the next thing I knew, he had his hands around my waist and was leading me toward the casino entrance. God, those hands felt good. I whimpered at the touch—it burned right through my clothing and pulled against my skin, and I had to fight the urge to rip my clothes off right then and there.

I glanced back at Remy, but all she did was wiggle her fingers and made a phone gesture with her hand. "Call me later," she mouthed, then gave me a thumbs-up.

I let the guy drag me out of the casino and into the cool night air. The doors shut behind us, and the sounds of people talking dimmed as the world got quieter, the noisy bustle of the casino exchanging for the relative quiet of the parking lot. A breeze touched my arms, helping me wake up a little. I couldn't concentrate—the Itch was throbbing too hard, and my head was spinning.

Then those hands twitched, resting a little lower on

my body until they were almost on my ass, and the world turned toward a red fog again.

"What did you say your name was again?" my new friend asked.

I shut him up with a kiss. It was better if he didn't talk at all, really. My mouth planted on his, my tongue diving into his mouth, and I pressed my body against his in an obvious invitation that he accepted. His hands slid lower, grasping my ass through my shorts and pulling me against his body. His mouth broke free of mine and he laughed again, that wonderfully delicious rasp. "You're one hot piece of ass, bitch." He pinched my butt, painfully.

Well, that was starting to kill the mood for me. Maybe I could live with the Itch for a little bit longer. "No talk," I mumbled. I tried to plant my mouth over his again in an obvious hint. Perhaps if I pretended he was Zane . . .

He wasn't so keen on the hint; he laughed again. "You're pretty hot for the cock, slut."

Okay, Itch or no Itch, I still had standards. I slithered out of his arms, wiping my mouth with my hand and staring up at him through the red fog. Damn, he still looked delicious, but there was a hard tilt to his mouth that I didn't like, now that I took a second look at him.

But God, I was throbbing painfully bad. So badly that I knew I wouldn't last until dawn, when Noah would arrive to lecture me. I hesitated. "What's your name?"

It came out all slurred and drunk. More like, "Whazzername?" The ground seemed to wobble and I flung my arms around him again, feeling strange and heavy.

He told me his name, but it didn't register. All I watched was that hard curve of his mouth as he smiled down at me. There was something I didn't like about it, and I finally realized what it was. "You don't have lipsh like my Zane," I said aloud, trying to focus. "His lipsh are wonnerful." So nice and full and soft against mine. "I mish him," I added sadly.

"Baby, I don't care who you miss, as long as you end up with me tonight." He leered at me and reached for me again. I slapped at his hand, but I missed and ended up slapping air, and his arms snaked around me again. The breath whistled from my lungs. "So tell me, sugar, does the carpet match the drapes?"

"You're gross," I slurred and planted my hand on his face, blocking his mouth when he dove down for another kiss. "Leaveme 'lone."

His hands dug into my flesh. "You were askin' for it, baby. So don't go blaming me when I give it to you."

"I don't think *la femme* wants to be with you," a cool voice interrupted, and the hard, hot hands were pried off my ass, leaving me to stumble backward. I smacked against the brick wall, scraping my oversensitive skin and sending shock waves through my body. I collapsed to the ground in a heap, too loopy to do more than sit and stare.

What was wrong with me?

Through the red haze of desire, I saw two men. The jerkwad who'd been pawing me confronted a much taller man that I didn't recognize. I could see only the back of his head, but he was dressed in dark clothing, and they kept moving so fast it was making my head spin. Had Zane come to rescue me?

I pushed myself off the wall, trying to stand upright once more. The world spun around me, and as I tried to take a step forward, my shoe slipped out from underneath me. I crashed to the pavement and smacked my chin, but that wasn't the part that bothered me the most. My legs began to cramp and clench, and the throbbing in my body was getting worse.

I couldn't focus. Something was horribly wrong—more than just the curse.

Moaning, I curled up around myself, hugging my legs close in a fetal position. I couldn't think or function—I was burning up inside. Somewhere in the back of my drunken, agonized mind, I heard the two men arguing and the quick shuffle of running sneakers on the pavement as someone left. I didn't bother to look, though. Nothing was as important as the heat sweeping through me and getting rid of it.

Gentle hands touched my shoulders, turning me over. A hand slid under my thighs, and I felt the cool breeze rush around me as I was lifted into the air. The crisp, starchy shirt my cheek pressed against was so cool in the night air that I snuggled up against it. The sensation was almost refreshing, and my body began to unclench a little.

"I've got you, *ma belle*. Relax."

I didn't recognize the voice, but the smooth, languid

hint of an accent tore at my already frayed nerves. My fingers dug into his shirt collar, clenched, and I huddled against his chest, willing for the Itch to go away and leave me alone. My flesh burned where he touched me, and everything hurt.

With every step he took, the sounds of the casino fled a little farther. Everything in me screamed with horrible tension, and the beer was just compounding the problem. One wrong move and I'd throw up all over my savior, so I kept my eyes squeezed shut. "Where are you taking me?"

His voice was a low whisper that soothed. "Back to your hotel, once you tell me where it is."

The part of me that worried about telling a perfect stranger where my hotel room was shut down when the next wave of Itch-induced tension shot through me, and my limbs clenched again. "Super 8," I bit out, then whimpered when he slid me into the backseat of a cab.

Through a drunken fog, I watched as the hotel approached in the distance. The lights of the Super 8 sign seemed uncomfortably bright as my new friend helped me from the cab, picking me up and carrying me out once more.

"My room," I mumbled.

"I'll take you to your room," he whispered in my ear, and I moaned with the pleasure that simple little sentence sent rocketing through my body.

I gestured feebly at my purse, hanging limply from

my arm. "Key's in there." I needed a lot more alcohol if I was going to get through this pain; my pulse hammered so hard in my body that it felt like someone was beating a gong.

My helper ignored me, sliding a key card into the nearest door. When he pushed it open, the cool air of the air-conditioned room hit me like a cocoon. I sighed with relief.

"Does the cold feel good?"

I nodded against my faceless hero's shoulder.

He laid me on the bed, and I felt the cool softness of crisp sheets under my sensitive body. I heard him across the room and the clicks of the dial as he turned the A-C down. The clothes on my body felt too warm, too over-heated. I wanted to feel the cool sheets all over me, and I plucked at my sleeve. "Hurts."

"Your clothes?" the soft voice whispered against my skin. He'd leaned very close to me, my solicitous hero. I could smell his breath near mine—a hint of spicy smoke and cloves—and it danced across my skin, teasing me. The succubus instincts in me made me reach for him as I would a lover, even as I opened my eyes to look at his face.

It was the tall stranger from the porn store. His beau-tiful, swarthy face with the amber eyes stared back at me, smiling as if he were amused by my drunken agony.

Instinct told me that I should run away from him. Scream, cry for help, anything to get me away from this bastard who intended me harm. Oh God, and I'd let him into my room. I'd even wrapped my arms around him and snuggled up against his chest.

I pushed at him, trying to get away. It was useless. I wasn't real strong even on my best day, and with the Itch raging through me, my body really didn't want him to go away. I wanted him to settle that heavy weight on top of my body and make sweet, forbidden love to me all night long.

He brushed a lock of hair off my forehead and gave me a hint of a smile, showing teeth of dazzling whiteness underneath. Nice, even teeth. No hint of fangs. "You look frightened, *ma belle*."

"Who are you?" The breathy growl caught in my throat. "What are you going to do to me?" The way it came out, it sounded more like an invitation than a frightened question.

He seemed amused by my drunken wariness. His hand stroked my hair, then the soft, overheated flesh of my arm, and the Itch began to switch from pain to intense pleasure. My breath hissed in my throat.

"You may call me Luc. And I'm here to help you, believe it or not."

"Forgive me if I choose to believe 'not,'" I whispered. "You've been following me." At the hint of a smile again, the throbbing started, more painful than ever.

"Believe what you like," he said, smiling wickedly as he lifted my hand. He flipped it over, examined it, and then kissed the palm. "I want only to help a beautiful woman in need. And you are in need. I think your friend back there slipped something into your drink."

He did? And here I'd thought it was just the alcohol and the Itch. "Bastard gave me a roofie?" I slurred, pressing my hand against his mouth again. No wonder he hadn't passed out like the pizza boy did when I touched him. Something in the drug was messing up my powers.

He nodded and pressed another kiss on my sensitive hand.

His touch sent shudders rocketing through my body. Even though I did not know or trust him, he was here and I needed him. I didn't pull away, just watched him with dizzy, lusting eyes.

Luc's hand stroked down my arm, gently massaging my tense flesh. The horrible, burning tension reduced, slowly replaced by throbbing desire—a welcome response. I arched under the gentle ministration, showing silent appreciation of his touch.

"Better?" His teasing whisper moved across my skin. "More?"

The right answer was "No" or "Help, police," but all I could think about was that soothing touch and the things it was doing to my desperate body.

His hand stroked across my shoulder, toward the buttons that ran up the front of my light, summery khaki top. "Do your clothes still hurt you?"

They did. Even now, the lace of my bra bit into my sensitized skin and made me miserable. I nodded, my breath sucking in as his long, tanned fingers hovered near the first button, then undid it, revealing a few inches of my pale skin. Those oddly yellow eyes stayed focused on my face, as if to reassure me that he was here for my pleasure, and not his.

One more button, then two, then another, and then the fabric parted and exposed my skin to him, the cups of my bra blindingly purple in the pale light of the hotel room. He looked down then, and the expression on his face changed slightly, from neutral to fascinated. "You are lovely."

"Comes with the job," I murmured, my back arching as I tried to aim my needing breasts toward his stroking hand. But he seemed oblivious to my wants, his dark hand splaying across my stomach, smoothing the soft flesh there.

I lay back, fascinated by that large hand against my skin as it circled my belly button, then moved down my side and slid under my back. With a deft motion, he lifted me into a sitting position, his other hand sliding behind my neck. "This will only take a moment, *ma belle*."

With those soothing words ringing in my ears, he slid off my unbuttoned top.

The cool air was wonderful against my flesh. The more clothing that I took off, the better I felt, even if the Itch hadn't been scratched. I sighed softly with pleasure and put my arms around his neck again, trying to pull him toward me for a kiss.

"*Non, chérie*," he said, flashing me another white smile that drove me wild. "You are drunk and do not know what you are thinking."

"I have a pretty good idea of what I'm thinking," I said, petulant, but let him lean away from me. After all, I couldn't explain to him that I'd boozed up because I needed sex really badly. Or that I was a succubus. Who'd been cursed.

Some things you just didn't discuss on the first date.

I didn't pull out of his arms, though, and he didn't seem to be in any rush to let me go. His hands smoothed up and down my back, stroking me and petting me as if I were a cat, and I arched with pleasure, my hips gyrating softly against the bed.

His amber eyes held mine as he undid the hooks on my bra, then helped me shrug the itchy material off my body. The last offending garment on my torso gone, he slid me gently back down onto the bed.

I nearly writhed with anticipation as his gaze glided over my body again. "You are very beautiful," he said, his hand sliding over my stomach again.

"You already said that," I slurred, though it didn't bother me like it normally did when men commented on my looks. Perhaps I was too far gone from the Itch.

I expected him to zoom in for my breasts, to put the moves on me, like any sane man would. But my mysterious stranger simply kneaded my skin, massaging away the awful tension and leaving a terrible ache in its place.

His jacket pocket began to vibrate.

A frown creased his beautiful face as he pulled the phone out of his pocket, flipped it open, and placed it to his ear. His other hand remained on my bare skin, caressing. "*Oui?*"

Silence. Then he said, "Safe. You should have no worries." Another pause and a smile. "I am looking out for our best interests, *mon ami*. Have faith." He snapped the phone shut and gazed back down at my flushed skin. "Friends. They always they call at the most inappropriate times, *non?*"

I wanted his hands back on me again, and I arched on the bed, suggesting so.

He took the hint. Phone put away, both his hands slid farther down my body and tugged at my shorts. They came off with one quick pull and were instantly discarded to the floor, leaving me only in my white cotton panties.

The sight of them brought a chuckle to Luc, and he touched the waistband lightly. "Not what I was expecting on a woman such as you."

"What do you mean?" I breathed, twitching as I waited for him to pull on the elastic Hanes Her Way band and expose my aching flesh to the air. I burned for him to fall over me and ravish me, to take away this endless torment.

But the phone rang in his pocket again, and his mouth thinned with displeasure. He took my hand again and kissed the back. "Tonight is not our night, it seems. I will leave you to get some sleep, *ma belle*. Perhaps next when we meet, you will not be so drunk and I will not be such a *chevalier*, eh?"

It was obvious I was going to have to seduce him to get any sort of relief around here. I slid my hands to his crotch and rubbed it enticingly. He might be saying "no" but parts of his anatomy were definitely saying "yes," if what was under my hand was any indication. "I need you," I said simply.

He winked at me, and leaned in and gave me a chaste kiss on the cheek. "Perhaps some other time, *chérie*. You have my card if you need me."

And just like that, he stood and left.

I guess what they said about granny panties scaring off a man was true.

CHAPTER NINE

Six hours later, I stared at the red numbers on the clock, hating life. And beer. In that order.

The worst thing about a succubus in a drunken stupor? You can't pass out, no matter what. I figured this out at some point after my erstwhile knight abandoned me. I spent the next few hours staring blankly at the TV as infomercials played on mute. My vision was still blurry, and my mouth couldn't seem to stay shut, and I drooled all over myself.

Yeah, real sexy.

Worst of all, there was no relief. The "help" that the mysterious Luc had given me faded within minutes, leaving me curled up on the bed, panting and writhing in frustration. The only thing that helped was the icy blast of the A/C as it roared in the corner. So I lay sprawled on top of the sheets, waiting for dawn and, I hoped, Noah.

I didn't know what I'd do if he didn't show up. Wouldn't think about it. Couldn't think about it.

My body was seizing in another round of horrible cramps when I heard my cell phone go off. My purse vibrated and the Aerosmith's "Angel" keened through the room, the high, tinny sound god-awful to my aching, hungover head. I rolled over to the edge of the bed, reaching for the phone, then promptly fell on the floor.

Ouch. That would leave a mark.

Fumbling through my small handbag, I located the vibrating phone and pressed it to my ear. "Hello?" I sounded as awful as I felt.

"Jackie?" Noah's voice sang into my eardrum, and my body responded with a wave of desire.

"Noah," I said, relief and need warring inside me. "I'm so glad you're here."

"I'm at the hotel. Where are you?" he said, his voice so loud that it blasted in my ear.

I winced, holding the phone away. "I assume you are cussing at me because you're worried?"

"Where are you?" His voice lowered, but it was obvious he was still stressed out. "I told you to stay here."

"Yeah, well, thanks, *Master*. So glad you're here to tell me what to do." God, Noah could be a dick sometimes, even though I knew he meant well. At least, I was pretty sure he meant well. "I'm here, in my room." Still on the floor, next to the nightstand. Still hating life.

"No, you're not," Noah said patiently. "I'm standing in your room right now, and you're not here."

I sat up and peered over the bed, squinting.

Well hell. This *wasn't* my room.

That made my bleary eyes open pretty fast. What the heck? It looked the same—all hotel rooms looked the same—except the coverlet was a different shade of "awful motel brown" and my bags were nowhere to be seen.

"Jackie?" Noah's concerned voice roared in my ear again.

Wincing, I stumbled over to the door and stared at the room rate chart on the back. "I'm still at the Super 8. Room 212."

"You stay in that room," Noah said, and the compulsion gripped me.

Like I could go anywhere even if he hadn't used the compulsion? I hung up the phone without responding, crawled back into bed, and pulled the pillow over my aching head. I'd give up two years of my immortal life to be able to take a nap right now.

Someone knocked loudly at the door a few minutes later and I groaned, burrowing farther under the blankets. "Who is it?" Maybe it was Luc, returning to finish what he'd never really started.

And wouldn't that just be awkward?

If Noah had problems with Zane, then he'd really have problems with a hot, mysterious stranger with amber eyes that made me hot just thinking about them—

The door opened and I heard heavy boots enter the room.

"Jackie?" Noah's voice was questioning, disapproving.

I peered out from under my pillow. "No yelling, please. My head hurts." It was nice to see that in my crazy world Noah never changed. He wore a dark polo shirt and crisp khaki pants, looking immaculate even at eight in the morning. His blond hair was perfectly waved, tousled just the way I liked.

My mouth watered.

He looked down at me, clearly frustrated. "What are you doing in this room, Jackie?"

I shrugged silently, and the covers slipped off, revealing my bare shoulder and the curve of my breast.

Immediately, Noah's face changed from exasperated to furious as he looked at my naked skin. "I see." His voice was tightly controlled. "Don't let me interrupt you. I should leave before your lover gets back." He turned away.

"Wait," I said, panic in my throat.

He turned tightly. "Tell me one reason why I shouldn't just leave right now, Jackie? It's obvious that my feelings are just a game to you."

I tried to sit up in the bed, but that simple motion seemed impossible. "Because I can't get up and chase after you." Walking to the door a few minutes ago had sapped my strength.

He paused, then returned to my side, staring down at me. "What's wrong, Jackie?" His bleached silver eyes roamed over my body with concern. Lucky guy, to be compelled only once a month.

I stared up at him in a misery of hurt. How could I tell him that I was cursed when he was still so angry at me? I didn't want to see his face turn from jealous concern to a look of disgust. So I pointed at my eyes instead, trying to dodge the subject. "Same old problem I've always had."

He sat down on the edge of the bed next to me, his lips twitching. "Drinking?"

Damn, I must look more wrecked than before. "Not drinking," I nearly growled at him, smacking him with my pillow. "The Itch."

He grew serious, his fingers lifting my chin and tilting my face toward his as he studied my eyes. "Your eyes . . . they're so dark they're almost purple, Jackie. How long has it been?"

I raked my hand through my hair in frustration. To my horror, a clump of it fell onto the bed. Oh my God. I was losing my hair after only one day of not feeding the Itch?

What would happen to me when the countdown got worse?

"Noah, I need help." My voice cracked hoarsely.

He noticed my fear and pulled me close to him. "It's all right, Jackie. I'm here now."

His tanned skin was hot against mine, and it felt good. He smelled delicious and familiar and so wonderful that I almost cried with relief.

Noah rubbed my back, stroking me, and the sensation made me—oddly enough—think of my interlude with Luc just a few hours ago. "Jackie, I want to apologize. I've been a damn mess lately. There's a lot going on right now, and I haven't been fair to you. First this thing with Zane—"

I didn't want to hear about Zane or anything else. I

put my hands on his face and turned his mouth toward mine. "Apologize later. Sex now."

Noah chuckled at my demand, brushing his lips gently against mine in a whisper-soft kiss. "I'm glad to see you haven't changed since I last saw you."

Oh, if only he knew. I yanked his expensive polo shirt from his waistband. He reached out to touch my bare breast with the back of his knuckles and I hissed at the painful sensation on my overly sensitive skin.

He stilled. "Jackie . . . are you in pain?"

God, I didn't want to get into this right now. If I told him about my curse, he'd give me the same cursory finger fuck that Zane had, then ditch me as well. But I *had* to tell him about it—especially if I could pass it to him. It was like having immortal herpes, but worse.

"I'm fine—"

He reached for the clump of my bright red hair that lay on the covers between us, and held it up to me. "This doesn't look fine to me."

"I'm cursed," I said, bursting into tears. "And now that you know it, you won't help me and my hair is falling out and my body aches all over, and if I don't have sex soon I'm going to shrivel up and die." My eyes squeezed shut so I couldn't see his horrified expression, and I blindly reached for the Kleenex box beside the bed. "And now you think I'm disgusting, too."

He caught my hand in his and brought it to his cheek, laying it against the whiskery stubble I felt there. He hadn't shaved this morning, probably because of his rush to come and find me. "Jackie Brighton, I could never find you disgusting."

"Not even if I'm cursed?" Somehow I doubted his assurances. I mean, two minutes after I mentioned my curse to Zane, he left me. It wasn't a coincidence.

Noah leaned forward to press kisses on my forehead and cheeks. "You're perfect, curse or no curse."

The soothing feeling of his mouth against my flesh calmed my locked-up nerve endings. "I have to keep having sex more and more often," I explained as he kissed my neck, his mouth sliding to my collarbone. "Remy says that I could starve to death in the middle of an orgy." The horrible image had been burned into my mind.

He bit gently at my shoulder, sending shock waves through my body. "And Remy's been cursed so many times before that she's the expert?"

"Well, no," I said, finding it hard to concentrate when he was nibbling on me like I was some sort of delicious fruit. "That's why we're going to New Orleans, to ask Delilah. She's a voodoo priestess and a succubus."

Noah made a sound of approval, even as he kissed the soft flesh at the bend of my arm. "Sometimes I don't give Remy enough credit."

I shuddered at the soft caress, digging my fingers into his scalp and winding them in his thick mane of hair. The slow, soft kisses were driving me crazy, the throbbing in my body reaching almost epic proportions. "Noah, can we please just have sex now? Foreplay is great and all, but my body *hurts.*"

His eyes were as blue as the ocean, telling me that his own urge was upon him, fueled by mine. "You need to come fast?"

My frantic hands unbuttoned his pants. "Understatement of the year."

Noah laughed. "Your wish is my command." His hand pressed on my shoulder until I lay flat on my back and he hovered over my naked hips, then leaned down and kissed my stomach again.

I nearly came off the bed with a hiss.

"Hurts?" Noah stilled over me.

Oh, but it was a good kind of hurt. "I'm okay," I said, my voice tight with tension.

His hand stroked down my hip and across my thigh, then parted them. He kissed the springy curls at the apex there, and I grabbed the pillow beside my head, clenching my fists to stop the moan building in my throat.

"Tell me if I hurt you," Noah said, his breath brushing over my heated flesh. My body tensed in anticipation and was soon rewarded. His thumbs parted my soft folds and he licked my clit, long, slow, and reverent, like a dying man with his last meal.

My breath exploded from my throat.

Noah froze and pulled away. "Are you okay?"

I put my hand back on top of his head and shoved it back down toward my thighs again. "Do that again." Oh, please, let him do that again.

He leaned in again, flicking his tongue against that most sensitive of spots. He swirled it around the tender flesh, teasing me with the soft, insistent touch, and then sucked.

My entire body locked into a spasm, and a scream of relief tore from my throat. Noah took that as a sign of encouragement, and continued to suck and lap at my clit until I stopped shuddering.

It took a while.

When my body finally uncoiled, the relief was immediate. The haze over my vision cleared, and the most languid, wonderful sensation rolled through me. No more pain and tension. No more aching throbbing. I sighed with contentment and reached for my lover, boneless and happy. "Mmmm, you're the best, Noah."

"Don't thank me just yet," he said, pulling me into a sitting position and pulling me into his lap. His erection—hard and thick—cradled between my hips as he pulled my legs over him. "Now that we've got the business out of the way, we have time to enjoy ourselves."

And then he proceeded to show me over the next two hours exactly what he meant.

CHAPTER TEN

S ometime later, I hopped out of the shower and dressed in the clothing I'd worn last night. It was wrinkled and reeked of casino and cigarettes, but my other stuff was down the hall. I finger-combed my tangled red hair in the mirror.

"Dr. Morgan has been calling my cell phone night and day," Noah said, pulling his shirt on over his head. "He seems to think we're having relationship troubles, and he's concerned that I'll pull my funding if we don't work things out."

I stilled, my eyes following his form in the mirror. "What did you tell him?"

Noah sat on the edge of the bed and pulled on one of his shoes. "I told him that the only way I'd continue to support the dig was if you shared my tent, regardless of whether you wanted to." He grinned at me, his eyes twinkling.

I went back to finger-combing my hair, relieved. "I'm sure, he offered me to you on a silver platter. 'Please, screw my newest archaeologist. She's a hot piece of ass!'"

"Surprisingly, no," Noah said. "He defended your

honor. Said you could sleep wherever you wanted, even if that meant with him."

"That's sweet . . . I think."

Noah's warm chuckle made me tingle all over again.

I glanced at his broad form in the mirror as he finished dressing. God, he was delicious. And so good to me. My legs felt boneless again, just thinking about the things he'd done to me a short time ago. Why did we ever fight?

He returned my gaze in the mirror. "So, how did you end up in this room?"

Oh. Right. We fought because Noah couldn't let stuff go.

I hesitated, not wanting to ruin our truce. "Someone helped me back from the casino last night. I thought he was taking me to my room."

Noah stiffened, then busied himself with tucking in his shirt. "He?" His voice was cold.

Irritated, I snapped, "Yes, and if I had done anything with him, I wouldn't have been in such pain this morning, would I?" I shoved my feet into my shoes. Count on Noah to ruin my good mood.

Warm hands touched my arms, and he pulled me against him. I stiffened, not wanting to be mollified, but it was hard to stay mad at someone as delicious as Noah. "I'm sorry, Jackie. It's hard for me to adjust. Despite our curse, Serim have issues with relationships."

The Serim? What did they have to do with me and Noah? He never talked about others of his kind, and

I'd never met any. I thought back to what Remy had mentioned earlier and wondered. Pulling back from his embrace, I studied his face. "Is something going on, Noah?"

He looked torn. "It's nothing I can't work out on my own. Don't worry about it. I'm just . . . unsettled. My kind does not share their mates."

Flattered and horrified, I pushed out of his embrace. "It's a good thing we're not mates, then. I'm just your indentured servant, and you're my master."

"It doesn't have to be like that."

"No? How should it be?" I stalked away to the bed and began to smooth the sheets, remembering all the careless commands he'd shot my way last night, forcing me to stay here. "When you say jump, I jump. When you say stay, I stay. When you say—"

"All right, Jackie." His voice was low, conceding. I felt him come up behind me and touch my shoulder. "We'll work out our problems later, okay? For now, let's just focus on you and your curse."

Just like that, my anger evaporated, and I turned to give him a quick hug and a kiss on the cheek. "Thank you, Noah. You're always there when I need you."

"Always." There was an odd light in his bleached eyes that I couldn't identify, but I decided not to bring it up.

"We need to get on the road before long. I think Remy has another engagement outside of Dallas this afternoon."

He clasped my hand in his. "Let's go get her, then."

We shut the door of the hotel room behind us, and I stared at the room number, thinking. I pulled my hand from Noah's and dug through my purse for a moment, fishing out the business card that Luc had given me, and extending it to him. "Have you seen this symbol before? I thought it might be one of yours."

Noah examined the card. He shook his head. "It's not angelic, if that's what you're asking. It's familiar, but I can't quite place it. Where did you get it?"

I took the card back from him. "Luc gave it to me in Colorado. He was here last night, too. I think he's following us." Why else would he be at a porn store in Colorado, then an Indian casino in Oklahoma later that same day?

"Luc, eh?" He plucked the card back out of my hand and flipped it over, reading the scrawl on the other side. His expression darkened when he read the threatening message. "What is this supposed to mean?"

"He was trying to warn me," I said dismissively and took the card back, shoving it in my purse. "So far he seems harmless." I just didn't know what Luc was up to.

"Is he a vampire?"

I thought back to Luc's bright white smile and perfect teeth. "I don't think so. He was at the porn store mid-morning. Long past vampire bedtime."

Noah pulled me possessively closer. A rush of warm heat slid between us, a nice feeling. "He could be dangerous, Jackie. I want you to be careful around him. Understand?"

I wanted to ask why one of the Serim would be interested in what I was doing, but I noticed the shuttered look on Noah's face. Whatever was going on, Noah wasn't sharing. "Want me to read his mind if I see him again? If he's immortal, it won't be quite as easy as a regular man—"

He shook his head at me. "It's too dangerous. If he finds out what you're doing, it could push him over the edge, make him act rashly."

Well, there was that. For some reason, men didn't like anyone rifling through their thoughts, hot succubi or no.

We grabbed a few doughnuts from the continental breakfast in the lobby. I was starving and polished off a neat dozen before grabbing a box while the desk clerk wasn't looking. Remy'd probably be hungry, too. And Drake.

Noah declined any doughnuts, having only coffee. "What's Remy's room number?"

I tucked the box under my arm and headed back out of the lobby and into the bright midmorning sunlight. "I'll show you."

We found Remy's room easily enough; I could hear her cries of pleasure from around the corner. Her room—114—had the "Do Not Disturb" sign hanging from the doorknob.

"Obviously she's not quite ready to go yet," Noah said, smiling ruefully.

"Not a big surprise there," I agreed. "Let's wake up

Drake, instead. I'll go get him if you'll get my things out of my room."

He took my room key and disappeared into 115 while I headed two doors down to Drake's room.

I knocked once and got no answer. "Wake up, Drake," I called through the door.

It was useless. The TV was on, blaring the local news loud enough to make me wince from this side of the door. I banged on the door harder.

It cracked open a bit; a bit of paper—a road map— wedged against the doorknob had kept it from shutting entirely. Fear prickled over me.

I'd seen enough episodes of *Law and Order* and *CSI* to know that this was bad news. Fearing the worst, I jerked the bit of map out of the door and swung it open.

The hot, sticky smell of blood was the first thing I noticed. His room was stifling—the air was turned off and muggy heat permeated the small room. I fumbled for the light switch, hoping that it would reveal some-thing different than what I was imagining.

The reality was much, much worse. Drake lay sprawled across the ugly coverlet on his back. His throat had been ripped open and he lay in a pool of dark blood. Worse, it looked like he'd fought whatever had attacked him. His arms and legs were mangled and covered in scratches, and blood sprayed the walls of the small room.

On the mirror someone had written in blood, I'M COMING FOR YOU.

Obviously a message for me and Remy. Or just me. And Drake had been the unfortunate recipient.

It was too much for my hangover, and the smell and the horror and twelve doughnuts in my stomach made me double over. Outside the door, I vomited on the sidewalk.

"Jackie?" Noah's questioning voice approached. He paused near me, and then I felt him go still and he cursed in a language I didn't know.

My body trembled, but my stomach was good and purged. I wiped my hand across my mouth. "Someone's trying to leave us a message."

"Your friend Luc?" Noah sounded grim.

"Not unless he likes eating people's throats." I swallowed hard.

I had thought the same thing, though: Who else knew that we were at this hotel? Knew what we were? Luc wasn't a vampire, nor a Serim, either, since I'd seen him in evening hours, as well. But if not Luc, then who?

My mind skittered back to Zane, but I shut that firmly out of my head. Zane would never threaten my life. He might be a bailing-out son of a bitch, but he wouldn't hurt me.

But there were a lot of factors in play that I was barely scraping the surface of. Angels. Demons. Vampires. Noah's kind, the Serim.

And Remy, with a possessed soul trapped inside her. Shit.

"Remy," I said weakly. "We need to check on Remy."

The sounds of lovemaking had died down, and Noah helped me to my feet. Her door was locked, but the room had fallen eerily silent. I knocked urgently.

No answer.

I wrung my hands, looking at Noah. "What should we do?"

"Step back." He pulled me to one side, grabbed the door handle, and shoved against the door with a mighty heave, using his shoulder as a brace. The door frame splintered and the door fell off its hinges.

I stared at Noah in surprise. Oh, my. That strength was a side of him I hadn't seen before. It made him a little more sexy and dangerous. It also made the Itch stir inside me again, but I clamped my thighs together.

Noah charged into the room ahead of me. "Get off of him, Remy!"

The bedroom was dark, and my eyes took their sweet time adjusting to the dim light. I heard someone crash against a nearby wall, and I flicked the light switch on.

Noah stood over the bed, an over-the-hill trucker staring up at him in disgust. Blood poured down the man's fat, unshaven neck. Across the room, Remy huddled near the wall, her eyes glowing eerily red. Blood ringed her mouth, and she panted heavily.

"What's the big idea, buddy?" The man yelled at Noah, struggling to sit up in bed.

I went to Remy's side, crouching next to her and using the hem of my T-shirt to wipe her blood-spattered face. "Remy?"

Those red eyes stared back at me, and a wicked grin curved Remy's pretty face. "Guess again," Joachim whispered from inside her body.

Aw, hell. I swiftly scanned the wrecked motel room. The bedding was tossed everywhere, but I found Remy's purse in one corner of the room and began to rummage through it.

Success—I found the holy water and held it aloft. Remy cackled wildly at the sight, her lips rolling back in an evil grin. "I've got what I need . . . for now." With that, the red color began to drain from her eyes, returning them to the sated silvery-gray I was used to. Her entire body went limp, and I guessed that Joachim had retreated again.

This time, though, Remy was aware of what had happened. She looked at me with horror and then bolted for the bathroom.

"Remy?" I followed after, shooting Noah a look.

"What's the problem with you people?" the man on the bed shouted. "Can't a guy and his date have a little fun around here?"

In the bathroom I watched as Remy chugged half a bottle of Scope, then scrubbed at her mouth again. "Don't let Zane fool you," she said to me, sounding sick. "Blood tastes awful."

"What happened?" I handed her a cheap towel from the rack and patted her back, trying to comfort her.

She wiped her face, looking weary in a way that I'd never seen before. "We were just enjoying ourselves.

I got back from the casino late after my date with the waiter, and George—"

"George is kind of disgusting, Remy."

She shrugged. "He's dying of cancer—I can taste it on him. I wanted to give him a send-off to remember." A disgusted look crossed her face, and she sat down on the edge of the tub. "We were having a nice little party when Joachim surges into my mind and decides that he wants to play, too. I think George was too drunk to care that I was drawing blood." She shuddered.

I gestured at the wall that separated her room from the one we'd just left. "Is that what happened to Drake? Joachim?"

She gave me a puzzled look. "What do you mean?" Remy stood slowly, an uneasy look on her face. "Did something happen to Drake?"

I eyed her skeptically. "You mean, it wasn't you—or Joachim?"

"I was sharing the whole experience this time—he didn't push me out of the way entirely. Just enough to take control, but not enough for me to miss out on what was going on." She shuddered again.

"Sir, I need you to sit back down," Noah said loudly from the other room. "Leave them alone—"

A hand grabbed my arm and tried to pull me out of the bathroom. I jerked away from him, the touch making the Itch stir and flare again. "Don't touch me!"

"Now, see here, miss," George said. Then his eyes widened and he dropped to the floor in a boneless heap.

A snore escaped him, even though his eyes stared up at the ceiling.

Not again!

Noah looked at my horrified expression, then down at the collapsed man. "What just happened?"

"My powers," I said, pulling my hands close to my chest so I wouldn't touch anyone else. "They sometimes go out of control and I wipe people's minds."

"The curse?"

"Yeah," I said in a small, ashamed voice. Now he'd really be horrified.

But Noah just put his hand out to me, helping me step over the sleeping man. "Come on, then."

"What do we do now?" Things had just gone downhill at a rapid pace. No one could see George's comatose body and Drake's murder scene and not think they'd been done by the same person. Remy was in trouble. I was in trouble, too. The police could think it was me.

"You've got to get out of here," Noah said.

"Good idea." The only other option was to wait around for the police to get here so they could grill us. And if we got locked up, waiting to be found innocent, I could die before I had sex again. Running was the only option. "I'll pull the car around, then I'll come back and get you and Remy—"

"I can't go," Noah said gently.

"What do you mean?" I frowned up at him as he helped Remy over George's sleeping body. "You just *got* here." He'd just returned to me and now he was going to leave me again? "We're still a day's drive from New Orleans. I won't last a day before the Itch kicks in again." Panic threaded through me.

But Noah shook his head. He already had his cell phone out and was holding it up to his ear as he urged me toward the door. "I've got friends in a few high places that owe me a favor. I'm going to call them and see what I can do to spin the damage control. It's best if you aren't here at all. Either of you." He gave me a stern look. "Understand?"

"But . . . but . . ." I wrung my hands, a stupidly girlish and weak thing to do. "What about my curse? And New Orleans?" I ignored Remy as she shoved me aside and began to toss her things hurriedly into her pink suitcase. "I *need* you."

A hint of a smile touched Noah's face and he pressed a quick kiss on my mouth. "You'll be fine, sweetheart. I'll catch up with you in New Orleans. You're looking for Delilah, right?"

Before I could respond, he turned away, putting a finger to his ear, his mind on the phone call. "Hey, Steve. It's Noah. Can you get the senator on the phone?

I hesitated for a moment, then reached up and gave Noah a quick peck on the cheek good-bye as he began to speak again. Remy was zipping her suitcase shut when I grabbed her by the hand. "Come on. Let's go."

I dragged her out of the hotel room and shut the door behind me. My suitcase and purse were discarded on the motel sidewalk where Noah had left them, and I bent over to pick them up.

"Holy shit," Remy breathed behind me. I straightened to see what she was staring at.

The door to Drake's hotel room was still open, and his blood-covered body was plainly visible on the bed. I grabbed the edge of my shirt and covered my hand with it, closing the door.

Remy's wide eyes stared at me, haunted. "It wasn't me, Jackie. I promise."

I took her hand. "I know," I lied. I didn't know what to think, but no sense in upsetting her further. "We've got to get out of here, like Noah said."

She nodded and we raced to the parking lot.

I tossed my suitcase in the backseat and climbed into the driver's seat. We had three-quarters of a tank, good enough to get us some distance between here and the motel. I started the engine and buckled in. "Hurry up," I yelled at Remy.

Remy slid into the front seat, and I could tell from the way her breath was catching that she was crying. I didn't have time to comfort her, though—not if I was going to get our asses out of trouble.

Even though I knew I shouldn't, I glanced back at the rooms. Noah's face was visible between the heavy curtains of Remy's room, watching me. He touched the window briefly, raising his hand to the glass, and then was gone, disappearing behind the drape again.

Yet another mess I'd left for Noah to clean up. The

thought ate at me as I backed the Hummer out of the parking space, threw it into drive, and peeled out of the parking lot, leaving my white knight behind—again. It seemed to be a bad habit of mine.

I didn't want to think about it. Or my curse. Or Remy, weeping quietly next to me, devastated that Drake was dead—and that she might have been the one to do it.

Instead, I thought about New Orleans. We just needed to get there in one piece, and I needed to trust that Noah would fix things. I just hoped that this time I hadn't gotten him into a bigger mess than he could handle.

Silence filled in the car as we drove through Oklahoma and into Texas. The sun was high in the sky overhead, the summer heat baking us through the windshield. I cranked the A/C on high. Remy stared out the passenger-side window at the flat, scrubby scenery as it rolled past. She'd stopped crying a while back, but her mood was still somber and her pale eyes were red-rimmed.

It felt like a much different road trip from when we'd first started. Now it was just two solemn succubi in the front seat. The men were gone. I wondered if the curse had a part in that, as well.

"I'm hungry," Remy said out of the blue, and looked over at me.

My heart fluttered at her words, thinking she meant for blood or the Itch.

Then she pointed at a billboard. "There's a Stuckey's at the next exit. Can we go there? I want a pecan log."

"Sure," I said, and pulled over to the right-hand lane. "But then we need to get right back on the road. Noah said he'd meet us in New Orleans, and I want to make sure we're there when he gets there."

"We'll get there," she assured me. "Don't worry. A couple of Slurpees and pecan logs won't delay us for long."

She had a point, and I was hungry, too. A pecan log sounded pretty damn tasty, and my stomach growled. "And maybe a pretzel or two," I added. "With nacho cheese."

"And chocolate," Remy said. "Chocolate always makes me feel better."

Me too.

I parked the Hummer as close as I could to the store, taking up two parking spaces.

"Keys?" Remy said, holding her hand out. "I want to drive next."

I handed them over. "Suit yourself. Just remember that we're in Texas now, so watch the speed limit." Because nothing caught the eye quite like a giant red Hummer going ninety down the highway.

She winked and gave me her usual saucy Remy smile. "I won't forget."

I was glad to see one of us was getting back to normal. Me? I was still pretty depressed over Drake dying and worried about Noah taking the fall for it.

The store was filled with all kinds of NASCAR memorabilia and the usual touristy crap, in addition to snacks.

After I grabbed a few bags of chips, some chocolate, and a few Dr. Peppers, I headed to the counter and put my stuff down.

The man at the register was older, fat, and wore a Stuckey's cap. He must shop in his own store. He gave me a friendly smile. "Want a lottery ticket?"

"No thanks," I said, trying to keep the smile on my face. With the luck I'd had lately, Lord only knew what would happen. I'd probably have to give money back.

He nodded and began to ring up my items, turning every once in a while to the TV that was on low volume behind the counter. I started to listen in to the news that was playing.

"*A grisly attack in a Super 8 in Ponca City, Oklahoma, left one man dead and another in a coma,*" the anchor-woman said in a serious voice. "*Police came upon the scene—*"

I froze.

"Seventeen thirty-two," the man said.

I ripped my gaze away from the TV. "I'm sorry," I said weakly. "How much?"

He repeated it and I held out my debit card carefully so that he wouldn't touch my fingers by accident, trying to listen as the anchor wrapped up the story.

"*One suspect is being held for questioning. Police say two others are at large, but they expect to bring them in shortly.*"

Oh jeez. That was us.

"Here you go," the store clerk said, handing me the receipt and my bag of junk food. I took it and nodded at him, scanning the store for Remy. I didn't see her inside, so I headed out. Maybe she was already in the car waiting for me.

That would be good. The sooner we got on the road, the better. The sooner we got to New Orleans, the better.

But as I emerged from the store, I noticed an immediate problem: The cherry-red Hummer was gone.

Fear flared through me. Remy had left me *behind*?

"Over here, silly," I heard her call from across the parking lot. Relief flooded me, and I turned to give her a real bitching out for scaring me like that.

And stopped.

Her hair pulled back into a long, sleek ponytail, Remy wore a new sundress (this one mint green) and waved from the door of a puke green El Camino, circa 1972. "Come on."

I checked the parking lot again. Still no sign of the Hummer. "Uh, Remy? Where's our car?"

She patted the puke-green door. "Right here."

"Last time I checked, we were driving around in a hundred-thousand-dollar car, not some five-dollar piece of crap."

"I traded the Hummer with some college boys that passed through." Remy smiled, refusing to take offense at my tone. She smoothed the door again, as if she could soothe it from my hurtful comments. "This ol' girl will suit our needs. It's perfect for . . ." She glanced around the parking lot to make sure no one heard. "Going under-cover."

Right. We'd just traded a Hummer for a rust bucket that probably wouldn't go fifty miles, much less five hundred. I sighed and moved to the passenger side. "It's a good thing you're rich," I muttered and jerked on the door handle.

It came off in my hand.

Remy cracked up. "This is *so Dukes of Hazzard*."

Just kill me now.

I threw my purse and bag in her lap and slid through the window into the bucket seat. "I hate you, Remy."

"Oh, you do not," she said cheerfully. "Think of it. Who'd look for us in an El Camino?"

She did have a point. I glanced at the back end of the car. "It's amazing that you were able to fit all of the luggage in the back of this car." Funny how I didn't see it anywhere.

Remy blinked. "Umm . . ."

The urge to cry grew stronger. "Let me guess. You forgot."

She started the car, the engine roaring—no muffler, from the sound of it—as it came to life. "I forgot," she called over the din. "We'll get new stuff in New Orleans."

"Better drive fast then, 'cause we're wanted women."

Remy gave me a thumbs-up. "We'll be there before you know it."

CHAPTER ELEVEN

The car began to smoke, and all the lights on the dashboard lit up as soon as we hit the eastern side of Dallas. We jerked over to the side of the road on Interstate 20 and skidded to a halt in the middle of construction.

I jumped out of the car, moving around to the front of the long hood.

"Is something wrong?" Remy said, sticking her head outside the window.

I fanned away the smoke, coughing. "Pop the hood."

The hood gave a rusty creak and groan, and as I pried it open smoke flew into my face, singeing my eyelashes with the heat.

Remy trotted to my side, her high heels clacking on the asphalt. "What are we looking for?"

Heck, I didn't know. The metal of the hood was so hot, it was burning my hands. I slammed it shut again. "I think we're stranded."

"Stranded?" Remy's brows drew together as she stared at me. Behind us, cars whizzed past. "What do you mean, stranded?" She looked down at the El Camino as if it had betrayed her. "The boys that sold me this car told me it never broke down on them."

"Gee, do you think they might have lied to get the free Hummer that you offered them?"

Her eyes widened. "Maybe."

Sigh. My hands went to my hips and I glared at the car. "So what do we do now?"

"Flag down a tow truck? Call the police?" She pointed at the road sign that gave a number for roadside assistance.

I shook my head. "We can't call the police. We're wanted for questioning in Drake's murder, remember?"

Her face fell, and she seemed to crumple from within. "I remember."

Ah jeez. I didn't need Remy falling to pieces on me. I forgot that Drake was her friend and sometime bed partner. I put my arm around her shoulders in a comforting half hug. "I'm sure it's fine, Remy. If they really wanted us for murder, they would have said more on the news. Someone must have figured out that Drake checked into the hotel with us, and they just want to ask some questions. That's all."

I hoped that was all. I was dying to ask Noah how he was doing, but calling him would be a very bad idea right now. If he was in custody, they might be able to track down my location from my phone signal and swoop down on us with a SWAT team. I wasn't sure if that was a realistic scenario or just something TV had fed to my brain, but either way, I wasn't calling him.

Remy gave a watery sniffle. "So what do we do?"

She was taking this harder than I thought. Alarmed, I stepped to the side of the road, glancing around. There had to be something we could do. Cars zoomed past, going well above the speed limit. The midday sun made the air shimmer over the asphalt.

I certainly didn't want to stay out here. On top of the heat, I was tired—tired of everything going wrong lately. The more I followed someone else's lead, the more it seemed to send me down the wrong path.

I thought for a moment, then decided to follow my own instincts.

Taking my Assistant T-shirt—I'd changed back into it and a pair of shorts when we'd left the hotel, since they were the only clothes I had left—I pulled it tight, knotting it underneath my breasts and exposing my unnaturally perfect torso. Then I rolled up the hem on my already-short jeans shorts.

"Are you doing what I think you're doing?" Remy said behind me, her tears replaced with amusement.

"Yep," I said, sticking my thumb out as I faced the highway, my other hand on my hip. I tilted my legs and torso so both my ass and my boobs jutted out, and pulled my hair out of its practical ponytail so the bright red curls would stream in the wind. "We're going to hitch a ride to New Orleans."

It was a picture-perfect pose, even if I did say so myself. I wouldn't think about the bad things that came with hitchhiking, like scary murderers or rapists. Remy and I could handle ourselves, and I'd wipe the brain of any man who tried to touch me (even if I didn't want to). Hitching seemed like the only way off the side of the road.

The first car to pass nearly got into an accident. Another car honked but didn't stop.

The third one pulled over.

Remy began to bounce up and down with delight. "A ride! Good thinking, Jackie!"

I felt proud of myself, too. The car that pulled over was a nice black sedan, nothing too fancy but clean, and it looked like it could hold us comfortably in the backseat. There were two guys in the front seat, which made me a little nervous, but we could handle them. One stepped out of the car.

And then I realized he was wearing a cop uniform.

"Aw crap." I looked over at Remy. "The curse strikes again."

Her eyes were wide, and she took a step closer to me. "Boy, you and that curse are something else. You want to go to Plan B?" She gestured at her forehead, miming that we should blank out his mind.

"Can I help you ladies with something?" The cop drawled as he approached us, his shoes clomping heavily in rhythm with the thudding of my heart.

I had to choose fast. My brain raced through the possible scenarios—we could overpower the one cop, no problem. The second one wouldn't be an issue, either, but then we'd have no way to get another driver to stop if we had an abandoned cop car next to us. And if we took their car, it'd be even worse news.

Our only other option was to go with them and hope for the best.

Remy gestured at her forehead again and I shook my head. We'd play this one straight.

"Hi, officer," I said, pasting a bright smile on my face and pulling Remy closer to me so I could watch her. "We're stuck on the side of the road."

He stood directly in front of us and glanced back at his partner, giving him a long, slow nod. What that meant, I had no idea, but I bet that it wasn't good. The cop put his thumbs in his belt and rocked backward a bit, eyeing the two of us. His gaze rested on my chest for a minute. "You ladies know that hitchhiking is dangerous? I wouldn't recommend it."

I hated the condescending tone in his voice. "We can handle ourselves."

His smirk indicated that he didn't think so. He thumbed a gesture at the car. "This yours?"

"Sort of," Remy chimed in helpfully.

The cop grinned, a slow spreading smile across his face that I didn't like at all. "That's real interesting," he said. "You know this car was reported stolen earlier this morning?"

Uh oh.

"That is such a coincidence," Remy said, giving him her best succubus smile. "Someone stole my car this morning and left me this rust bucket."

The officer smiled behind his dark sunglasses. "Then you won't mind coming with us to the station and answering a few questions."

"Of course," she chirped, grabbing me by the arm. When the officer turned away, she leaned in to me, offended. "Did you see how he treated me? He didn't even check me out once. Count on us to get a gay cop."

The officer turned, his face purpling with rage. "What did you say?"

I groaned.

A short time later, I found myself in a small Podunk jail in a Podunk county in East Texas. The police officers had moved Remy to a different cell. I could hear her arguing with the guard.

They'd decided to separate us after the excessive amount of whispering we were doing. My whispers consisted of demanding that Remy not mess with the guards' minds (and thus get us into deeper trouble than we were already in), and Remy's whispers consisted of arguing with me. Neither side was productive.

Officer Hawkins gave me a surly look as I thumped down on the bench in the small cell. I'd managed to avoid being touched by either of the police officers, but mostly due to luck—and the fact that they wore motorist's gloves. My guess was that he thought they made him look cool, because it certainly wasn't due to the steamy weather. He even wore one of those ridiculous beige hats and oversized mirror sunglasses, like the kind you only saw on *Walker, Texas Ranger*.

"You sit there," he said, pointing at me, "and you be quiet. And if we find out that your story matches up with your friend's, then we'll decide what to do with you."

Fat lot of good that was going to do me. I glared at the man. "You're not being very fair about this. I told you we didn't steal that car."

"I'm supposed to believe that your friend there traded away a brand-new Hummer for that piece of shit I found you girls driving?"

It did sound pretty stupid. "You don't understand. She's rich. She's a porn star."

The officer just laughed at me. "Sure, lady. And I'm the Queen of England."

I bit back a sarcastic remark and slumped on the bench. Frustrated to my core, I swung my foot in a rapid circle, trying to think. I couldn't stay in jail. I'd be a wreck if it took twenty-four hours to get us out of here. I eyed the tall, grim policeman on the other side of the bars and shuddered. Nope. I still had a few hours before he started to look good.

"So how long am I going to be here?"

He looked over at me, squinting. "The police in Oklahoma have asked us to detain you for questioning."

"Don't I get a phone call? Or a lawyer, or something?"

The policeman glared at me for a long moment, then grudgingly said, "You get a phone call."

I perked up and shot off the bench. "Really?"

I almost thought he was pulling my leg until he came over to my cell and started to unlock it. My hands nearly trembled with excitement and I folded them under my armpits lest I accidentally brush against him and steal his mind. Arms tight against my chest, I bowed my head, meek, when he opened the door to my cell and stepped out.

"One call," he said, his voice gruff. "So make it a good one."

I nodded, my thoughts racing as Officer Hawkins led me through the small police station and over to his desk. There was an old phone—the entire sheriff's office was a dusty dump of a building—and he handed it to me, the cord wound into a messy knot.

Who to call? My partner in crime—literally—was on the other side of the jail. Remy would be no help. My boss? Heck, no—if Dr. Morgan found out I was in jail, I'd lose my coveted job in a heartbeat, no matter if he had the hots for me. It was still daytime, so Zane was out of the question. My thoughts turned to Noah, but I hesitated. If Noah was still in police custody from this morning and I called him, that would implicate me.

"Well?" The policeman stared at me.

I thought hard. "Can I see my purse for a minute? I need a phone number from a business card." While I hated the thought of calling Luc for help, it was my only option."

The cop got up and returned a few minutes later with

my purse in a plastic bag. The inside was covered with a powdery substance, and I gave him a suspicious look. Either they were dusting for fingerprints or testing for drugs.

Within a few moments, I had the business card and I dialed.

Luc answered on the first ring.

"This is Luc." The trace of French accent was there, even in his greeting. A wave of accompanying warmth rolled through my body, and my eyes closed involuntarily.

"It's me," I said, then felt a bit stupid. "Jackie."

"I know your voice," he said softly.

I squirmed in my seat even as warning bells went off in my mind. This man was very bad news for me. Very bad.

And I totally wanted him. Damn the Itch.

"What can I help you with, *ma belle*?" His voice jerked me back to reality.

"I have a bit of a problem," I said. "A jail sort of problem."

"I see," he said, his voice smooth and tinged with a hint of laughter. "Perhaps this would be the Cherokee County Jail? Yes?"

How the heck did he know that? *Was* he stalking me?

I resisted the urge to hang up, though my senses tingled with fear. I needed this creepy asshole's help, whether I liked it or not. I didn't have anyone else to turn to. "That's the place. Can you help me?"

"I am but a stone's throw away."

What the hell did that mean? "So, uh, is that a yes or a no in mystery speak?"

"Oh, it's definitely a yes."

Goose bumps prickled through me. "So how soon can you get here?"

He only laughed, the sound throaty and seductive, and yet grating on my nerves.

A hand loomed in front of my face suddenly, reaching for the phone. "If all you're going to do is flirt, you're done with this phone call," the officer said in a surly voice.

I flinched back, holding the phone against my neck to keep it away from Officer Hawkins. "Wait, I'm not done—"

But he was determined, and his fingers brushed mine. Even as I jerked away, I felt that slight *snap*, like a rubber band being pulled tight and released, as his eyes rolled back in his head and he collapsed to the floor.

Oh jeez. Not good. Not good at all.

I hung up the phone, forgetting all about Luc and his flirtatious nonhelp. I now had a much bigger crisis at hand. I stood over the fallen cop and hesitated for a moment.

His phone rang, and I jerked up, my heart pounding. The phone rang again, and I glanced around, a guilty look on my face.

Crap!

"Dammit, answer your phone, Jimmy," called another man from a nearby cubicle.

It rang again, and I grabbed the receiver and then

dropped it back down on the hook, hanging it up just as quickly. At my feet, Jimmy snored soundly, comatose. I stepped over him and grabbed my purse back off his desk, tucking it under my arm. I had to get out of here.

A quick shuffle of the desk did not reveal the keys to Remy's cell. I checked his belt, and yanked the key chain off of it. Success. I clamped the keys against my palm so they wouldn't jingle and trotted back to the holding area, ducking my head when I passed the rows of cubicles in the background.

The holding area had a passcoded door blocking my way in. Luckily, Officer Jimmy's badge was on his key chain, so I swiped it and opened the door. Remy was inside one cell, seated across from an old homeless woman. In the next cell over, a man who stank of alcohol fingered his crotch as he watched Remy. Lovely.

Remy approached the bars with a relieved smile when she saw me. "Thank goodness. This place is more boring than your job. You here to spring me?"

I glanced at the door, uneasy. "I have a problem, Remy." I leaned in and whispered to her. "I sort of mind-wiped the cop by accident. He's lying under his desk right now."

She flinched a little. "That's not good."

"Understatement," I agreed, glancing warily back at the door. Someone was bound to see the downed police officer soon.

Remy waved a hand, dismissing my worry. "Calm down. I'm thinking." She drummed her fingers on her chin as she pondered our problem.

I gave the other prisoners an anxious look. "Can you think a little faster, Remy?" The man was eyeing me with all the restraint of a bulldog and, well, the woman smelled. Bad. I pulled out the keys and began trying them on the door.

"What are you doing?" Remy wrinkled her brow.

What did it look like I was doing? Knitting her a sweater? "I'm busting you out of here."

She reached through the bars and put her hand over mine. "Don't do that, Jackie. We're in enough trouble as it is—no need to add a jailbreak to things."

I stared at her. "I can't stay here, Remy." I pointed at my eyes. "Bad news in a few hours, if you catch my drift." At her blank look, I added, "Urse-cay? Uccubus-say?"

A look of comprehension dawned on her face. "I know you can't stay." Remy patted my hand. "Look, I'll slip into their heads and work my mojo. I can make them think that you were released before coming into custody. And I'll be out by the end of the day. No worries." She seemed supremely confident of the fact.

"How do you know for sure?" I was skeptical of that. "What if they want you for murder?"

"Sweetie, no one can resist a succubus when she turns on her charms." Remy gave a toss of her long hair and shifted her stance, at once becoming flirty and seductive. "I'll have my record—and yours—clean as a whistle by the end of the day. By cleaning *their* whistles." She winked at me and put her hands on her hips. "You can count on it."

Hoo boy.

I glanced at the door again as someone walked past. They were going to notice me here soon enough, and then I'd be in big trouble. "Do you want me to wait outside for you?"

"No, I've got some promo I should probably do in Dallas. I'll head back there once I'm free, and then I'll meet you in New Orleans tomorrow or the day after. Okay?"

Uncertainty washed through me. Now she was going to leave me alone, too? "I . . . I guess so. But how will I find Delilah? I don't know my way around New Orleans." I wasn't sure that I was ready to fly solo.

"Just ask for the LaFleur house in the Garden District. You can't miss it." She thought for a moment, then added, "Or ask to see a voodoo priestess. That'll get you to her, too."

"LaFleur house," I repeated, staring at her through the bars. No way was I getting involved with voodoo. Not with my bad luck. "Got it."

"Now get out of here," she said, shooing me. "Before you get caught again."

"You're a good friend, Remy. I don't know if I say that often enough." Hell, now I was getting all sappy. My eyes even watered.

She gave me a beaming smile. "Us Sucks have to look out for each other. Now scoot. I'll be fine."

I nodded. Heading for the door, I quietly went through into the main office. A couple of cops had their backs turned to me, so I held my breath and took a few steps backward, ducking in between the cubicle rows nearby.

A female cop turned the corner and glared at me. She reached for my arm. "There you are—"

Alarmed, I pushed her away.

Too late. Her eyes rolled back and she collapsed against me. Aw, *crap*. Not again. I caught her sliding body on the way down and helped her to the floor so she wouldn't break something, staggering under her dead weight. Well, that was one way—a most unfortunate one—to shut her up.

Remorse slamming through me, I stepped over her sleeping body. I couldn't focus on that now. I'd focus instead on a way to reverse the mind-wipe. There had to be one; I refused to think otherwise.

I ran out the front door of the station into the gravel parking lot. The late afternoon heat was sweltering, and thick pine trees in the distance blocked even the slightest breeze. I took a few steps forward, my feet crunching on the gravel. What to do now?

As I stood between two police cars, frozen in indecision, a dark blue sedan pulled up alongside me. A rental, judging by the green sticker on the bumper. It drove past, then stopped, then backed up.

The passenger side window rolled down, and the driver looked over at me.

Luc. Just as sexy and mysterious as before. He smiled behind dark sunglasses. *"Bonjour, ma belle."* Angling his chin, he gestured at the passenger door. "Won't you join me?"

All my senses flared with warning, but I put my hand on the handle and opened the door anyway. It was either this or go back into jail and try to explain why those cops were unconscious. Like it or not, I had to pick Luc.

He smiled as I slid into the car. "Going my way?"

"To New Orleans, actually." I buckled my seat belt and locked my door, glancing at the police station. "Can we get out of here?"

"But of course," he murmured, putting the car in drive and flying out of the gravel parking lot.

I watched the sheriff's office recede in the distance and felt a twinge of guilt for poor Remy. I hoped she'd be okay.

I hoped *I'd* be okay.

I crossed my arms over my chest and looked at Luc. "So where are you taking me?"

"You are so untrusting," he said with a hint of a smile in his voice. His gaze never left the road. "Did you not say that you need to go to New Orleans?"

Of course, I was untrusting; the guy was stalking me, and it was desperation that made me use him. That, and I just really liked sitting close to his lovely body, damn the Itch. "Correct me if I'm wrong, but isn't New Orleans about five hours from here?"

"You are wrong," he said, and glanced over at me, taking off his sunglasses. His smile flashed, his white teeth blinding in his swarthy face. "Six and a half hours."

"Picky, picky." Darn it, but he was pretty.

Those amber eyes smiled at me again, and he casually ran a hand through his long hair. "You said to correct you if you were wrong. I did so. You seemed to want it."

Boy, did I want it.

My legs throbbed with want, my loins throbbed with want, and I wanted so much that I was in danger of attacking him. I clamped my legs together tightly, shifting on my seat. My purse was biting into the flesh of my arm, I clutched it so hard. Need shot through me, thick and violent, and I eyed the car seat. No bucket seats, just one long bench. I could slide over and he could put his hand between my legs while he drove—

"Jackie?" He gave me a smooth, studied look. "Are you well?"

I blinked a few times, dragging my mind out of its wonderful fantasies. "Huh?" My nipples were hard against my T-shirt, and I clutched my purse against my chest to conceal them.

He studied me for a moment, the smile curling his mouth again, and giving me another hint of his perfect teeth. "You act as if you are scared of me."

"Scared of what I might do to you," I agreed, then flushed with embarrassment. "I mean, scared of what you might do to me." Yeah, like the cat wasn't out of the bag there.

He merely smiled. "You know I have no wish to harm you, *ma belle*."

"Then why are you stalking me? How did you know to be here?" His mesmerizing hotness waned for a moment. "Why are you are following me?"

And oh God, did he know about Drake?

But Luc didn't lose his cool. "You seemed like a woman who is in need of a friend. I had some time on my hands, so I followed you. That is all." He flicked a glance back at the road and pulled his sunglasses out again, putting them back on and concealing his amber eyes. "We have a mutual friend, you know."

"We do?" That would explain why he was following me, at least. "Noah? Zane?"

Luc chuckled. "If I told you, it would spoil the fun, *cherie*."

"Go ahead. Spoil my fun. There's not much of it to be had on this road trip."

"No? I enjoyed our little rendezvous the other night." His voice dropped low, and with it, my heart dropped into my thighs and began to pound there. "You did not seem to mind my attention then."

Lord help me. "I was drunk," I said, sounding feeble even to my own ears. "Don't use that as a yardstick for our friendship, okay?"

The smile didn't fade from his face. "Are we friends, then?"

I didn't know what else to say to that. "Something like that." I cleared my throat and looked out the window. "I'm trusting you to get me to New Orleans."

"I am flattered that you have put your trust in me."

"Don't be too flattered just yet," I said.

CHAPTER TWELVE

Luc seemed content to drive in silence. The sun went down, the moon rose, and the stars came out. Headlights flashed as cars passed us, and still we drove on. Once we reached New Orleans, then I could rest.

Being in the car for so long with Luc was strange. The clock on the dashboard was broken, so I had no idea how long we'd been driving. I felt all tense and keyed up just being near him, but he didn't try anything. Every once in a while, I'd catch him looking over at me, but he'd just smile and turn to stare back out the windshield. It was as if he was going out of his way to make me comfortable.

However, "comfortable" was nearly impossible, given my rising Itch.

At first, I thought I could ignore it long enough to get me to New Orleans. But as we drove further into the night and through the Louisiana woods, I began to have the sneaking suspicion that I wouldn't make it. My body ached with need, and even the air conditioner blowing full blast on my skin wasn't helping.

I needed sex. Again. And boy, was I getting sick of

this. It frightened me, too; Remy's prediction was coming true.

Something vibrated in my lap, setting off a tidal wave of sensations. A moan rose from my throat, even as I jerked my purse up and searched for my BlackBerry.

Luc glanced over at me, watching me with interested eyes as I shifted in my seat. "Are you well?"

"Fine," I snapped, staring at the lit-up screen of my phone as it vibrated in my hand again. Zane was calling.

I hesitated for a moment, wondering if I should answer, or be a bitch and let it go to voicemail. Need won out, though. I wanted to hear his voice. I hit the Receive button and put the phone to my ear. "Hello?"

"It's good to hear your voice, Princess." Zane's smooth voice sounded tired. "How's the road trip going?"

"Why do you care?" Part of me wanted to unload my problems to him, but Luc was listening to every word I spoke.

"Because I care about you—"

"You sure have a strange way of showing it," I said. "Where are you right now?"

There was silence on the other end of the line for a heartbreaking moment. Then, "I can't tell you, Princess."

My mood went straight to Hell again. "What do you mean, you can't tell me?"

"You wouldn't understand." He sounded so weary and sad. "I'm sorry I had to leave you. It's . . . complicated."

It figured that he'd automatically assume that I wouldn't understand. "Yeah, you're right," I said, trying to hide my hurt. "Nothing in my life is complicated at all."

"Jackie, that's not what I meant—"

"Just shut up, all right?" I refocused, pinching the bridge of my nose hard, determined not to cry. Screw crying. I shoved the depressingly lonely thoughts out of my mind and stared at the highway ahead. "So what were you calling for, Zane? Did you need something?"

There was a pause on the other end as he registered my defensive tone. "I guess I wanted to know that you were all right," he said softly. "With the curse and all."

The curse that had caused him to reject me like I was a piece of trash. "I'm just fine," I said, my throat tight. "Since you've abandoned me, I've found other company to help me with my needs. All of my needs, if you catch my drift."

"I do." Zane gave a soft laugh, and it sent a bolt of longing through me. Damn, I missed him. "Well, say hi to Noah for me, Princess. I guess I'll have to wait for another day to steal you away from him."

"Noah's not here," I said, rubbing my thumb on the side of my BlackBerry. "I've got someone new with me." I glanced over at Luc's handsome, lean profile.

As if on cue, Luc took one hand off the steering wheel and put it on my thigh. His fingers kneaded my flesh suggestively as he looked over at me.

A slight whimper of desire escaped my throat. There was no mistaking the look in his eyes.

"Someone new?" The tone of Zane's voice became guarded. "Anyone I know?"

My hearing grew distant, my mind distracted as Luc's long fingers caressed my flesh. He'd turned his eyes back to the road, but his fingers continued their easy massaging of my flesh, and it was distracting the heck out of me. "Someone really hot," I said dreamily into the phone, my breath coming in short bursts. "I should probably go."

Luc glanced over at me again, and his thumb grazed the inside of my thigh. "You should definitely go," he said, that hint of French accent in his voice melting my resolve.

"Jackie," Zane said warningly, all amusement gone from his voice. "Tell me who you're with. You need to be carefu—"

"See you later, Zane," I said, and ended the call.

That magical thumb brushed along the inside of my thigh again. "Is that your boyfriend on the phone?" Luc's voice was cool with amusement. "He is worried that you are here with me, *non?*"

"Ex-boyfriend," I said, my hand sliding over his to stop that maddening circle he was doing with his thumb. "And I don't care about what he wants right now."

"Bien," said Luc. "Neither do I."

Gravel crunched under the car's tires and I stared out the windshield, realizing that Luc had pulled the car over to the side of the highway. He had pulled off at an exit, and I could see a gas station amid the trees a couple hundred yards ahead, the yellow light of the sign bright in the distance. Over where we were parked, though, it was quiet and dark, the car nearly hidden from the road by the tree branches hanging overhead.

Luc turned the key in the ignition and the lights died, and the world grew dark and silent between us. The only sound was my rapid breathing. His thumb ran along the soft skin of my thigh again. "Will it upset your boyfriend that you are here with me, *chérie*? Alone?" He made the word *alone* sound very suggestive, and I knew what he meant.

My mysterious swarthy stranger was giving me an out. If I said something, he'd lift his hand off my thigh and we'd go on our merry way. If I didn't—well, even the most oblivious of succubi could guess where this would lead.

I studied Luc in the darkness of the car. He was a stranger. *Stranger danger, stranger danger,* my mind kept chanting, but the Itch overrode all sense. I needed sex, I needed it as quickly as possible, and Luc was easy on the eyes.

Damn easy on the eyes. He looked very different from both Zane and Noah. Both of them had the wide shoulders and strong upper body meant to carry wings. Luc was more slender, streamlined—though still sexy and masculine by my book. Elegant rather than overpowering. His eyes looked dark in the starlight and his lean face studied mine, as if he were making the same assessment about me. There was something different about his features—a tilt to his eyes and a grace to his cheekbones that made me think he wasn't native to . . . well, Hell. Like I had a clue where he was from?

"You're French?" I blurted out. It suddenly mattered to me that I pin him down and figure out what he was.

"I come from everywhere," he said, with a hint of a smile. "My family comes from a long line of gypsies."

"Gypsies?" I echoed. Modern-day gypsies? How weird.

How very, very *hot*. The haze of desire clogged my brain, fogging my thoughts and making my focus shrink to a very small portion of the world—the space between us in the car.

I tossed my phone to the floor of the car and slid closer to Luc, my mind made up. He said nothing as I slid over, merely watched me with a hint of an amused smile playing at his mouth.

My hand slid onto his thigh and I squeezed it. Lean or not, he was packing enough muscle to make me shiver with delight at the discovery. He smiled at me then, his hand sliding over mine and rubbing it, a silent encouragement. Now that the initiation was set, he'd let me be the aggressor.

I rather liked that. "If we do this, we do it by my rules," I said, eyeing him hotly.

"Agreed, *chérie*."

I slid over closer until my thigh was pressing against his. He hadn't moved a muscle, still leaning back and regarding me as I approached. I smiled, then, and leaned over his lap. My breasts brushed against his thigh and my long, curly hair played over his legs. I ducked my head under the steering wheel. The faint sound of him sucking in a breath made me tingle with pleasure. Casual though he might pretend to be, he was into this, too.

My hand reached under the seat and I hit the release. The entire seat fell backward another half foot rapidly, jerking us both and startling Luc. "Let me fix it," he began.

"Don't," I said softly, and sat up. There was now enough room between him and the steering wheel for me, and I flung a leg over him and moved onto his lap. It was a tight fit, but that suited our purpose just perfectly.

We both inhaled at the same time as my body settled onto his. My hips bore down on his at the junction of his thighs. The hard length of his cock slid against my apex in just about the most perfect way possible, and I rubbed against him, delighting in the feel. The steering wheel pressed against my lower back, forcing my hips hard against his, and I leaned forward, my breasts in his face.

The sudden desire to strip down and writhe on his lap struck me, and the mental image was so delicious that I peeled my T-shirt over my head. His hands slid to my back, holding me steady as I pulled it off and tossed it on the seat.

Luc leaned forward then, his hands reaching up and tangling in my hair and pulling my face down to his for a kiss.

The intimacy of that bothered me, and I pulled back. "No," I said. "Kiss later. Help me undress now." Maybe that would distract him. Lord knew it was distracting me. I took his hands and pulled them to my flesh again, guiding them up the column of my back until they touched my bra. "Help me take it off," I said.

He pressed his face between the mounds of my breasts, and I felt his tongue lick the valley between them. "Your body is perfect, *ma belle*. I could not get it out of my mind, the feel of it beneath my hands."

His words brought a rush of exciting memories to mind, of being stroked and soothed and petted over every inch of my skin as I lay on the hotel bed, quiescent beneath him. Oh yes. I'd liked that very much.

Luc nipped at the swell of my breast even as he unhooked my bra, eliciting a whimper of delight from me. His mouth slid over the swell, caressing it with his lips as he worked the lacy garment off my shoulders and then tossed it to the side.

I rotated my hips against his, feeling very naughty as I straddled him, topless in the moonlight. The car windows were fogging with the heat of our breath, and I felt like a schoolgirl about to get caught making out with her boyfriend in the backseat.

He bit at the swell of my breast again, then looked up at me. "Your move, *ma belle*."

"Put your hands on me," I said softly, reaching for his soft cotton shirt. I toyed with it, teasing his nipples through the thin fabric. "Touch me like you did last night."

A groan arose as my fingers teased his nipple, and his hands slid over my bare arms, massaging them with his palms. Heavens, that felt nice. I gave a soft sigh of pleasure and stroked his chest in time with the gentle touches he gave me. His hands slid around to my back, and he stroked them up and down my spine in a languid fashion. Every time his hands descended close to my ass, I'd raise my hips up and down, mimicking the motion. It was driving me crazy.

His hands pushed me forward suddenly, and I collapsed against Luc's chest, my breasts falling against his face again. He pinned me against him, his hands holding me tight as he nuzzled against my breasts, and his mouth latched on to one of my nipples.

I gasped in delight, my hips cresting in response as the sensation took over. God, but he was good with that mouth. His teeth played with my nipple, rolling it against his tongue and biting down just hard enough to make me cry out. He teased the taut peak until I was squirming against him, locked in his arms, and then he switched to the other breast to begin the same maddening, delicious process all over again.

"Do you like that, *ma belle*?" He grazed the nipple with his teeth and gazed up at me with hot eyes. Luc's hips rose under mine, reminding me of what we were barreling toward. "Do you like my lips upon your beautiful body?"

As wonderful as his lips were, I wanted him to talk less. When he spoke, it made me realize that I was betraying Zane and Noah with my actions. If he was silent, I could just revel in the sensation and think about things later. So I simply brushed the tip of my breast back into his mouth in a silent urge.

He took the cue, capturing the peak again and sucking hard, flicking his tongue against the tip, his eyes focused up on me. It was oddly erotic to watch him suck on my breast, feeling his hips moving under mine.

The sucking stopped and his mouth released the sensitive tip. Exposed to the air, it tightened as the rush of cool air touched my skin. He blew on the peak, then touched it with his fingers. I moaned again, wiggling in his lap.

"Answer me," he breathed against my skin, his lips hovering close to my nipple. Close enough to tantalize me, far enough to drive me mad. "I want to hear you say it."

Frustrated and needing, I put my hand over his mouth and rotated my hips again suggestively. "This is my party," I said softly.

That lit a wicked gleam in his eyes. "Is it, *ma belle*?" He put his hands around my waist and lifted me off of him, sliding me back onto the passenger side of the seat.

My arms and legs seemed to be everywhere all at once, and I flattened on my stomach, trying to adjust myself in the cramped confines of the car. Confused, I tried to sit up.

He was undressing, ripping his shirt off his body post-haste. Then his hands wrapped around my waist again and I yelped in surprise as I slid back into his lap, this time facing the steering wheel. His hard cock pressed against my ass and Luc grasped my hips again, then separated my legs so I was straddling him again, my legs splayed over his. I gasped, clutching at the steering wheel to hold myself steady as the new sensations swam over me.

Oh, this was very, very nice, too.

My shorts and panties still separated the two of us, and I knew he still wore his pants—his clothed legs were hot and hard under mine. But it didn't seem to matter much as his hands roamed over my back again, sliding over the bare skin and throwing my long, thick hair over my shoulder. Then, both of his hands reached around my front and grasped my breasts, kneading them roughly.

I moaned loudly at that, leaning backward against him. My nipples were trapped between his fingers, and he coaxed them even as he kneaded my flesh.

His hips jerked against mine, driving that hard, cloth-covered length against the spread of my legs. "Tell me that you like it, *ma belle*." The aching nubs of my breasts were teased again, coaxed into points as my bare back slid against his chest. The friction of our bare flesh against each other was erotic as hell, and I moaned again, low in my throat. He stopped, his hands frozen on my breasts.

I writhed in his lap, knowing what he wanted. I wouldn't give it to him, either. This would be on my terms. I wouldn't beg—I'd demand. "Touch me again."

He did, though not in the way I expected. Instead, one of his hands slid down the front of my stomach, sliding to the waistband of my shorts and unbuttoning them. His other hand flicked my nipple again, reminding me.

Then his hand slid into my waistband and past my panties, his fingers digging into my flesh as he searched for the hot folds that covered my sex. They slid against my overheated, damp flesh, eliciting a strangled moan from me and a groan of delight from him. "You are so wet for me, *ma belle*." His fingers stroked down my cleft again, a long, deep stroke even as he pinched my nipple. "So wet and hot."

When his fingers fluttered over my clit and then moved on, I lost my death-grip on the steering wheel and placed my hands over his and guided him back. "Now, Luc." I leaned back against him again, my hips jerking in response. "Touch me there again."

My entire body tensed as he seemed to hesitate over the spot, his actions driving me wild. Then, he circled my clit with one long fingertip. Once, twice. I felt him kiss my shoulder softly, then nip at the side of my neck.

I shattered. Rocking against his hand, feeling his teeth graze against my collarbone, I felt the orgasm roll over me and I cried out loudly with the intense release. He continued to rub against my clit, letting me ride the wave of the extended orgasm as my hips rocked against his, and he whispered against my neck in French.

"Oh, my God," I panted, rolling my hips against him one last time as he slid his fingers over my flesh. That was one of the most intense orgasms I'd ever had, and to think that I'd had it with a veritable stranger was almost shameful. Almost. The burning, obsessive yearning of the Itch was gone, though, and my body felt lazy and warm.

Luc kissed the back of my neck again and thrust against my spread hips, still whispering in French.

That jerked me back to reality, and I blinked for a few times, struggling to right myself.

I was sprawled in a stranger's lap, his hands still down my panties as we steamed up his car. And I still hadn't made it to New Orleans. And while I frolicked with the sexy Luc, Remy and Noah were languishing in jail.

I slid off Luc's lap, reaching for my shirt. I needed to get dressed, recover for a minute, clear my head, and think. Fresh air. Definitely needed fresh air.

He reached for me again, jerking me back against him. "Jackie, *ma belle*," he growled against my ear, his fingers searching my shorts for my clit again. "Not yet, my sweet." Luc nudged his erection against me again, reminding me that one of us hadn't had our fill.

For some reason, that annoyed me. I squirmed away, prying his hand out of my pants and sliding down the car seat. I glared at him as I panted for breath. "Stop it."

He gave me a burning look, his mouth thinning to a slash. "What are you doing?"

I jerked my shirt over my head, ignoring my bra. No time for trivialities right now. "You said we'd do things my way, right?"

"*Oui.*" One single, clipped syllable.

Good. He remembered. "Well, we just did it my way.

I'm done now." I tried to keep the smile on my face. "Thanks—it was awesome." I dug around on the floorboard, reaching for my purse.

He stared at me for a moment, then barked a laugh. "You are quite the little fucking cock tease, Jackie." There was a scary undercurrent to his voice that I didn't like. "Do you find this amusing? To leave me like this?" He gestured at the erection that strained against the front of his pants.

"Not amusing, no," I said, clutching my purse to me. What to say now? I still needed to get to New Orleans, and he was massively pissed at me.

His eyes had gone cold and hard, his shoulders heaving as he struggled to catch his breath. Luc's glare was intense, and his eyes never lifted from my face. That cold stare frightened me like nothing before, not even Zane in his most vampiric moments. There was something about Luc that made my skin crawl at times, and now was one of those times. My internal tuning fork was twanging like mad.

Something about Luc was bad news.

His hands clenched into fists, and he watched me, waiting.

Desperate for an excuse, I looked around the car. The yellow light of the gas station gleamed in the distance, and with it, I had an idea.

"Condoms," I said suddenly. "I don't have any condoms." I pointed at the gas station. "We need to get some." I hoped my smile didn't look as fake as it felt.

He ran a hand down his face and then reached for me again. "You do not need condoms."

Crap, did he know my secret? I decided to bluff, letting him run his hand over my front again. "Yes I do," I said, trying to stay focused as he roamed over my body. "I don't want to get pregnant." My stomach growled in the silence, and I added, "And I want something to eat. We haven't eaten in hours." Which was, like, a record for a succubus.

Luc gave me a hard look. "Condoms," he agreed, though the dangerous edge was still in his voice. "Then you come back and we finish this."

I nodded, then leaned in to give him the kiss he'd seemed to want so badly earlier. It only added fuel to my feeling that there was something wrong with him. The kiss felt . . . odd. It would have been an amazing kiss if it had been Noah or Zane to give it to me. But the taste of him was slightly . . . off. I hid my distaste, smiling at him to break the tension. "Yum," I lied. "I'll be back to get me some more of that." I stroked my hand along his cock to emphasize my point.

His eyes flared again. "Hurry," he gritted.

"Right. I'll hurry," I said as I opened the car door and slid out, my purse clutched to me.

The night air hit me like a brick wall—bracing and windy, it was just the wake-up I needed as I emerged from the steamy car. With my head clear, I picked my way through the gravel and headed toward the gas station in the distance, not looking back. My ears strained to hear the sound of other footsteps on the gravel, or the thunk of Luc's shoes on the road, but there was nothing but my own panting breath and the sound of crickets chirping in the trees.

That little episode had just taken a turn in ways I didn't want to think about. Maybe if I lingered in the store long enough, Luc would calm back down and we could finish our drive without it being awkward.

I mean, sure, I'd used him, but it wasn't like he hadn't set himself up for it. He'd said he'd play by my rules. My rules involved relief for Jackie but not relief for Luc. Tough nuts.

Besides, I was getting a little tired of everyone using me. I wanted to be in control for a change.

Okay, a lot tired, I mused as I tromped down the side of the highway. And it sucked. If all the other immortals were going to think of themselves first, I needed to do the same.

Time for Jackie to be in charge of Jackie.

The gas station wasn't far away, and soon I was under the bright lights. My shorts (and panties) were still damp with the heavy petting we'd done in the car, but thanks to khaki and the length of my T-shirt, it wasn't noticeable. I kept my purse clutched to my chest to hide the fact that I wore no bra.

Inside the gas station, it was nearly deserted. One old man hung out behind the counter, and he gave me a quick, friendly wave as I entered. I waved back, then headed to the back of the store, trying to think through my muddy thoughts as I grabbed a few bags of Doritos and all the Twinkies I could carry. I was starving.

I lingered inside for as long as I could, scanning the parking lot. For some reason, I kept expecting to glance outside and see Luc's car in front of the store, but it was still down the road, waiting patiently.

After grabbing a soda and a small package of condoms, I put my stuff on the counter and smiled at the old man. My hands were sweaty from nervousness and I wiped them on my shorts. I really, *really* didn't want to go back to the car and Luc. I kept thinking about that off taste in his kiss and the hard edge his voice had taken. It killed any sort of desire I felt for the man.

"You seem a little nervous, young lady," the old man said as he pecked at the ancient cash register and rang up my things. "Is your young man not treating you right?" He eyed the condoms, then eyed me.

"I'm fine," I said, trying to shut down that conversation. "Just tired." I glanced at the counter, drumming my fingers. Refocus. Refocus. A thought occurred to me and I smiled at the clerk. "Do you have a map of New Orleans here?" We'd be there soon, and thinking about New Orleans got the other, more dire thoughts out of my mind.

Like whether or not I'd have to end up having sex with Luc after all.

The old clerk squinted at me. "New Orleans? No, ma'am. Why would we have that?"

I wrinkled my brow in surprise. "Because it's the biggest tourist attraction in the state?" Though judging from this small, rinky-dink gas station, they probably didn't get a lot of tourists passing through.

"In Mississippi?"

Was he senile? "No, sir. Louisiana."

He shook his head. "You're in Mississippi, young lady. Just east of Jacksonville. Louisiana's about an hour and a half back in the other direction."

That didn't make sense. I grabbed a nearby newspaper and stared at the top of it. *Clarion Ledger*, it read, with Mississippi printed beneath in very hard-to-miss letters.

Oh, dear. "We must have taken a wrong turn," I said as I put the newspaper back on the stand.

The old clerk chuckled at me. "Not likely, miss. You would have had to miss a lot of road signs to go that far out of the way." He bagged my things and smiled at me. "Twenty-three ninety-five, please."

I counted out the money and handed it to him. How on earth had Luc missed the turn south to New Orleans? If what the old man said was true, we'd missed it hours ago. Long before lust had started to cloud my mind, much less his.

Either Luc was a really poor navigator, or he hadn't intended to take me to New Orleans after all.

Cold washed over me, and I forced my trembling hand to take the change and receipt the old man held out to me, careful not to touch his bare skin. "Thank you," I whispered. I grabbed the bag off the counter and stood there, uncertain. I couldn't go back to Luc.

Couldn't have sex with him, couldn't let him carry me off to the wilds of Mississippi.

He was a very dangerous man, I realized suddenly. A stalker, and I'd merrily climbed into the car with him and expected him to take me to New Orleans.

I was such an idiot.

I turned to the man behind the counter. "I need help," I said, pitching my voice low. "I have to get away from my boyfriend." Without looking out the window, I gestured with a slight nod of my head down at the highway. "He's out there waiting for me."

The old man nodded and gave me a faint smile, as if girls escaped from evil dates through his gas station every day. "I understand. There's an exit in the back, through the stockroom door."

Grateful, I smiled at him and threaded my way back through the dusty aisles. "You won't tell him you saw me?"

"Didn't see anybody," he agreed.

CHAPTER THIRTEEN

There was a dirt path behind the small area designated for receiving, and I ran down it, clutching my grocery bag and purse. The path descended into the woods and I followed it, trying not to think about scary stuff like wolves and bears and things like that.

After all, I couldn't die from a grizzly bear attack. It'd just hurt like a bitch. And I didn't even know if grizzlies lived in this neck of the woods—so to speak.

I ran down the path for what seemed like forever until it branched down the side of a hill, and I paused. If Luc tried to follow me, I was going down the exact way he'd expect me to. And the path wasn't too hard to find behind the gas station. Sucking in a deep breath, I eyed the woods to the right of the path and took a step off. I could go cross-country for a bit.

As it turned out, cross-country sucked.

My cute ballet-style sneakers weren't made for heavy hiking, and by the time I'd gone a couple hundred yards, my ankles were hurting and my shoes were filled with mud. A stick jabbed me in the leg and I swore, resolving to take a plane on my next road trip across the damned South. Damn Remy and her nitwit ideas.

"Jackie," Luc's voice called in the distance.

Shit.

I dropped to the ground, ignoring the mud and the branches that dug into my skin. It didn't matter if I was sitting in a nest of snakes—I was not getting up until Luc was gone.

Sure enough, he paced down the path a few moments later, shining a flashlight as he looked for me. I ducked my head, hiding behind the foliage and keeping my body as low to the ground as possible.

"Jackie," he called again. "Where are you, *ma belle*? Come back. We are almost to New Orleans."

Lying bastard. I clenched my hands, resisting the urge to choke him. Better yet, smack him on the forehead and wipe his mind—

Wait. I froze in place, thinking hard. My hands had been all over Luc a short time ago and he hadn't shown any signs of succumbing to my curse.

Which meant that Luc was something supernatural.

Which explained why my internal tuning fork went nuts every time I saw the guy.

Which explained why I was alternately attracted to and utterly frightened by him. What was he? A demon? No, demons were female, I reminded myself, thinking of Mae. He wasn't an angel or a vampire, since he wasn't affected by night or day.

So what the heck was he?

And why did he want me?

My stomach growled, reminding me that I hadn't eaten in hours. I unwrapped a Twinkie very slowly and ate it, careful to make as little noise as possible. I wasn't getting up from here until I knew it was safe.

When sunlight broke through the trees, I sat up and dusted myself off, surveying the damage. Snack cake wrappers and empty chip bags littered the area around me, but at least I was still safe. Luc hadn't returned last night—he'd searched the path for well over an hour, and then disappeared. I had been tempted to follow him to see if he was going to leave, but I forced myself to remain in the dirt and wait him out.

I looked like quite a sight, too. My legs were scratched, bug-bitten, and covered in mud. My porn star's assistant T-shirt had big muddy blobs across the boobs and stomach where I'd laid in the dirt, and I had no bra. My hair was a tangled mess, but at least I had my purse. And since the sun was up, I could call Noah.

Except—I didn't have my phone. I searched my purse three times before I remembered tossing it down on the floor of the car and then climbing into Luc's lap. Well, drat.

I eyed the path. Guess this was a good time to see where it led. I thought about heading back down to the gas station, then nixed it. If Luc was still nearby, he'd find me for sure. In my muddy, nasty gear and my red hair, I'd stick out no matter where I went.

So I decided to head farther down the trail and see where it led. Couldn't be any worse than the situation I was in.

After a half hour of walking, I came upon a small cabin—a tiny stroke of luck in what was turning into one long, ugly streak of misfortune. From the looks of the shanty, it wasn't more than eight feet by eight feet on the inside. There was no car pulled up, or even a place to park a car.

Hesitant, I knocked on the door.

No answer.

I pried it open and peered inside.

A deer head stared back out at me.

I jerked backward in surprise, then relaxed when I realized the deer head was stuffed. I opened the door farther and stepped inside, glancing around.

It was a hunting lodge of sorts. A few bags of old and moldering deer corn lay in the corner, along with a metal coffeepot and a camp stove. The window had a small hole cut out of the corner, the perfect size for sticking a rifle through and shooting game. Bambi's head was the only decoration on the wall to my right.

To my left, however, was a spare set of camouflage clothing. A quick check under a table scored me some boots, and a cap hung on a hook. Perfect. I changed clothes and left the few dollars remaining in my wallet on the table as a thank-you.

The pants and top were musty and smelled like old, wet dog, but they were clean and mud free. No one would look at me too oddly when I went into town, though they might question my sense of fashion. And I was determined to find a town around here.

I rummaged through the rest of the cabin but found nothing else worthwhile. No phone, no TV, no food or drink. I eyed the deer corn for a moment, then decided against it. Even I wasn't that hungry. When I was done in the cabin, I grabbed my purse and shut the door behind me.

The path to the cabin had forked, and I followed the new path for a good while. It must have been three miles and the oversized boots were determined to rub my feet raw, but I was descending some big-ass hill, so I felt like I was getting somewhere.

Unfortunately, that somewhere was right back down to the highway. I came out next to a sign that declared how many miles it was to the next town. Damn—much too far to walk. I hesitated in the woods, then glanced back at the road. I couldn't stay here; I had to take my chances with a lift.

For the second time in what seemed like a string of really bad coincidences, rather than a road trip, I pulled my shirt tight against my breasts and struck a sexy pose, sticking my thumb out. Oh, please, let someone be into chicks dressed like a centerfold for *Guns & Ammo*.

Once again, the succubus genes didn't let me down. Within five minutes, a truck pulled over. I approached the side as it idled, eyeing it suspiciously. It was fairly new as far as trucks go, and enormous. Bumper stickers about fishing and beer and ex-wives covered the back end, ruining what might have been an otherwise fine-looking vehicle. The passenger-side window was rolled down and I peeked in, hoping to God that it wasn't Luc.

It wasn't. It was a dirty-looking man of indeterminate years, wearing a red cap that sported a rebel flag. And he was eyeing me like he'd just hit the jackpot. Lucky me.

"Hey," I said, smiling faintly. "You a cop?"

"Naw," he said, his eyes widening at the sight of me. He glanced around, then leaned over. "How much?"

I frowned. "How much for what?"

He licked his lips nervously and leaned over a bit more, hanging off the steering wheel. He smelled like he hadn't seen a shower in weeks. Heck, maybe he hadn't. "How much for . . . you know." Licked his lips again, eyeing me. "A hummer."

Oh, ew. He thought I was some sort of hillbilly hooker? Please. I curled up my lip to spit back a fine retort, but stopped.

I could get to New Orleans in a nice truck like this.

It was time for Jackie to look out for Jackie again.

I turned the lip curl into a smile, putting on my best Hi-I'm-a-Redneck-Whore look. "Five bucks for you, sugar," I drawled. "If you want the full kit, it'll cost ya twenty-five."

His eyes bugged and he opened the passenger door for me. "What do you get for twenty-five?"

"A muskrat up your ass and a video of it on YouTube." I smiled sweetly and took his hand.

He collapsed with a heavy snore.

I glanced around to see if anyone was looking, then grabbed him by the front of his shirt and hauled him to the passenger side of the cab. Guilt returned, but I forced it away. I'd just ripped his consciousness from him, but thinking about the fact that he wanted me to blow him for a car ride made me feel better. Jackass. Besides, I refused to believe that the condition wasn't reversible.

I climbed into the truck and buckled in. Lucky for me, this big monster was an automatic, and I leaned over and picked through the glove compartment to see if there was anything useful. A handful of uncashed lottery tickets—along with a tin of chewing tobacco—spilled out onto the floor. I picked up the first ticket—a five-dollar winner. The next ticket was a twenty-dollar winner.

I smiled, glancing over at my sleeping passenger. "New Orleans, here we come."

With a road map, some instructions from a helpful man at another gas station, and a few bucks in my pocket, I was soon headed back in the right direction. I cut south through Mississippi and crossed over Lake Pontchar-train's long Causeway, constantly checking my rearview mirror for cops. It was silly to think that someone might report the truck stolen, of course. My redneck friend had been riding alone, and he wasn't able to tell anyone what I'd done.

Thinking about the people I'd zapped made me physically ill, and I had to press a hand over my mouth as I drove, concentrating on the road with ferocity. Focus on saving myself first and then I could worry about saving everyone else I'd screwed up.

I abandoned the truck in a parking lot on the outskirts of town and reported a flat tire, so someone could find my sleeping passenger and take him to a hospital. I called a cab from a nearby store and had it take me to the French Quarter. New Orleans, finally. The relief that shot through my system was palpable.

There had been over seventy dollars in uncashed lottery tickets in the glove compartment, and I'd redeemed them all before crossing the state line back into Louisiana. Now with the rest of the money in my pocket, I stopped at a nearby café and ordered coffee and something called a beignet.

Beignet must be Cajun for sugary-delicious, because I ate four of them before stopping myself and saving my money.

A few people were giving me weird looks, probably due to the commando gear, and I decided that the next course of action was to get some new clothes if I wanted to keep a low profile.

Or call Noah.

The Itch was rearing its ugly head, and I knew it was only a matter of a few hours before I'd be in dire need once more.

This was a matter of life and death, so Noah first,

fashion later. *If* Noah was even around. He'd said he'd meet me in New Orleans, but if he was still in jail, I was screwed. I had Delilah's name and knew that she lived in a district somewhere in town, but I couldn't remember anything other than that. Drat.

"Excuse me," I said, heading back into the café and wiping my fingers on a napkin. I smiled at the woman behind the counter. "Can you tell me some of the districts around here?" Maybe if I heard the name, it'd ring a bell.

She gave me an uncomfortable look, as if she'd like nothing more than for me to leave her shop—and her— alone. "Districts?"

I must have looked like more of a mess than I'd originally thought. "Never mind," I said. "Where's the closest internet café?"

The barista pointed me across the street and I headed over there, renting an hour's worth of computer time. I drummed my fingers on the mouse, thinking. A quick Google search of New Orleans maps had revealed a hell of a lot of districts, but I didn't remember which one was Delilah's. The Garden District sounded about right, but there were two of them on the map, and a ton of houses in those areas. I wasn't quite sure where to go next, so I Googled Noah's business and found the phone number.

His assistant answered the phone. "Gideon Enterprises, may I help you?"

Crap, what was his assistant's name again? I thought for a minute, leaning against the pay phone. "Hi, uh, is

Noah there?" Should I mention that I thought he was currently in jail?

There was a pause on the other end. "Mr. Gideon is currently unavailable. Is there something I can help you with?"

"Oh, um," I hesitated for a moment. "Do you know when he'll be available? I really need to talk to him."

Another pause. "Is this Miss Brighton?"

Uh oh. "Maybe."

Relief broke through his voice. "Mr. Gideon will be so happy you called. He's been checking his messages every hour and asked me to let him know as soon as you called."

Oh, thank God. "So he's okay? He's not in . . . jail?"

"No, ma'am. The police had to release him when they had no evidence against him."

That was great news. "Is he there?"

"No, he's in New Orleans looking for you. He's rather upset that you haven't called him in the past twenty-four hours."

"I lost my phone." I fiddled with the heavy metal cord of the pay phone. "Can you give me his number?"

"I'm texting his BlackBerry right now. Is there a number he can reach you back at?"

I gave him the number on the pay phone and hung up. The moments ticked by excruciatingly slowly as I stared at the phone, waiting for it to ring. What if this was one of those stupid pay phones where you couldn't call back? What if Noah was still pissed at me and wouldn't call now that he knew I was alive and kicking? What if—

The phone rang.

I leapt forward and jerked it off the hook. "Hello?"

"Jackie?" Noah's urgent voice was the most beautiful thing I'd heard in days. "Where are you?"

"The French Quarter." I was so happy, I was ready to break down and cry. I almost did as I sniffled out the name of the street corner I waited on. "Where are you at?"

"I'm coming to get you right now. Don't move from that corner until I get there."

The compulsion took a hold of me and I felt my legs lock into place. This time, however, I didn't mind Noah's bossiness. "I'll stay right here," I promised. "Just come get me."

Once we hung up, I sat down on the curb next to the phone, waiting. It was damn hot out, the midday sun beating down on me like I was a baked potato in an oven. My clothes smelled and they weren't exactly cool summertime gear, so I grew nice and sweaty while I waited. Add the humidity of the Louisiana bayou, and it was downright miserable. Jazz music rolled down the street, laughing tourists wandered up and down the French Quarter, and I might have enjoyed myself if I wasn't so damn hot and thirsty. The coffee shop across the street taunted me as people walked out sipping iced lattes.

But I couldn't go there; the compulsion from my master wouldn't let me. I pulled my grubby hunting cap down over my forehead, squinted at the sun, and waited.

I'd been sitting there for what felt like hours (okay, maybe it was a half hour, but it was a long half hour) when a shadow fell over me, blotting out the sun and offering a modicum of relief. "Jackie?"

My heart gave a happy thud. I jumped to my feet and flung my arms around Noah. "You're here!" I buried my face in his neck and breathed in his scent.

Noah was warm and delicious and so strong. His arms wrapped around me and he pulled me close to him, enveloping me in his embrace.

We stood there for a long moment, and the heat of the day no longer mattered. All the awful, terrible things of the past few days, the curse, Zane's disappearance—nothing mattered as long as Noah had his arms around me. I slid my arms around his neck and burrowed closer against him. "Thank you."

Noah chuckled, his breath light against my hair. "No need to thank me. You know I'll always come through for you."

I did know that, even if it was a subtle jibe at Zane. I chose to ignore that, wedging my body against his and letting his hair tickle my nose. "It still deserves a thank-you, though."

He touched my hair, then pulled a small stick out of it and tossed it to the ground. "Why is it that whenever I see you, you're covered in debris and smell bad?"

Oh, he just *had* to bring up the fact that he'd run into me after I'd crawled out of a Dumpster, once. I stepped back with a scowl, though I kept my hands on the soft knit of his shirt. He was not going out of my sight. "Never tell a lady she stinks."

Noah touched my nose and smiled. "When I meet a lady, I'll remember that." Before I could protest that, he eyed me with surprise. "So should I ask why you're in hunting gear?"

I thought of the trucker, and Luc, and all the other awful things that had happened in the past few days, and shuddered. "Probably not."

"I see." His hand slipped around my waist, supporting me. Noah wouldn't pry. "But perhaps you'd like a shower before meeting Delilah?"

"No," I said grimly. "No more delays. I want this curse gone before I lose my mind."

He eyed my clothing and chuckled. "She might think you already have."

CHAPTER FOURTEEN

I expected Delilah to have the most outrageous mansion in New Orleans. After all, Remy was only a few hundred years old and she had a palatial house that screamed money. So I was surprised when our cab pulled into the Garden district and stopped in front of a pale pink gingerbread house with a white wraparound porch and overgrown trees. It looked old and mysterious, like New Orleans itself.

Frowning, I turned to Noah. "This is Delilah's house?"

He gave me a puzzled look, sliding his hand from my shoulders to pay the cab driver. "Yes. Is there a problem?"

I eyed the old mansion. "It's so . . . normal." Subdued. Quiet.

"Not everyone has the same tastes as Remy." He slid out of the cab and offered his hand to me to help me out.

True enough. I mean, if the world was full of flighty, porn-star succubi . . . I slipped my hand into his and let him help me from the car.

I waited on the sidewalk as he shut the door and then

put his hand around my waist again. I was surprised at the possessive move—Noah wasn't a big one for public displays of affection, but I welcomed it. It was nice to know that he wanted me close to him, smelly hunting gear or no. I hoped I wasn't too out of place at Delilah's pretty, antique house. Noah was dressed in a short-sleeved, buttoned-up shirt with the collar open. No tie or jacket, so that was a good sign.

Noah led me up the flagstone walkway, and we paused on the porch and rang the doorbell.

Nothing.

I glanced around at the house, trying not to worry. There were potted plants scattered all over the veranda, and a rag rug. A cat lazed in a wicker rocking chair, enjoying the heat.

I flicked a look over at Noah. "Are you sure we're at the right spot?"

If Martha Stewart came to the door, I wouldn't be surprised one bit. But a voodoo priestess succubus? Come on.

Noah simply gave me a faint smile and glanced at the door, waiting. He seemed pretty sure that someone would come to it soon.

Me, I wasn't so sure. I stuck my finger on the doorbell and let it ring again. Then one more time, just to make sure they heard it.

He swatted my hand away. "Jackie, stop it."

"We're kind of in a hurry, Noah," I said peevishly. "The least she can do is answer the door." Didn't anyone around here have the same sense of urgency

I did? Didn't anyone care about the seriousness of my curse? I went to put my finger on the doorbell again . . . and couldn't. Noah's last words had been a command.

The door to the old house opened and a girl came to the door, her butter-blond hair in coiling ringlets that bounced on her shoulders. She wore a puffy white blouse and a pleated pink skirt. She looked about eighteen if she was a day, and plucked iPod earbuds out of her ears as she glared in my direction. "Can I help you?"

"Yeah. Is your mom home?"

Noah made a strangled noise, and the girl gave me a cold, withering look that could have frozen Bermuda.

A few things clicked into place. Aw, hell. "You're Delilah, aren't you?"

She smirked, flouncing her hair with practiced precision. "Of course."

I could tell this was going to go real well. I pasted a big fake smile on my face. "Hi there. I'm Jackie."

"I know who you are," she said loftily, eyeing me with distaste in my hunting gear. "Noah's told me all about you." She glanced over at him and smiled again, a coy look with a possessive edge that I did not like at all.

I stepped a little closer to Noah and put my hand around his waist. Must not lose temper. I need Delilah's help. "That's great that you know Noah," I said in my chirpiest voice, glad that my curse didn't involve the inability to lie. "Did he tell you about my problem?"

"Yeah. He mentioned that you have the supernatural equivalent of an STD. Way to go."

I could feel my face grow hot and my entire body tensed. If she said one more thing in that bratty voice, I was going to lose it.

"Jackie, don't," Noah said, as if sensing my anger. "We need Delilah's help."

I turned to glare at Noah. Another damn command. "Can you quit it with all the master bullshit? It's really getting tiresome."

Delilah's expression changed from smug loftiness to confusion. "Noah, you're her master?"

Noah ruffled his blond hair and gave her a sheepish look, the color rising on his face. "It's not what it seems."

Not what it seemed? Exactly what did he mean by that? That we weren't lovers? Master and succubus? My fake smile masked my hurt. "He just likes to dominate me in front of others," I offered, linking my arm in his again. "Part of a little sex game we like to play."

Delilah's jaw dropped as she looked back to Noah.

I thought Noah was going to swallow his tongue.

"Enough, Jackie." He turned back to Delilah, a faint flush on his face. "It's not what it seems," he repeated.

"No, I would guess not," Delilah snapped, and a flicker of jealousy crossed her face as she looked over at me. "Come in, then, the both of you."

Interesting that Delilah wanted Noah and was jealous of my relationship with him. All succubi were sired by a Serim. Was it bothering her that Noah and I had a strong connection? My hand firmly planted around his waist, we followed her into the house.

Inside, the Southern mansion motif continued. A large, sweeping white staircase took up the most of the foyer, and antique furniture graced the rest of the room. Flowers bloomed on a nearby table, and a blond male servant dressed in a suit moved down the hall, a feather duster in hand.

Between Remy's maid, Ethel, and now Delilah, it seemed like no supernatural cared to do their own housework.

"Nice place," I murmured. Too bad it didn't look like it belonged to her. I'd been expecting something a little more . . . scary. Voodoo-ish. Not Southern genteel.

"Thanks," she said, the malice gone from her voice and a hint of pride returned. "It's been mine for the past century and a half."

Delilah led us into a sitting room. I sat on the edge of an old-fashioned sofa with a circular back and little wooden legs. Noah sat next to me and put his hand on my knee, conveying our relationship to Delilah. She noticed but said nothing, perching delicately on the edge of a velvet settee across from us. "So tell me what brings you for a visit, Noah? It's been so long since we've seen each other." There was a definite purr to her voice, one that made my hackles rise.

"Jackie needs your help, Delilah. She has reason to think that she's been cursed, and we need your help to lift it." Noah's voice was even and smooth. He explained my symptoms and Remy's mention of Victoria and what had happened to her.

Delilah sat quietly, legs crossed and hands folded in her lap. I was pretty sure she knew the entire story already, but she listened to him attentively, her eyes roaming over him in a possessive way that I definitely did not care for.

When he paused, she raised her hand and gestured. The blond male servant came forward with a tray of lemonade in a sweating glass pitcher, and placed it on the coffee table between us. Delilah said nothing until she was handed her drink, and sipped it in a ladylike fashion.

The servant offered us lemonade as well, and I took a glass, holding it but not drinking. Noah declined.

Delilah swirled the lemonade in her glass a while, and silence fell in the room. She eventually glanced over at me, tilting her head slightly. "It does sound like the same curse that felled Victoria." Her pretty, round face was emotionless, her gray eyes cold. "Which I find interesting in itself, as it is a very specific curse. A curse upon your curse, if you will. A double-curse can be administered only by the most powerful of creatures." She sipped her lemonade again. "There is something you are not telling me, then. Who is your enemy?"

"My enemy?" I swallowed. "Um, well, I know I'm on Uriel's shit list right now."

Delilah's lips twitched. Whether she was going to smile or frown again, it was hard to say. "Everyone on earth is on Uriel's bad side. But I am positive that it wasn't him."

"I don't know." I mean, she hadn't seen how pissed he was about the whole Joachim-halo thing. But Delilah was the expert. If she said it wasn't Uriel, then it wasn't Uriel. "There's the vampire queen, but I haven't seen her in weeks." Thank goodness.

Delilah inclined her head in a nod. "Perhaps a minion of hers, then?"

"Zane," Noah growled beside me.

"No," I protested, startled. "Zane wouldn't hurt me. I know he wouldn't. Besides, the vampire queen kicked him out, remember?" I frowned at Noah. "Don't blame this on him, just because he's not here."

"Zane . . . as in, the vampire?" Delilah said mildly, arching an eyebrow at the two of us.

"Her vampire master," Noah agreed in a cold voice. "She has a blind loyalty to him that I don't understand."

I smacked Noah on the arm. "It's not blind faith."

He drew back and nodded crisply. Noah's expression didn't change, but I knew my words had hurt him.

"I don't think he did it," I said softly, trying to soothe him. "Zane was horrified when he found out I was cursed."

Delilah inclined her head again, like a queen receiving court. "Anyone else?"

Luc's slender, haunting beauty flashed through my mind. As oddly compelling (and alternately creepy) as I found the guy, I'd met him only after I'd been cursed. I was strangely reluctant to bring him up in front of Noah, too. He'd been so possessive and worried about me lately. To mention that I'd nearly had sex with another guy—a total stranger, to boot—would hurt him. "I've seen one guy a few places, but I don't think it's him. I only met him after I was cursed." I downplayed it deliberately, watching Noah's face tense at the mention of Luc. "I'd say it was him, except for the fact that I haven't done anything with him. Or to him." Much.

A hint of annoyance flashed across Delilah's face. "You are not giving me much to work with, I am afraid. No strange gifts? No charms left where you might find them?"

I shook my head. "Nothing. It's like I've been cursed out of the blue."

"No one is ever just cursed out of the blue," Delilah said with a lofty smile. "A hoodoo curse involves a lot of power and effort. Someone did this to you, and deliberately. You must have pissed them off royally."

That sounded like something I would do. "Hoodoo?"

"Magic." Delilah stood slowly, placing her glass of lemonade on the nearby table. "I must pray to the loas and ask them for their assistance on this matter."

My brow wrinkled. "Pray to the what?" If that was some term for angel or demon, count me out. I tensed just thinking about it.

"They are the spiritual advisors of those that practice voodoo." She seemed irritated by my questions. "I will ask them for their advice about your situation. You must give me complete, uninterrupted silence for the next few hours as I go to pray."

Right. To the voodoo hoodoo gods. Or loas. Or whatever.

"We'll leave the house," Noah assured her, a faint smile creasing his face. He stood up and touched her shoulder in a soft gesture that made my blood boil with jealousy. "Thank you so much for your help, Delilah."

"But of course. And I insist that you both stay with me instead of at a hotel," Delilah said, graciously as she gazed up at Noah with what could only be called adoration. "My house is always open for friends."

"We'd appreciate that," Noah said, squeezing her shoulder before dropping his hand. "Same room as always?"

"Same as always," Delilah agreed, casting a smug little look over at me.

Obviously, Noah had stayed here before. I clenched my fingernails into my hands, reminding myself that he was with me now. "Before we leave, can I take a shower or borrow a change of clothes?" Because lordy, I smelled bad.

Delilah's mouth curved into a smile. "Of course." She gestured at the sweep of stairs. "You may have the guest room," she stated, obviously not wanting me staying with Noah. "There is a shower in your room, and some clothing. Please help yourself."

"Come, Jackie," Noah said, taking my hand. "I'll show you where the rooms are."

I glanced back at Delilah as he led me out of the

room. She was watching us leave hand in hand, a frown marring her pretty face.

She didn't like that Noah was with me. Not at all.

Despite the fact that Delilah had put us in separate rooms a good distance apart (the point of which was not lost on me), I wasn't displeased with the quarters. The old-fashioned bed in my room was large and lush, and the closet was full of normal clothing, skirts and feminine, flowing blouses like the one she wore. None of them were her size, which made me wonder.

There was also a mirror on the ceiling, which made me wonder as well—for all of two minutes. This was the house of a succubus, after all. Even if she looked like an angelic high schooler, Delilah needed to have the same amount of sex I did.

Well, the same amount of sex before I'd been cursed, that is.

I picked up the landline phone on the edge of the bed and called Remy's cell. No response—it went automatically to voicemail. Maybe she was still in jail. Worry niggled, but I pushed it aside. Clean shower and clothing came first.

I rummaged through the dresser and closet. I found some panties that fit, a bra that was a cup too small but would still work, and a light, lemony chiffon blouse and matching skirt that would be nice and cool in the humidity. Now to shower. I headed down the hall.

To my deep happiness, Delilah did not skimp on the expensive soaps and shampoos, and within moments, I stripped and had climbed into the claw-footed tub. The showerhead was a few inches too short for my height, but I didn't care. The hot water felt delicious over my skin and I let out a groan of delight, closing my eyes and letting it run over my head.

"Room for two in there?" A hand touched my waist.

I screamed.

Noah clapped a hand over my mouth. "Shhh," he said, a hint of a laugh in his voice.

I was glad he found this funny, because it had scared the heck out of me. And now I had water in my eyes. I blinked rapidly and slapped him on the shoulder, my hand lingering when I noticed that he was naked and rather warm. Mmmm, nice. That took a lot of steam out of my anger. "You scared the hell out of me." The words sounded more like a caress than a rebuke.

Noah noticed that, too. He smiled at me and wrapped his arms around my waist, pulling me closer to him. His mouth brushed mine for a whisper-soft kiss. "I thought . . . we might . . . have time . . . for a quick . . . kiss or two," he said between nips at my mouth. "We can take care of the curse before we have to leave for a few hours."

My arms wrapped around his neck and I pulled his body close. His wet skin felt delicious against mine. My nipples were already hard as they brushed up against his chest, and I could feel his hard, thick erection against my belly. "Just a few kisses?"

His hands slid down to my ass and kneaded it. "For starters. After that, I figured it wouldn't matter if she was mad at us or not."

"You have a point," I said, nipping his shoulder suggestively. "Want to soap me up?"

His eyes flared to blue as they met mine. "I thought you'd never ask."

I handed him the washcloth and body wash.

Noah tossed the washcloth aside, then poured a big handful of body wash into his hand, his eyes on mine.

The Itch flared with hunger at the thought of his slippery hands sliding all over my body, and I bit my lip to keep from attacking him.

He raised his hand to my shoulder, dribbling a bit of the body wash on me, then slid his hand around the other side until the liquid dripped down my skin, smelling of gardenia and soap. His hands smoothed it onto my skin, rubbing my flesh gently.

"My breasts are rather dirty," I said helpfully.

"Are they?" He chuckled and his soapy hands slid to my waiting nipples. "Very dirty," he agreed softly. "This might take some extra time." His slick thumb flicked across one hard peak, his other hand circling the globe of my breast.

I groaned at the sensation, my hands moving back behind his head again, the urge to pull his mouth down against my body overwhelming. "Noah," I said with a small, needy whimper.

"Shhh," he whispered, teasing the tips of my breasts

with his fingers. The soap made them slippery, the flesh gliding over mine. "You asked me to clean you up, remember?" His fingers slid from my nipples and his hands circled my breasts, teasing their heavy weight and sliding over my skin, down my waist. "My dirty girl," he said in a low, teasing voice.

Lord, but that drove me wild. I tugged at his hair at the base of his neck, my nails digging into his skin to let him know how I felt. "Dirty all over," I said softly.

His wet hand slid between my legs. "Here, too?"

"God, yes," I breathed, wriggling against his hand.

His fingers slid between my wet folds, searching, and when he hit upon my clit, I moaned, shuddering.

"Feel good?" he asked, sliding them against it in a teasing back-and-forth motion.

I nodded, not trusting my voice as I clung to him, my breath coming in shuddering gasps as he teased the flesh between my legs, playing with my clit until I felt the quick body-shudder of an orgasm. Hard, fast, and overwhelming with relief. A sob escaped my throat as I came.

"That's it, Jackie," he said softly, sliding his hand away and then kissing my forehead.

I nestled against him, letting him put his arms around me and stroke my back, the hot water pounding on us. It felt nice to be held by someone I trusted, after the horrible week I'd been having. To feel the relief pour through my skin and know that I was free of the mood swings and hormones for the next few hours. And to know that help was just a few hours away.

I looked up at Noah and gave him a kiss, a smile on my face. "Best shower I've had in a long time."

"Kind of smelled like the only shower you've had in a long time."

I grinned. The heat of his erection still pushed against my body, nudging me with its insistent warmth. Noah would never ask for anything, though. That was just the way he was—all about others. All about me.

I reached over and grabbed the bottle of body wash, pouring a large handful into my palm. "My turn," I said with a wicked smile, then took a step backward.

Noah's body was big and tanned all over. I loved it: loved the thick play of muscles in his upper arms and torso, loved the thin line of darker blond hair that led to his groin. He let me smooth my soapy hands all over his body, his eyes closed as he enjoyed the sensation. My fingers slid over his shoulders, then lower to his shoulder blades, only to be met by a mass of rough scar tissue.

He hissed at the touch and jerked backward. "Don't, Jackie. Not there."

Not where his wings had been ripped from him.

I nodded and slid my hands back toward his front, playing with the flat discs of his nipples. The tips were hard and I flicked my fingertips across them, liking the reaction that got. It encouraged me to do more, and I slid my hands over his hips, then dropped to my knees in the shower in front of him. His quick intake of breath shot a thrill through my body. With my hands anchored on his hips, I tugged him closer to me, until the head of his cock hovered just inches from my mouth. The spray of water pounded on my body, on the back of my head, and showered me with distracting heat. I looked up at Noah, my eyes sultry compared to his blazing ones. "Dirty here?"

His jaw flexed and he remained silent, though his hand went to my hair, digging into my wet locks. He wouldn't tell me that he wanted my mouth on him, on the thick cock that twitched and jerked so close to my mouth, the head gleaming with wetness that had nothing to do with the shower. But the hand in my hair was all the encouragement I needed to know that he wanted it very much indeed. I leaned forward a little and brushed my lips against the salty head of his cock.

Noah's breath exploded and he swore softly.

I took him into my mouth. The thick head of his cock at first, teasing it against my tongue, playing with it. His fingers dug into my wet hair, encouraging me to go deeper, and I did so, letting the length of him slide along my tongue, stroking him deeper, farther, until I was filled with the thick length of him inside my mouth. The head of his cock butted at the back of my throat, and I pulled back, then released him to let my lips play on the tip of his cock again.

"Sweetheart," he groaned over me.

I wasn't sure if that was a "keep going" or a "stop it," but I was going to take it as an encouraging sign. My hands slid around to his ass, feeling the muscles in his buttocks as I slid my mouth down and over his cock again, pumping him with my lips and the warm, sucking cavity of my mouth.

A few minutes later, he groaned my name loudly. So much for silence.

Best shower I'd ever had.

CHAPTER FIFTEEN

We parted ways to dress. I opted not to bother fixing my wet hair—the humidity would just make it a curly mess—So I dragged it into a wet ponytail at the top of my head and dressed in my borrowed skirt and blouse.

Noah met me again in the hallway, his silver eyes gleaming in a proprietary way at the sight of me. He leaned over to give me a quick kiss on the cheek and took my hand.

"Any word from Remy?" I asked. "I left her a voicemail, but no answer."

He shook his head. "We can try her again when we get back. Delilah's getting started, so we need to leave. Let's go, and keep it quiet."

Like I couldn't be quiet? He didn't have to tell me, much less make it a compulsion. I glared at Noah but let him lead me down the staircase and toward the front door.

The sounds of chanting filled the house, concentrated back at the sitting room that we had left. Delilah's high voice rose in the sound of a language that

I didn't understand. The hair prickled on the back of my neck and my natural curiosity got the best of me. I slowed, craning my head to look even as Noah shoved me toward the door.

Delilah knelt in the middle of her quaint, old-fashioned living room. Hangings had been thrown over all the windows, and she sat in darkness before a candle-covered altar. Her face glowed in the darkness, deathly serious, and as I watched, she lifted a stick of incense, chanted more, and waved it in front of a few figurines.

Shivers ran down my spine. I let Noah pull me out of the house, glad to be out of there and back in the open, bright sunlight of a New Orleans summer afternoon.

"She's creepy," I said to him as we emerged onto the street. "And it's not just because she's practically jail-bait."

Noah laughed. "Not 'jailbait.' Delilah's body is stuck at a human age of nineteen or so, but she is extremely old. Very set in her ways—the old ways of New Orleans. She knows a lot about voodoo and ghosts and vampires. My kind, too."

"Yeah, I noticed she was rather into you," I said cattily as we crossed the street.

He only smiled at my jealousy. "I remind her of her sire. She was deeply in love with him when he was destroyed by a gypsy warlock."

"You know, this 'warlock' word keeps coming up, and I'm afraid that it's freaking me out a little." Poor Delilah. I almost felt sorry for her. Almost.

"Warlocks take magic and twist it for their own needs. They've been around for as long as my kind and vampires. Longer, maybe." He raised his free hand to hail a taxi. "Don't worry about warlocks. They're too rare for you to fret over."

"Where are we going?" I asked him as a cab stopped.

"Back to the French Quarter. We're going to have some wine, some good Cajun food, and enjoy some music."

"That sounds like a date," I said suspiciously.

He gave me a smile. "Don't you think it's time we had one?"

My heart melted, just a little. "I think so," I said, squeezing his hand.

I eyed the plate of crawfish in front of me with dismay. The beady eyes stared back at me. "I'm supposed to eat this?"

He grinned at my expression. "They're called mudbugs. What did you think it was?"

"A cute name for something without limbs?" I poked one with my fork, and I could have sworn it moved. I shuddered. "I ate all those beignets at the coffee shop earlier. I'm not that hungry." Dang, but I was a bad liar. Just the smell of hot food was making me drool, mudbugs or no.

Noah ignored me, cutting into his food with precise motions. "You break off the head and suck out all the juices. It's supposed to be excellent."

Yeah, well, I noticed he'd stuck with safe ol' lobster tail. I batted my eyes at him and tried to look pitiful. "Can I have a bite of yours?"

He shook his head and held his silverware in front of his food protectively. "You eat like a horse. If I let you have a bite, it'll be gone before I even get a taste."

I poked the creepy-crawlies in my dish and scowled. Suck head, indeed. I eyed my handsome date. "You know, Noah," I said, my voice soft as I slipped off my shoe and ran my foot up his leg. "If you wanted to see me suck head, all you had to do was ask."

His face purpled and he jerked in his chair, choking on his food. His eyes flared from silver to blue with desire as he stared at me.

I laughed evilly and removed my foot. "Gotcha."

"I can't take you anywhere, can I?" He said with a half smile, and flagged the waiter down. "Can you please bring a second lobster tail? And more wine?"

"More wine," I agreed happily, finishing off my third glass. I gave Noah a dopey smile when he pushed his lobster tail toward me. "You're a sweet man, you know that?"

He shrugged, a hint of a smile playing at his mouth. "Just your everyday fallen angel lusting after a busty redhead with her foot in my lap."

I broke into giggles and pushed the plate back toward him. "Here, we can share until he brings the second one."

Noah poured me a new glass of wine. "Or I could feed you."

My own eyes flared with desire at that. Noah really

knew how to push my buttons. I raised my glass of wine to him in a toast. "To New Orleans."

Noah lifted his glass. "To amazing company."

I blushed and sipped my wine. I had to admit, going on a date with Noah in the French Quarter was the most fun I'd had in a long time. Jazz music played in the background, and a festive mood filled the restaurant. I watched him over the rim of my wine glass. Maybe we'd have time for another shower before Delilah was finished with her ritual.

I put my glass down as the new lobster tail was brought out for us. Noah thanked the waiter and I tilted my wine glass back again, enjoying the taste. I wasn't much of a wine drinker, but Noah had ordered the most expensive bottle of something white, and it was extremely tasty.

Out of the corner of my eye, I saw something move and I glanced over, thinking it was another server. A man walked past the bar and turned into a door in the back. He paused in the doorway and met my eyes with a smile before disappearing through it.

I instantly recognized that lean, tall body, the almost too-pretty face, and the amber eyes.

Luc had followed me to New Orleans. He knew where I was.

My stomach churned, and my internal tuning fork—which had been vibrating so pleasantly—jarred me with uncomfortable sensations.

"Noah," I said, placing my napkin slowly on the table

and focusing on the uneaten food there. "We have to leave."

He reached across the table and touched my hand. "Is everything okay?"

I shook my head and whispered, "No."

The playful half smile on his face vanished in an instant. "I'll find the waiter and pay the bill," he said, getting up from the table. "Stay here, sweetheart. I'll be right back. You scream if anyone touches you. Understand?" He came around to my chair and kissed my forehead quickly, then disappeared into the crowd in search of our waiter.

If anyone touched me, I'd wipe their minds.

I wasn't sure if that was part of the escape plan or not. It was nice that Noah sprang into action, though— no protests, no questions, just implicit trust. Gratitude rushed through me, reminding me that no matter how much Noah irritated me at times, he was there when I needed him.

I could see Noah from my chair at our table. He waited by the end of the bar, talking with the waiter as he handed him a credit card. His gaze flicked back to me twice, but other than that, there was no sign of distress.

Me, I was a bundle of nerves. I stared at the door in the back of the restaurant, waiting for Luc to appear again. Waiting for him to approach me or do something. Anything. Every time the door swung open and a waiter came out, my breath caught in my throat.

"Ready to go?" Noah's hand touched my arm and I stifled a yelp.

"Ready," I jerked to my feet and tucked my hand in his arm. "Get us a cab, fast." I clung to him, scanning the crowd.

He led me out onto the busy French Quarter streets. The crowds had come out as twilight loomed, and the festive lights dangling from every roof were lit up. Before, I'd thought the crowd in the streets was fun. Now it just seemed dangerous. Luc could be anywhere, could step around any of the laughing, drinking couples and grab me. I stared at the setting sun with anxiety—Noah would be down soon for his evening nap, and I'd be alone with Delilah. With Luc somewhere in the city, looking for me.

It wasn't until we were safely in a cab again and heading back to the Garden District that I exhaled.

"Tell me what's wrong, Jackie," Noah said, his voice low, his still-blue eyes searching mine.

"I'm being stalked," I said. "Someone's following me. They have been since Colorado."

He looked at me thoughtfully. "I thought you said it was nothing?"

I winced. "Well, I thought it was nothing. I thought I'd ditched him back in Mississippi." I clasped my hands in my lap and stared down at them. "Plus, I didn't want you to know about him," I mumbled under my breath.

"What was that last part?"

"I didn't want you to know about him," I repeated

louder. "You can be a bit jealous at times. I didn't want you to know about him because I'm not exactly thrilled about it. Okay?"

Uncomfortable silence fell in the car. Noah's mouth drew to a tight line of anger. "He was in the hotel room with you. Back in Oklahoma."

"Yes." I flinched when Noah looked away from me, a muscle flexing in his jaw. "We didn't do anything, though, Noah. Remember how bad I was in pain when you found me a little while later?" I touched his arm softly, trying to soothe him. "I think he was just trying to help me, in some weird way."

Noah glanced back at me. "Then why are we running from him?"

"Because he's the one I hitched a ride with to get here. And I ran when I found out he had no intention of taking me to New Orleans after all." I shivered in recollection.

"What was he planning on doing with you?" His voice was cold, angry. Even murderous.

"I don't know. I didn't stick around to find out."

He exhaled, then he put his hand over mine. "We'll talk to Delilah and see what she thinks. If he's not a vampire or a Serim, that doesn't mean that he's not dangerous. Warlocks are human, too."

Good to know, I suppose.

Back at Delilah's house, we found the young succubus still in front of her altar. After we had left, she had pulled up the old-fashioned carpet over the wooden floors and had drawn all kinds of symbols in white chalk on the floor around her. It made the hair on my arms stand on end, but I followed Noah into the room anyway. Her chanting had stopped, and she turned to us with a grave expression as we entered.

"Sit," she commanded, gesturing at the sofa. I plunked down in my seat. Noah sat as well, though with more grace.

Delilah's eyes were dark blue with the Itch, and she frowned as her gaze roamed over me, searching my appearance. "The loas do not tell me much about your curse," she said, studying me. Her gaze flicked over me one last time and she turned back to her altar, where small figurines and dolls were intermixed with the incense sticks and candles. A Virgin Mary figurine loomed over all of it, her arms spread in a benevolent gesture to encompass the altar. As I watched, Delilah snuffed one of the candles with her fingertips. "They tell me that your curse was cast by one who knows you."

Well, that was kind of a big Duh. Can't see a lot of strangers cursing other strangers just for shits and giggles. "So what else do they tell you?" *Anything helpful?* I wanted to add, but kept my mouth shut.

"The curse was not placed upon *you*." Her blue eyes met mine, and the faint smirk returned. "As I thought, it was passed to you by another."

"But how?"

Delilah's smirk grew bigger. "Surely you can guess. I

don't have to explain something like that to you, do I?"

A Suck-to-Suck conversation about the birds and the bees? I narrowed my eyes at her. "Thanks, but I'll pass on the enlightenment. And that's not what I meant. I was cursed back when I was still in New City. Days before all of this." I waved my hand, gesturing at her living room. "So I don't see how all this works."

"Don't you?"

Noah gave me an odd look. "Are you being deliberately obtuse, Jackie?"

"No." I scowled at him. "If I received the curse while in New City, the only people that touched me were you and Zane. And neither of you would do that to me."

Delilah picked up something from her table and held it out to me, her palm extended. "Here."

I took it, wrinkling my nose as she handed it to me. It was a clump of hair, a few long strands of blond. "Um, thanks?"

She gave me a frustrated look and gestured with her hand. "Place it in your own hand, palm up."

I did as she told me to. "I really don't see—"

"That hair belongs to Noah," she said, interrupting me. She pulled a small vial from her altar and removed a stopper. The faint smell of herbs touched my nose. "This is an oil, specially blessed by the loas. It will show if Noah has ever been touched by a curse." She grabbed the tips of my fingers to ensure that I wouldn't move my hand, and sprinkled the oil over the strands of hair on my palm.

Nothing.

I resisted the urge to wipe my hand. "So, what happens now that we've watered it? Do I grow a new Noah overnight or something?"

Delilah raised her chin, glaring at me for poking fun of her magic. "If Noah had been touched by a curse, you would have known."

"I'm really not sure this voodoo stuff is working." I grabbed a Kleenex from a nearby box and began to wipe down my oily hand.

"Voodoo is the religion. Hoodoo is the magic, you idiot," she hissed at me. "And it *is* working."

I bit the inside of my cheek to keep my temper in check. "Any way to prove it?"

She reached forward and jerked at the now-dry ponytail that draped over my shoulder. Her fingers snagged in my hair and I yelped.

"Ow! That hurt—" My hand flew to my hair as I stared at her. Delilah took the clump of stolen hair in her hand and shook the oil over it. A faint flicker edged over her palm, like fire. The room filled with the smell of burning hair and the strands curled and writhed on her palm.

My skin prickled. "Give me the oil." She must have switched bottles when I wasn't looking. That had to be it.

Delilah handed me the vial of oil. I looked over at Noah. "Sorry, Noah," I said, and reached over and jerked on his hair.

He hissed, getting up from the couch and taking a step away. "You could have asked, you know."

I guess I could have. Grumpy, I took Noah's hair and shook the oil all over it. Nothing again. "So . . . maybe it works," I admitted, a little freaked out.

"You have been touched by a curse," Delilah said calmly. "Noah has not."

"Then that means . . ." I trailed off, unwilling to say it aloud.

"I'm sorry, Jackie," Noah said. "Zane cursed you."

CHAPTER SIXTEEN

I thought I handled it pretty well. After all, finding out that your vampire lover has cursed you gives you a permission to shriek and cuss. Maybe even sob loudly.

But I handled it like a pro. I let my lower lip wobble for a while, but I refused to cry. I was tired of crying. He'd asked me to trust him, and I'd trusted him so much that it hurt me.

My lower lip wobbled a bit more.

Noah was back at my side in an instant, pulling me against him. "Hey there," he said softly. "No crying. Let's just think about a solution, okay? We'll figure everything else out later."

He was right. I looked back to Delilah. "Why haven't I passed the curse to Noah, since it's passed with bodily fluids?"

A flush crept over Delilah's round cheeks—whether she was angry or embarrassed, I couldn't tell. "Curses don't work that way. Most are geared toward one specific person, and one person only. It's kind of like a key." Her pale eyes flicked back to Noah, and I could almost see them turn bluer. "The curse will be transferred continually, inactive, until it hits the intended target. Once it does, boom. The curse is in play."

So someone had deliberately set out to curse me. Oh, Zane. I gave a heartbroken sigh. "So how are you going to get it off of me?"

"The curse isn't a *hoodoo* curse," she said, putting the emphasis in for my uneducated benefit. "I can't remove it. There's all kinds of magic out there. Witchcraft, warlock magic, shaman magic—religious magic is just one small piece of the puzzle. It could be any kind of magic."

"So how do we figure out which kind it is?"

"We bring your sire here." Delilah's expression was cold. "You lure him here, confront him, and force him to reveal the one who laid the curse."

Somehow I doubted Zane would be up for that. "That's our only option?"

She shrugged. "We could always have someone cast an even greater curse on you. That would negate your current curse."

Gee, what a solution. "I'll pass, thanks."

Dark fell, and Noah retired to his rooms to sleep off the evening hibernation. I hated to see him go, but I knew that he would have stayed with me if he could have. It left me alone with spooky Delilah and her servants.

I hung out in my room for a bit, lying on the bed and trying to wrap my brain around the fact that Zane had betrayed me. Again. I still didn't believe it; my mind kept flashing back to our last face-to-face conversation. When I'd told him about the curse he'd been just as puzzled—and surprised—as I had been. If he'd given it to me, surely he wouldn't have reacted like that. But the evidence was stacked against him, even if I wasn't much of a believer in voodoo-hoodoo-whatever. It was hard to trust him when everything kept pointing to a betrayal.

And he'd abandoned me. I couldn't work past that.

My stomach growled, pulling me out of my heartsick misery, and I decided to help myself to Delilah's kitchen. Cookies always made me feel better. Cookies and milk.

I wasn't the only one in Delilah's kitchen. To my surprise, four other women loitered around the breakfast bar, sipping coffee and laughing at a shared joke. All of them wore short skirts, high heels, and skimpy tops. They eyed me as I entered the room and headed for the fridge.

"You a new girl?" one asked, her voice blunt and unfriendly.

"Look at her hair," another whispered. "No way that's a natural red."

Bitches. "It is *so* a natural red," I argued, grabbing the milk out of the fridge and placing it on the counter. Supernatural red was still natural for me. "And why do you care?" I opened a cupboard, trying to figure out where she kept her cookies.

A tall, lean girl with pale skin and a poof of dark, curly

hair—the prettiest of the lot and the leader if I had to guess—gave me a sneer. "Delilah didn't tell us there were any new girls."

"Maybe Delilah likes me better than you." Doubtful, though. Delilah and I got along about as well as two rabid wombats. "What are you guys? Voodoo groupies?"

The girls just glared at me. I sighed and turned back to my food hunt. The cupboard revealed nothing but health food: wheat pasta, diet popcorn, baked soy chips, rice cakes. Bleh. Like a succubus needed to diet? I grabbed the chocolate-flavored rice cakes and tore them open. Mmm, disgusting. I forced myself to wash it down with a double-swig of milk.

I was in the middle of another swig when the leader sized me up again, scowling at my boobs. "Ain't enough johns tonight to go around for all of us."

Milk sprayed out of my mouth. I choked for a moment, then wiped my dripping chin. "What?"

She lifted her chin. "You heard me."

I was saved from having to answer by the kitchen door opening, and Delilah breezed in, wiping the corners of her mouth. Her eyes were bleached silver, and she was followed closely by her handsome blond butler, whose shirt buttons were done up wrong. He bent his head at the sight of the women in the kitchen and slipped past Delilah, a blush on his cheeks.

She swatted him on the ass as he walked past and grinned at the women. "Hey, girls."

Weird. Delilah looked way too young to be treating men like a piece of meat. Even if her eyes seemed a bajillion years old.

The leader inclined her head at me. "Who's the new ho?"

"Ho!" I sputtered.

A bright, delighted grin crossed Delilah's face. "She's one of ours, so quit worrying. Do you have any clients lined up ahead of time?"

As I ate my horrid rice cakes, the girls discussed clients that had already booked time with them this evening. So Delilah was a madam, as well as a voodoo priestess. I'd forgotten about that. Guess she had picked up a few little hobbies over the years.

A knock came at the back door and another girl stepped inside, a puzzled look on her face. She held a hand to her neck.

"You're late, Lucy," Delilah snapped. "If you're late again, I'm going to dock you one night's work."

Man, harsh taskmaster. Poor Lucy looked rather distraught.

"I'm sorry, Miss D," she said, on the verge of tears. "I was coming up the walk and this other woman distracted me."

"One of those pamphlet carriers again?" Delilah frowned. "Do I need to call the police?"

Wow, Delilah was all business. I shoved another rice cake into my mouth, interested. This was better than TV.

Lucy dabbed at her neck again. "No, some freaking weirdo," she said. "Red eyes."

The rice cake lodged in my suddenly dry throat and I choked. As I coughed, trying to breathe, Delilah shook her head at Lucy. "What are you talking about?"

"The girl with the red eyes," Lucy said, puzzled. She touched her neck again, her fingers red. "She bit me."

I shoved past Lucy and out the door. Delilah's backyard was quiet, the oleander bushes and magnolia trees obscuring my view of the street. I descended the steps to the small walkway that cut through the grass, scanning my surroundings.

"Get away from me, lady!" a man yelled in the street, and I bolted in that direction.

Remy was there, her eyes bright red as she wrapped her arms around a tourist in a golf shirt. The balding man struggled to get away from her, clearly unnerved by her eyes. Around them, passersby were slowing down to stare.

I rushed forward and grabbed Remy by the arm, trying to pry her off the tourist. "I'm sorry," I said, jerking on my fellow succubus. "She's on a bad acid trip."

"Tell her to leave me alone!" the man shrieked, shoving his hands in Remy's face. The laugh that rumbled out of her throat wasn't a normal one.

"Joachim," I said in her ear, trying to distract the spirit possessing her. "Stop it! If you cause a scene, you'll get locked up. And then you won't be able to bite anyone at all."

Remy's hands flexed and she released the guy, sending him tumbling backward and the two of us sprawling in the street. A car honked.

I sprang back to my feet and dragged Remy/Joachim to hers. She smiled at me, red eyes unnerving, and tried to pull me in for a kiss. I slapped her hands away. "What are you doing?"

"Need to feed," the deep voice rasped from her throat. "Blood. Sex. Need." She reached for me again.

Oookay. People were stopping in the street to stare. I grabbed Remy's arm. "Blood. Sex. Sure thing. Let's go inside and make wild crazy whoopee. I'll let you bite the crap out of me. Deal?"

Remy's strong hand grabbed my arm and began to drag me toward Delilah's house. Her grip was much stronger than it should have been, and it dug into my arm as she pulled me through the backyard.

Once inside and through the front door, the girls emerged from the kitchen to watch as red-eyed Remy began to drag me up the stairs.

I clung to the banister, trying to stop my forward motion. "A little help here?"

Remy jerked on my arm so hard, I thought it was going to fly off. Could I regenerate an arm? I didn't want to find out.

Delilah stepped forward, a puzzled frown etching her young brow. "What's wrong with Remy?"

Another vicious jerk by my possessed friend nearly sent me tumbling backward. I wrapped my arm around the banister and clenched my hands together, forming a closed circle. She was going to break my arm if this kept up. "Long story," I panted, as Remy gave my arm another tug and growled. Her hand dug into my hair. "She's possessed."

The girls backed away. Delilah turned and ran back to the kitchen.

They were leaving me here with Remy? Alone? My grip slipped and I tumbled backward. Remy gave a grunt of approval and began to drag me up the stairs by my hair. "Hey!" I yelled back at the cowards hiding in the kitchen. "Help me!"

Remy crashed through the upstairs hallway, my legs flailing and kicking as she pulled me behind her. With her other hand, Remy grabbed me by the shirt and hauled me into my bedroom, which was the first one down the hall.

Remy's face suddenly loomed over mine, all red eyes and creepy smile. "Blood and sex now."

I shrank away, my shoulders raising up to protect my neck from her teeth. They weren't long like a vampire's, but it didn't matter. What she lacked in fangs she made up for in batshit-crazy, and I didn't want to be mauled. Or have sex with my best friend. *Ew.* I closed my eyes as she leaned in closer and planted my hand against her face, trying to shove her away.

There was the faint hiss of something burning, the smell of smoke, and Remy roared in my face. My eyes flew open to see Delilah looming over the two of us, a large silver cross in her hand and a canning jar of white stuff in the other.

She pressed the cross to Remy's shoulder again and

smoke rose from her skin. An unearthly scream rose from her throat.

"Get back," Delilah said in a calm voice.

Remy shrank back, hissing and drooling. Her lips bared her nonexistent fangs and she growled low in her throat.

"Get back," Delilah said again with more urgency, wielding the cross in front of her.

I realized she meant me, and I scuttled across the wooden floor behind her as she forced Remy to retreat. The growling and hissing continued, and when I hit the doorway, I got to my feet and stared at the two of them.

Delilah had backed Remy into a corner of the room. She hovered in the doorway of the closet, edging away from the cross with a hiss. "Get that away from me," the ruined voice growled.

"Back!" Delilah said again, and Remy retreated into the small closet.

As soon as she crossed the threshold, Delilah tipped her jar over, spilling a thick line of powder onto the floor. She muttered something under her breath as she covered the entire threshold of the closet with the powder line.

Then she relaxed, and turned to smile at me. "You okay?"

I eyed her warily, staring at the closet behind her. I fully expected to see Possessed Remy leap through the door and maul the crap out of her. "I'm fine," I said slowly, edging forward a few steps. "What did you do?"

Delilah tucked the jar back under her arm. "Rice powder. Old hoodoo trick. Your enemies can't cross a threshold that has rice powder—or brick dust—over it."

I edged forward a little more, staring into the closet. Remy huddled in one corner, her red eyes glaring at me as she stared at the rice powder line. Large, raised welts in the shape of the cross dotted her shoulder.

"Why did the cross hurt her?"

"Whatever's inside of her is unholy. I don't suppose you know what it is?"

"It's a long story."

"Try me."

I tried to gather my thoughts. "If I told you that, last month, we were trying to retrieve a halo for the vampire queen from one of the original Serim who became a vampire before he died, and when the halo broke, Remy absorbed him and now she's possessed—would you believe me?"

She didn't blink an eye. "Yes."

Right. These people had weird lives. "Then I guess that saves me the long story."

No matter how much I coaxed and pleaded, Joachim would not release Remy. He simply stared out at me from the closet with sullen, angry red eyes. I left my room so I wouldn't have to look at her. I didn't have any idea how to help her, and it upset me.

We'd tried more holy water but when we splashed Remy with it, it had no effect.

My friend was gone.

Downstairs, the girls and their "business" were in full swing. As dark fell, men began to show up at the house, disappearing for hours at a time with the girls into various bedrooms. So many men showed up that I stopped keeping track. The girls avoided me—I wasn't sure if it was jealousy over the looks I got from some of the men, or because of the weird supernatural stuff that had gone on earlier.

I sat in the kitchen alone, ate more rice cakes, and tried to think of a plan. There were still hours to go before dawn. I needed to get Zane here as quickly as possible so we could figure out what to do about my curse. I'd need to call him tonight so he could fly in and be here by tomorrow.

Which meant that I needed a plan ASAP.

So I sat in the kitchen and made lists on Delilah's Hello Kitty stationery, staring at my pen. What could I possibly tell Zane to make him come after me?

"Problems?" Delilah came and sat next to me, reaching for one of the rice cakes. "You look like someone just stole your lunch money."

"Close," I said. I scratched off the latest thing I'd written on my list: *Remy possessed and needs help.* Zane wouldn't care if Remy was possessed. He only cared about me. "I can't think of anything that would bring Zane running here to New Orleans."

"Have you played the girl card?"

I frowned and looked up at her. "Girl card?"

She took a dainty bite out of the rice cake and looked over my list, then handed it back to me. "Yeah. You know." She paused for a moment, then broke out into a large, theatrical sob. "Oh baby," she wailed. "I'm so scared. Please come help me."

Taken aback, I stared at her. It had sounded so realistic. "I'm a terrible liar. He'd see right through that in a heartbeat."

"Yeah, well," she said, and pointed at my list. "It beats number six here—'Tell him Noah has abandoned me and I need to have sex.' That's just stupid. If that was important to him, he wouldn't have left you in the first place."

I scowled at her and jerked the notepad back across the table to me. "I know that. That's why I scratched it off." Even I knew a lost cause.

"Tears. That's your ticket," Delilah said as she stood up again. I have seven hundred years of experience under my belt, and tears have never failed me once."

"Well, sure," I said, disgruntled. "You look like you're in high school."

"I was eighteen when I died," she shot back at me, irritated. "So don't even start."

As she stalked out of the room, I muttered, "Jailbait."

"Heard that!" she said. "And the sun's coming up soon, so you'd better hurry."

I headed into the foyer and picked up the phone. It

was now or never. Bracing myself, I dialed Zane's cell number.

The phone rang once, twice. When it clicked over to voicemail, my heart plummeted. Was he screening his calls?

It wasn't hard to fake tears for the message. Hell, I didn't fake them at all. When the phone beeped, I began to speak, my voice husky and full of tears. "Zane? Please, pick up the phone. I'm in New Orleans at Delilah's and I'm . . . I'm scared. Someone's following me and I don't know what to do. I'm scared he's going to hurt me. I need you." My voice broke and I sobbed into the receiver. "Please, Zane. Please come find me. I'm so scared . . . I'm at Delilah's. I . . ." I hung up after that. What else could I say? I love you? Miss you? Come see me, you double-crossing, cursing bastard, you?

Wiping my eyes, I headed back into the kitchen. Suddenly exhausted, I sat and buried my face in my hands. It had been such a long week, and it got longer by the minute. Noah would be up in an hour or so. Nothing to do now but wait and see if Zane got my message.

The phone in the foyer rang. I leapt out of my seat and slammed over to it. The caller ID on the screen showed Zane's name. Torn, I wrung my hands. What should I say to him when I picked up? More tears? Lie to him? Tell him the truth?

The phone stopped ringing. Eagerly, I watched the

machine to see if the voicemail light would flick on.

Nothing.

"Was that him?" Delilah hovered nearby, arms crossed over her chest.

I nodded, not wanting her to see how disappointed I was. "He didn't leave a message. I don't know if he'll come or not."

She lifted her shoulders in a gentle shrug. "Hard to say. Vampires are tough to read."

"Very," I agreed softly. After all, Zane had me fooled for weeks now.

The phone rang again.

Delilah and I looked at each other, and she came to my side. The red light on the machine flickered like mad when the phone rang again, and Delilah smiled.

"Should we answer it?" I said, a bundle of nerves. I frayed more with every unanswered ring.

"Nope," she said, smiling. "He's checking to see if it's really my number or not. Let him leave a message. It'll make him wonder."

After six rings, the answering machine picked up. "This is Delilah LaFleur," a youthful, bouncy voice said. "Leave a message after the beep. Thanks!"

"Delilah!" Zane's voice nearly screamed into the receiver, startling me. "I know you're there, you little bitch. Put Jackie on the phone."

A faint smile curled her mouth. "I see he remembers me."

My heart broke at the panic in his voice, and I

itched to reach over and grab the receiver. I took a step forward, but Delilah shook her head at me. "If you want him to come after you, let him worry. Best thing for it."

She was right, but it didn't make my heart any easier. I wrapped my arms around myself and listened as Zane screamed into the answering machine.

"Delilah! You put her on the phone right now. Right now! *Right fucking now!*" Zane panted for breath for a moment. "If I get there and you've let one fucking hair on her head get hurt I'm going to make you regret it," he said in a low, terrible voice. "Don't you let them hurt her. Do you hear me? *Do you hear me—*"

The phone beeped, and the message cut off.

"Oh my," Delilah said with a drawl, fluttering her hand over her heart. "Sounds like he's got it bad for you." She gave me a saucy wink. "Looks like we'll be seeing him, after all."

That should have made me feel better. Instead, I only felt worse. Zane had been so worried and distraught. It made me wonder if he'd truly been the one to curse me, or if Delilah was playing me for a fool.

But Delilah's magic didn't lie. Did it?

"I think I'm going to go lie down for a bit," I said hoarsely.

Delilah gave me an odd look. "Sure." We both knew that succubi didn't sleep, but she didn't ask, and I didn't explain.

As I headed up the stairs, she cleared her throat, and

I could hear her shoes on the wooden floors. "Jackie, wait."

I turned around and glanced down at her. Delilah's youthful face was frowning up at me, and she crossed her arms over her chest, troubled. "How did . . . how did you talk Noah into turning you?"

I wasn't sure if that was supposed to be offensive or flattering. "I didn't talk him into anything. We had sex after Zane bit me, and boom—next thing I knew, I was a succubus. It was a bizarre coincidence."

"Some coincidence," she said in a dry voice. "I was just wondering." She looked as if she wanted to say more but hesitated.

"What is it?" A gnawing filled my stomach. "What do you know?"

Delilah shrugged, her curly blond hair flowing down over her shoulders. "I thought it was outlawed to make new succubi. It's been a Serim rule for a hundred years now. But maybe they repealed it."

"Maybe," I echoed, disturbed by the thought. Was Noah in trouble over me? Delilah didn't seem willing to part with more information, so I trudged up the stairs. Inside the guest room, I flopped down on the bed and stared up at the ceiling. All I could think about was Zane's terrified voice on the phone, and how guilty it made me feel.

Soft, rapid panting hit my ears, and I opened my eyes and rolled over. The closet door was open and Remy crouched near the shoes, her long black hair a mess over her face. Red eyes stared out at me, inhuman. Her mouth was open as she panted, and drool hung from her lower lip. As she caught me looking at her, she smiled, and the drool-string wobbled.

Well, now that was pleasant.

Looking at Remy would only cause me to tense more and I left so I wouldn't have to stare at the living embodiment of things I'd ruined. And I wondered, briefly, if there was something that Noah wasn't telling me.

CHAPTER SEVENTEEN

I t was a long, excruciating day.

The girls had left Delilah's house by the time I emerged from my quiet room, plagued by bad thoughts. I smelled coffee, and coffee sounded wonderful.

I met Delilah in the kitchen as she counted out stacks of money on the table and made notes in a day planner. She gave me a faint smile and turned back to her work. "Coffee's fresh if you want some."

"Thanks." I headed over and poured myself a cup. There was no sugar or creamer on the counter, so I opened the cabinet overhead. Several canning jars of more suspicious white powder were shelved there. "I suppose it's too much to hope that this is sugar?"

"I don't keep sugar," Delilah said, not looking up.

Figured. Black coffee, coming right up. I needed a caffeine rush to take away the pounding in my head. I returned to the table, pulling up one of her bar stools. "That your money from last night?"

She nodded. "The girls pay me a fee to give them a nice place to set up and to keep them safe. It works out well."

It worked out very well, judging from the amount of money on the table. "Am I the only succubus that isn't in a sex-related line of work?"

She only smiled. "You're an archaeologist, right? Noah told me about that. He likes smart girls, you know. He's very proud of you and your job." Her mouth had a wistful curve to it.

Huh. I wondered what else Noah had told her about me. "Do tell."

But she changed the conversation. Delilah reached into her pocket and pulled out something hidden in her fist. "Here—these are for you."

I held out my hand and she dropped a pair of necklaces on it. One was a heavy, ornate silver cross on a chain. It looked very old and very expensive. The other was a small bag that smelled musty and had lumps sticking out of it.

"Okay, I'll bite," I said, looping the cross over my head. "I get that the cross is for protection from vampires. What's this other thing?"

"More hoodoo magic," she said. "It's called a *gris-gris*."

I pulled open the knot around the top of the bag and stared inside. An old penny, some dirt, some herbs, and some other crap I didn't recognize. "It looks like trash."

She frowned at my distaste. "It's powerful magic, so don't knock it. That will keep you safe from any supernatural thing that wishes you ill. Well, except for a succubus." Delilah continued to stack the money, her hands busy. "I had to handle it, after all. Couldn't very well ward it against myself."

"As long as you don't start frothing at the mouth and try to bite my neck, we'll be fine." I slipped the bag over my neck. It looked hideous.

"Ha ha," she said, then glanced up. "Hello, Noah." Her voice changed to a sweet, sing-songy tone that put my nerves back on edge.

"Good morning, Dee," Noah said from behind me.

Dee? When the heck did she become Dee to him?

I was mollified when he pressed a kiss to the top of my head and sat next to me, rubbing his eyes. I wished for a moment that we were alone, so I could ask him about the disturbing conversation I'd had with Delilah, but she didn't seem to be going anywhere. Figured. I pushed my nasty black coffee toward Noah. "Here. Looks like you need this more than me."

Noah bent his head over the coffee cup, sniffed it, and handed it back to me. "Pass. So what were you two talking about? How to fix Remy's situation?"

Guilt shot through me. "More like hookers and money," I said, glancing over at Delilah. "I don't know how we'll fix Remy's situation, frankly."

"Wait him out." Delilah picked up a stack of bills and rubber-banded it in half.

I frowned at her. "You're kidding, right?"

She rolled her eyes and sighed, looking startlingly young for a moment. "No, I mean it. Wait him out.

Demons hate to be trapped. Give it a few hours and he'll let her go."

"Remember the whole halo thing? He wasn't a demon—he was an angel. Once." Something niggled at the back of my mind. Something I was supposed to do. The word *demon* kept tripping through my brain . . .

Oh, right. I'd nearly forgotten the promise I'd made to Mae. "Which reminds me," I said, trying to recall her message. "There's something I nearly forgot to pass along."

"Oh?" Delilah picked up another stack of money, her voice bored. "And what's that?"

"Do you know a demon named Mae? I made a deal with her to find out about my curse." Delilah's hands slowed and her head shot up. "I'm supposed to tell you that she's invited—"

"Jackie, no!" Delilah grabbed my arm just as I reached for my coffee.

The hot liquid slopped over the edge of the cup, burning my hand and splattering on the countertop. "Ow," I yelped, trying to jerk my hand away from hers.

"What have you done?" Delilah cried, her nails digging into my arm.

A loud boom shook the house. The windows shattered and glass rained in on us from every direction. I dove under the breakfast bar. My head smacked against the tile floor, jarring my brains, and for a moment I thought I'd died in a bomb explosion. The thick, noxious scent of sulfur filled the room, and heat radiated. I opened my eyes and sat up, terrified that I'd been caught in a fire.

No fire. Just one big, scary-looking demon in the middle of the kitchen. Mae wore another power business suit—this one bright pink—and stilettos. Silvery-white curls framed her face in angelic halos, nearly masking the red gleaming from her eyes.

"Aw," she said at the sight of me, a wicked smile curving her face as she cocked her head. "And here I didn't think you'd be dumb enough to go all the way through with it, sweetie. My apologies for underestimating you."

Beside me, Noah struggled to his feet, blown off balance by the force of Mae's entrance. Glass tinkled to the floor as he moved. It caught the demon's attention and she glanced over at him. With a quick flick of her wrist, he flew against the wall and crashed with a groan.

"A Serim? Here?" Mae tsked and looked down at Delilah, who lay on the floor, staring up at the demon with hate. "Your taste in friends is sorely lacking, my dear. You know you'll get a nasty reputation if you hang out with his kind."

I scrambled to my feet and rushed to Noah's side. He leaned against the wall limply, his head lolling to one side, and my hands swiftly ran over him. There were a dozen cuts and blood everywhere, but he seemed to be fine otherwise. Dazed and half out of it, but fine. "Jackie," he mumbled under his breath.

"Shh," I said, putting a finger to his lips to silence him and moving to stand in front of him and shield him.

As luck would have it, Mae was watching me with

avid red eyes as I turned. "Interesting," she said with a soft purr in her throat. "Your sire, I assume?"

I leaned back against Noah as Mae stepped over the glass shards in her delicate, strappy pink heels and crossed the floor to us. My body jammed up against Noah's, I squeezed my eyes shut when Mae got in my face, waiting for the worst.

Her chuckle blasted sulfuric breath in my face. "Don't worry, little one. You did me a favor, and I don't forget those sorts of things easily," she said with a sultry tone.

I stared at her. "What do you mean?"

"I'm quite impressed," Mae said in a blithe tone, studying me for a moment longer before moving back toward Delilah in an unhurried, long-legged stroll. "Most of your kind don't keep their word to demons. But I like you, Jackie. You kept your word. I'll be sure and put in a good word for you downstairs."

Just what I needed. A demon's word of recommendation.

"How?" Delilah coughed, grabbing a hold of the edge of the counter to pull herself up. "You can't be here. This isn't unhallowed ground."

"It is now," Mae said, smirking. She strolled over to Delilah and slammed her fist down on her fingers. Delilah shrieked and fell back to the floor, rolling in pain. "Your little friend saw to that."

Delilah shot me a look of hate from across the kitchen floor. "What did you do?"

"Nothing!" I protested. "All I did was deliver the message."

I should have guessed. A demon bargain was never without strings attached.

"Delivered the message," Mae agreed. "Then you spilled your coffee. Inviting a demon into your home and making an offering of food or drink is enough to change any ground to unhallowed." A smile touched her lips, quirking her mouth. "No upside-down crosses or unholy prayers needed."

This was *very* bad news.

"Now, speaking of unfulfilled promises," Mae said, her sights turning to Delilah once more. "I think there is the small issue of a certain succubus who promised to destroy an angel or two on my behalf three centuries ago . . . and then didn't pay up."

"I'm not killing anyone for you," Delilah said, struggling to get up from the floor. From the way she flailed, something unseen was holding her down.

"I know you won't, precious," Mae cooed, standing over her. "That's why I'll have to take matters into my own hands and take over your body."

I had to do something, this was my fault. "Wait," I said, stepping forward. Noah groaned, but didn't follow me. I glanced behind and saw him pinned to the wall in the same fashion that Delilah was pinned to the floor. Not good.

Red eyes focused on me, narrowed. "Is there a problem?"

The way she said that made my skin crawl, but I forced myself to take another step forward, scanning the kitchen for anything that would help me take down a very angry demon. "Don't touch her," I said, a warble in my voice. "I need her to help me."

"Sweetcakes, I don't care about you," Mae said, turning away from me again. She loomed over Delilah for a moment, then planted one shoe over the girl's hand and slowly ground her heel over it.

Delilah screamed in pain.

I darted forward, not thinking, and tried to shove Mae off of Delilah. The demon's flesh burned against mine when I touched her, like touching lava itself. My hand blistered and I screamed, jerking back away from her.

Mae jerked backward as well, baring her long, sharp teeth in a hiss. "Idiot." She rubbed her arm where I had touched her, as if my touch had hurt as well.

"The *gris-gris*," Delilah said from on the floor. "She can't hurt you."

Gee, I guess a blistered palm was just a nice howdy then.

"You shut your mouth, whore." She reached down and hauled Delilah up by her long hair. Dee's eyes were wild with fear, and she writhed in the demon's grasp. "I can see you're obviously not going to stay on my good side, darling Jackie. A shame. You'll regret that later."

With one last ugly look at me, Mae turned to Delilah and planted her mouth on her.

Delilah's knees buckled and she sagged against the

demon. The smell of sizzling flesh filled the room and Delilah's cheeks glowed orange, as if lit by a fire within. The demon stilled, pressing the girl's body against her, locked in a smoking embrace. As I stood there her body began to pale and dissipate, and Delilah's grew brighter with intensity.

She was absorbing the demon. Soon she'd be possessed, just like Remy.

Remy—of course!

I darted across the kitchen and reached for the Mason jar of white rice flour in the cupboard.

Since it had trapped Remy, I figured it could work on Mae, as well. I unscrewed the cap and glanced back at the two women locked together, just in time to see the last wisp of smoke from Mae's shifting form drift into Delilah's mouth. The succubus stood there, her eyes fluttering backward, skin steaming and red. Blisters rose on her face, everywhere the demon had touched her.

I rushed forward and began to pour the powder on the floor. Within moments, I had a clumsy circle poured around the frozen Delilah, and I waited. Would it work on her, or did I have to be a voodoo priestess?

As I watched, Delilah gave a great shudder and the blisters disappeared leaving only a pink flush to her skin. Her eyelids fluttered and then opened. Her eyes gleamed red, then rested on me.

Delilah/Mae smiled, slow and sure, and my heart began to pound in my throat. If she came after me, the *gris-gris* wouldn't protect me. It didn't work against succubi . . . and judging from the smile on her face, Mae knew that.

She took a step forward, and flinched as if she'd run into a wall. Confusion clouded her face, and she looked down at the circle on the floor, and then back at me.

"Let me go, precious. You don't want to do this."

Instant relief shot through my body. She couldn't come after me. "No. Let Delilah go."

"You and I had a deal," Mae said, her sultry voice odd coming from Delilah's mouth.

I clutched the jar closer, expecting her to burst forth and come claw my eyes out. "As you reminded me before," I said, "the deal was just for the message. Anything else would be a second deal."

The demon stared at me, her lips twitching as if she were amused by my retort. "Do you want to make a second deal? Name your price."

"I'll pass for now, thanks."

The demon snarled, an unearthly sound, and Delilah's body writhed. "Let me go," she screamed again at the top of her lungs, flinging herself against the circle's invisible wall.

She was going to hurt Delilah if she kept that up. I took a step toward the circle, wincing as she flung her body against it once more, screaming at the top of her lungs.

"Jackie, no." Noah stood up, extending his hand out to stop me. "Don't touch her."

I hesitated, looking over to him. "She's going to hurt Delilah."

He shook his head, trying to shake free the fog in his mind. "She wants you to *think* that she is. Remember, Delilah is a succubus, like you. She can't be permanently injured."

I willed myself to glance back over at Delilah's "cage" and shuddered when she stared at me with avid red eyes, grinning.

"So what do we do, then?"

"We wait. Demons can only manifest on this plane for a short period of time."

Like Joachim, Mae didn't seem as if she was in a hurry to get out. "Er, how short?"

"It depends on the strength of the demon."

Mae was a lower-class demon, but she still looked strong enough to make us miserable for weeks. "I need her help tonight. Remember? The whole vampire-showdown thing?" God, first Remy, now Delilah. It sucked to be a Suck around me. "Is there a Plan B?"

"There is." Noah pulled out his cell phone. "We call an exorcist."

CHAPTER EIGHTEEN

M orning turned into afternoon as Noah made a few calls, trying to line up an exorcist to make an emergency visit that day. One priest was busy, two wanted nothing to do with us, and the fourth hung up on Noah when he mentioned the address. I guessed that Delilah had a bit of a reputation around here.

Eventually, though, Noah got an exorcist from Baton Rouge to agree to drive into the city and perform the dirty deed. So we hung out in the kitchen and waited.

I perched atop one of the countertops, wiggling my bare feet. "Are you sure you got all the glass out? They still hurt." I'd stepped in a lot of broken glass in my race to the rice flour.

Noah wore a pair of glasses and was shining a flashlight on my foot. "This is the fourth time I've checked your feet, Jackie," he said, a husky note in his voice. He was probably remembering that round two of the glass removing had led to some hot sex in his bed (since my room and the kitchen were both occupied by demon-possessed Sucks).

It was almost a shame the exorcist was on his way. I

could have stood for another round of bed romping to take my mind off the fact that twilight was rapidly falling and Zane would be here soon.

"I promise you, there's no glass," Noah said, interrupting my thoughts. "And your feet will stop hurting soon. You heal fast."

That was true; already, the soles of my feet were growing new skin. The wounds would probably be entirely gone by morning.

I looked over at the bloodied Delilah in the ring of powder. "*She's* not healing very fast." It worried me.

"She's currently possessed by a demon. That tends to affect your recovery."

Mae/Delilah simply smiled at me and rammed herself against the invisible wall again, causing blood to gush from Delilah's nose.

I wrinkled my own in distaste. "I think she's just doing that to bug me."

The demon laughed and ran her nails down her face.

Yup. Definitely doing it to bug me.

I looked back to Noah. He looked so serious with his glasses on—very Clark Kent. I slid one foot out of his grasp. "Can we talk about something?"

He sat back on his heels and looked up at me. "Of course."

Unsure how to approach the Serim law thing, I hesitated. What if Noah wouldn't tell me his big secret? "Delilah was telling me—"

Something black moved past the broken window, in

the front yard. I stilled, my breath catching in my throat. Was it Zane? So early? I caught a glimpse of black clothing before it disappeared around the shrubbery, and part of me cringed even though my heart pounded.

The doorbell rang.

I exchanged a look with Noah and hopped off the counter and onto the newly swept floor, taking great care to avoid Delilah's circle.

Noah put a hand on my arm. "Stay behind me." He grabbed one of the kitchen knives and tucked it into his hand, then strode into the foyer.

Hesitating only for a moment, I trailed behind him. Part of me really didn't like cowering behind him. After all, Zane thought he was coming here to rescue me, right? But the entire thing still made me nervous. I clutched the *gris-gris,* grabbed a knife of my own, and headed after him.

The doorbell rang a second time. Noah checked the peephole, then glanced backward at me. "It's the priest."

"Oh." I waved my knife at his knife. "Might want to put that away, or he's going to think today's daily special is priest gumbo."

He handed it back to me. Like I was supposed to do something special with it? I glared at Noah for a moment, then hid both behind my back as Noah opened the door.

Now if everyone could please ignore the redhead with the giant pair of knives.

Noah greeted the priest with a smile, opening the

door wide and extending his hand as if greeting a long-lost friend. "So glad you could make it."

The priest was a rather small, easily dismissed type. He probably weighed ninety pounds soaking wet and barely topped five foot. His eyes were curious as he gazed at me and he lifted his ginormous Bible a bit higher. "Is she the possessed one?" His gaze fixed on the *gris-gris* pouch around my neck, then went down to my waist.

I looked down, following his gaze. The knives were sticking out at awkward angles from behind my back. Total concealment fail—whoops. I brought them forward and gestured at the kitchen. "Not me. My friend in there is the one possessed. She's the one in the hoodoo circle."

The priest's eyes widened. Noah scowled at me and gave me a subtle shake of his head. Right. No voodoo hoodoo mojo in front of the fragile priest. Got it.

"Come on," I said, leading the way to the kitchen, trying to seem nonchalant. I tucked the *gris-gris* into my shirt just to be on the safe side.

Mae/Delilah crouched in the kitchen, still trapped. She stood when we entered, hissing and baring her teeth at the sight of the priest. Her wild red eyes turned to me and narrowed. "You do not want to do this," she snarled. "You will earn my undying enmity if you do this to me."

"You're gonna have to stand in line," I bluffed, faking courage I did not feel at the moment. I waved one of the knives at her and moved forward, trying to provoke her. "I've got quite a few enemies at the moment."

Noah stepped to my side, pulling me away and taking the knives. At the brush of his skin against mine, my knees went weak and I collapsed against him. "Jackie," he said softly, so the priest couldn't overhear us. "Move back. You don't want her to touch you—your curse is getting worse. Even right now your eyes are almost fully blue again."

And we'd only had sex about three hours ago. It was definitely escalating.

Noah nodded at the exorcist. "We're ready."

The priest stared hard at me, then back at Noah. "Very well." He took off his glasses and rubbed his nose, then opened his Bible. "I shall begin."

I couldn't take my eyes off of Delilah. "Go ahead."

"I'll have to ask the both of you to leave the room," he said in his mild voice. "You're agitating the demon, and that will make things all the more difficult."

Relieved, I headed for the door. I certainly didn't want to be around to watch this. "Great. Call me when you're done."

Noah shut the door to the kitchen behind us, looking more calm than I felt.

The priest began to chant in Latin, his voice carrying through the thin wood of the door. Mae immediately began to scream, her howls of outrage echoing in the house.

I winced, covering my ears to block out the ungodly noise. "Do you think she'll be okay?"

His face was pensive, but he nodded. "Delilah's

strong. This isn't the first time she's been possessed by a demon, and it probably won't be the last."

Geez. "You know, someone should have told me when I became a succubus that I'd manage to piss off every supernatural I run into."

A faint smile curved his lips. "You've got a knack, that's for sure."

Lucky me.

Mae's wails turned into angry screams as she cursed at the priest in an unknown language. An unnatural wind whipped through the foyer, smacking my hair in my face. Twilight was almost here. "Maybe we should go upstairs and wait?"

The next hour was long and excruciating. I went in to check on Remy, but Joachim was agitated by the exorcism going on downstairs, and he babbled in the same strange language that Mae spoke. It made my skin crawl, so I headed for Noah's room and hung out with him. I was too nervous and edgy to do more than sit on the edge of the bed.

After a while the screams began to die down, and so did the massive tension headache throbbing at the front of my brain. For the hundredth time in the past hour, I glanced out the dark window, hoping for a sign of a dark wing or the gleam of pale skin. Nothing.

Noah stifled a yawn. "It sounds like they're almost done."

We traipsed down the stairs, and I made Noah go ahead of me to check out the kitchen.

Inside, it was a nightmarish mess. Dishes were strewn across the floor, leaves had blown inside the windows, and everything was knocked off the walls. Bright green splatters of what looked suspiciously like puke dotted the walls.

In the midst of this, the sweating priest packed up his things as calmly as if he were finishing a day at the office. Delilah huddled on the floor panting, her long blond hair plastered to her face. She still remained inside the circle.

"Is everything all right?" Noah motioned for me to stay back.

I didn't listen, following him inside and heading for Delilah. She seemed frail, young, and certainly weaker than I'd last seen her. Was the demon gone for good?

"Dee?" I knelt outside the circle, guilt swimming over me. She looked like she hurt really badly.

The young succubus looked up at me, her eyes back to their normal washed-out gray. "You suck," she said, wiping her mouth with the back of her hand.

"I know," I said, glancing at the priest. "Can I let her out now?"

"Hand her your cross. That will be the true test," he said.

I hesitated for a moment, then pulled it over my neck and handed it through the circle, wincing. If Mae was still in there, she'd bite my hand off like I was a big piece of demon kibble.

But Delilah took the cross from my hand and pulled

it over her head. It rested against the neck of her filthy shirt, and she tucked it under, holding it close to her skin. "No burning. No pain. Can I get out of this circle now?"

At the priest's nod, I stood and dragged my foot through the white powder, breaking the heavy line.

"Come with me, Father." Noah took the priest by the arm and gave me a meaningful look. "I'll write you a check and we'll get you on your way."

That was code to me for "Keep Delilah out of trouble." I wanted to ask why we weren't going to send the priest up to see Remy, but I suspected that it wouldn't help her anyhow.

After all, Joachim had been inside Remy for weeks and didn't show any signs of leaving. I suspected that it had something to do with him being bound to this plane because of his curse. Where did a Serim or vampire go when he'd been kicked out of both upstairs and down?

Delilah stood and stretched as the men left the room, coming to my side. "That's better." Delilah jiggled her hands, shaking out her limbs like a runner. "God, I feel disgusting."

"You don't look so hot, either," I said with a faint smile. "Throw-up definitely doesn't go with the décor in this kitchen, by the way."

"Which reminds me," she said coolly, clenching her hand into a fist.

As I stood there smiling with relief like an idiot, she pulled back and slugged me in the face.

Lights popped in front of my eyes and I went stumbling backward. For a small girl, Delilah had one hell of a right hook. And when she jumped on me and pounded me with a left, I collapsed to the floor.

"You stupid bitch," she seethed, climbing over me like a monkey and slamming her fist into me again. "You let a demon into my house? Stupid, stupid idiot!"

The room spun crazily, a mass of red and black stars. I shoved my hand in her face, trying to get her off of me, but she was slippery with sweat (and God knows what else). I squirmed underneath her, trying to free myself.

"Get off of her," a new voice yelled.

Cool air swept over me as Delilah went flying. She crashed into the refrigerator and slid to the ground.

Zane moved into the room and stared down at me, his eyes glittering. His dark trench coat swirled around him, creating a dark aura. His eyes were red and wild and he breathed hard, staring down at me, his fangs bared.

I flinched, scooting backward until I hit the kitchen island. My hands flew to my bloody face and mouth, wary. Two other vampires stood behind him, dressed in black leather and scowling down at me.

Zane started toward me looking as if he wanted to comfort me, but at Delilah's groan of pain, his face changed and he leapt onto Delilah.

I scrambled to my feet as the other two vampires behind him separated and headed deeper into the house, leaving me alone with Zane and Delilah.

Both of whom probably wanted to kick my ass.

The sound of choking reached my ears, and I stumbled forward. Zane crouched on top of Delilah, choking her, his body tense with rage.

"Zane," I said, putting my hands on his shoulders. "Stop it! You're hurting her!"

He ignored me, lost to everything but hurting Delilah. Her eyes bugged, and she stared at me, her face purpling. She shot him the middle finger even as he choked her, glaring at the both of us.

Okay, she couldn't die, but it looked like it hurt like a bitch, and it was scaring me. When Delilah's fist clenched in his hair and yanked a handful out and he didn't react, I freaked. I slammed my hand into Zane's shoulder. "Stop it! Zane! Listen to me!"

I might as well have been talking to a rock. He ignored me. I grabbed his collar and heaved. "Zane!"

The hissing sizzle of burned flesh broke through the near-silence and Zane flew off of Delilah, slamming into me. I was knocked back to the floor. With a groan, I forced myself to sit upright, holding a hand to my head.

Zane had backed against a nearby wall, a hand to his cheek as he touched the cross-shaped welt rising there. His fangs gleamed in the light and he panted as if trying to recover. Against the fridge, Delilah held the cross in front of her, her gaze darting back and forth between me and Zane.

He hesitated for a moment, clearly torn between the two of us—anger and lust—and then bounded to my side. He helped me to my feet, and when I stood staring at him with uncertainty, he leaned in and cupped my face in his hands. "Jackie, Princess," he said, his voice soft as he ran his thumbs over my bruised skin. "Are you all right?"

"I'm fine," I said, forcing myself to push his hand away. "Don't touch me."

He scanned my face with worried eyes, then nodded and pulled away. "Get your things, Princess. We're getting out of here." His gaze went to Delilah and his lip curled with disgust. "I'm here now. Everything's going to be okay." He slid his hands over my shoulders possessively.

His casual ignorance rankled, even though it hurt my heart. I slid out of his grasp. "No, it's not okay. I can't leave with you." I moved away from him to go stand at Delilah's side.

She finally seemed calm, glancing at me, then back at Zane. Her hand slid into her pocket, probably searching for another cross.

Zane stared at me, obviously confused. "Jackie. You called me. You asked for my help."

I nodded, lifting my chin a little. "I *do* need your help. I need you to tell me who cursed you, and then let you pass it on to me." There. I threw it out in the open.

"You think I was the one that was cursed?" His scowl grew dark, and he took a step toward me. "You're being ridiculous. I've never had a curse."

Delilah extended her hand, displaying the dark hair she'd pulled from Zane's scalp in their struggle. She removed the small bottle of oil from her pocket and sprinkled it over the hair. Tendrils of heat arose from her palm, wispy smoke and the smell of burning hair filling the kitchen. "You were touched by the curse at some point," she said calmly, as if none of this bothered her.

At the sight of the smoke, proof of Zane's lies, big, fat tears rolled down my face. I turned back to him. "How could you do this to me? I trusted you."

"You don't really believe this crap, Jackie?" Zane stared at Delilah with cold eyes, then looked back to me. His lip curled a little. "You expect me to believe these parlor tricks?"

Calmly, Delilah discarded the burning hair and plucked out a few strands of her own. She shook the oil over them. Nothing happened.

She looked over at me, and I took a step backward. "*I'll* get the hair this time."

I pulled a few strands out, handed them to her, and watched as she repeated the process. My hair reacted the same as Zane's: The smell filled the room, twice as powerful as before. I pinched my nose to block the smell.

"That doesn't mean anything," Zane said.

"It means everything. It means that you've somehow passed your curse on to me."

He shook his head, his brows drawn in anger. "Jackie, I didn't curse you."

"No? Then tell me how it happened." Fuming, I shoved past him. I'd get Noah in here, and maybe the three of us could bully Zane into removing the curse. My heart ached.

"Jackie," Zane said, following after me. His hand touched my arm, but I shrugged it away and stumbled out into the foyer.

The two vampires stood there, holding the small priest between the two of them. Noah lay collapsed on the floor at their feet.

Panic surged through me, and I immediately fell to Noah's side. "Noah!" I touched his face, my heart thudding painfully. "What did you do to him?" If Zane's men had harmed him . . .

I brushed my finger under Noah's nose and was relieved to feel his breath, warm and regular. A quick glance showed that he hadn't been harmed. Just his evening hibernation. Thank God. My heart thudded painfully and I pulled his heavy, limp body back toward me.

One of the men kicked his unconscious form in the side. "Idiot Serim, to leave himself open and unguarded in our presence." They exchanged fanged, unpleasant smiles.

I glared up at them. "Don't you touch him," I said, raising a fist. The vampires ignored my anger, looking to Zane for approval.

My blood went cold and I turned back to Zane. "I thought you were an outcast."

He glanced over at the others, then back to me. "I'm back in her majesty's good graces." Zane did a little mocking bow to take the sting out of his words.

They still hurt. I brushed my fingers over Noah's cheek to assure myself that he was all right. He was the only one I could count on. "But I thought—"

Zane grabbed me by the arm, pulling me back to his side. "It's complicated, Princess," he murmured. "Now come in the kitchen so we can discuss this like adults."

I shoved away from him, anger surging through me. "Are you kidding me?" I took an angry step backward. "*You're* the one being childish here. Thanks so much for running out on me, back to your bitch of a queen."

"Watch your mouth," one of the vampires behind me warned in a low rumble.

Zane reached for me again, obviously intending to drag me away by force if necessary. "You're being foolish," he began, his voice low.

I took a step backward, tripping over Noah's prone form. My hands flew up and I felt a pair of hands grab my arm, trying to stop my fall.

Oh no—the priest. I barely had time to see his face out of the corner of my eye before he fell over on top of me, out like a light.

"Damn it!" I said, trying to shove his small form off of the succubus-sandwich I had become, trapped between Noah and the priest. "Not another!" I glared up at Zane from my uncomfortable position. "Look what you made me do."

Zane grabbed me by the arms as the two vampire goons pulled the priest off of me. One of the vampires shook the poor little man so hard I thought his neck would snap, trying to wake him up.

"He's out," the other said. "Think he's a Serim, too?"

"He's not a Serim, you nitwit," I said, shaking Zane's hands off of me. "*I* did that to him. I'm cursed, remember? Your boss here knows all about it, because he won't even touch me without fear of getting cooties."

"Cursed?"

I buried my face in my hands and moaned. "This is very, very bad. First the pissed-off demon, now the priest."

"Jackie," Zane said between gritted teeth. "I'm going to ask you one more time. We can have this conversation privately, or we can end it right now." His scowl was dark as he glared at me.

I struggled to my feet, frowning at him. Delilah stood in the kitchen doorway, watching us. Her eyes were narrowed and she had something moving in her hands.

"Well?" Zane said, crossing his arms and staring down at me, waiting for an answer.

Uncertain, I dropped my gaze to Noah. I didn't want to leave him.

Zane grabbed me by the hips, flinging me over his shoulder. "It looks like I'm going to have to *make* you listen." He began to head up the stairs.

CHAPTER NINETEEN

I slammed my hand onto his back. "You bastard! Put me down!" From my upside-down position, I could just barely make out the two vampires. The thick red curtain of my stupid hair blocked everything else except the two men collapsed on the floor. I hoped that Delilah's plan involved saving Noah from the two vampires.

"Put me down!" I screamed again as Zane climbed the stairs, ignoring my blows. I might as well have been tickling his ribs.

We got up the stairs and he turned into the first doorway at the top—my room. As soon as we were inside, he shut the door behind us and dumped me on the floor.

Outraged, I got to my feet. Arrogant ass! My hand flew to his face, a slap—but it never connected.

He caught my hand and rubbed his thumb against my palm, then released it. His hands slid to my face and cupped it gently, kissing my mouth with the tender lips I remembered. "Jackie, Princess . . . are you okay?"

I took a wary step backward. "That depends," I said. "*Make* me listen? If you're planning on beating me, we might have to have a little talk."

He shook his head. "That was just for those goons' benefit." He gave me a lazy, heartbreaking smile.

"So you're posing for your friends now? That's disappointing." Very disappointing.

"Come on, Princess." His easygoing smile seemed a little strained. "It's so they report to the queen that everything is hunky-dory. You know I'd never hurt you."

I crossed my arms, staring at him as if he were a stranger. Hell, maybe he was. This wasn't the Zane I knew. "Actually, I *don't* know that you wouldn't hurt me. Remember? You cursed me."

"I swear, Jackie, I didn't know anything about it. I promise." He stuffed his hands in the pockets of his coat, almost as if he didn't trust himself around me. Anguish ripped across his face. "And I can explain—"

"I doubt that very much," I snapped.

Zane's lips tightened. "Do you know the trouble I had to go through to get here? The hell I went through because I thought you were hurt? In trouble?"

"It doesn't feel so great, does it?" My hands clenched into fists.

He scowled at me, his teeth bared to show his fangs in a rather unfriendly manner. He took a step forward . . . and then stopped, staring at something over my shoulder. "Is that . . . Remy?"

"Sort of," I said, unwilling to turn around. I could feel her creepy eyes boring into the back of my neck. "Long story. Don't change the subject now. Let's get back to how you betrayed me."

An exasperated look crossed his face. "I didn't betray you—"

A loud crash sounded downstairs, followed by Delilah's angry bellow. The voices of the two vampires rose, as well. It sounded like they were inches away from killing each other.

Zane cursed, raking a hand through his hair in exasperation. "Will you stay here a moment while I check things out downstairs?"

I didn't feel like being obliging. "No."

He glared at me for a moment, then reached over and pulled me against his body. I struggled for a moment, but then his lips locked on mine and I forgot everything but the feel of his mouth. His breath was warm and sweet, without a hint of the coppery tang of blood. His tongue swept into my mouth, igniting the Itch from a low, burning spark into a full-blown inferno.

Zane groaned low in his throat, his hands sliding to cup my face, thumbs stroking against my cheeks. His tongue delved deep into my mouth, tasting me, insistent and warm. Each thrust of his tongue was a suggestion, until my body was tensing and coiling with each thrust.

The kiss broke off entirely too early, and Zane touched my chin, then smiled. "Better?"

I regained my senses and slapped him in the arm. "Why is it suddenly okay to kiss me?"

His mouth slid into a sardonic smile. "I figured you

can't get any madder at me." He glanced at the door. "Wait for me here? I promise I'll tell you everything."

Dazed by the kiss, I shook my head, my movements slow. "If you leave, I'm not staying."

"Jackie, please." A hint of a smile tugged at his mouth. "You said you trusted me, remember?"

And he'd betrayed that trust. "No. Either we talk now, or we don't talk at all. I don't need someone who abandons me just when I need him."

Something crashed below, and Zane hesitated, clearly torn between staying with me and answering to duty.

A male voice screamed an epithet downstairs, and duty won out over lust. He sighed and pulled my arms away from his neck. "Can you hang tight for a few minutes, Princess? I promise I'll be right back." He took my hand in his, turned it over, and kissed the palm.

"You always say that," I muttered, but I sat down on the edge of the bed as he disappeared out of the room and down the hall. My knees were strangely weak after that kiss, and I pressed a hand to my forehead, feeling the flush creeping over my skin.

At least Zane was here now, which meant the Itch could be taken care of soon. Even better, he'd kissed me on the mouth before he'd left, so maybe he was over the whole "passing the curse" thing.

After all, *he'd* passed it to *me*.

I listened to the shouting voices downstairs, wiggling one of my feet in anxiety. The Itch made my entire body restless, and I couldn't sit still. I hummed to myself, trying to block out the sound of Remy's loud, harsh panting in the closet.

Noah—he was downstairs in the midst of all that chaos. My lust had nearly made me forget about him. I lurched for the door.

A hand clasped my arm, warm against my bare skin. I jerked in surprise, but it was too late.

Unnatural darkness fell over me.

CHAPTER TWENTY

Having the tables turned on you really sucked.

I sat in an ice cream shop with a black-and-white checkered floor, staring at the table in front of me mournfully. It was a beautifully set table, with crystal water glasses and fine silver, and the prettiest embroidered napkins. Empty sundae glasses were lined up in front of me, obscene with their sparkling cleanness. It was obvious they'd never held a lick of ice cream in their lives.

"Is this Hell?" I asked the guy across from me.

The priest shook his head, his hands clasped across his chest. "I think it's all in your head."

"If it was my head, there'd be some dang ice cream." I picked up one of the shining spoons and sighed, glancing around. The mini-jukebox on the table played Chuck Berry, just like in the movies.

Across from our booth, at the counter, sat everyone that I'd accidentally sucked the brains out of. The pizza dude. The fat dude who'd been porking Remy, George. The redneck in the truck who thought I was a hooker. The two cops.

I picked up a napkin and pretended great interest in it, not making eye contact with the lineup that glowered at me. "So uh, you guys have been in here the whole time?"

The priest inclined his head slowly. "That's what they are telling me. We seem to be stuck here in limbo. And it's somehow directly connected to you."

I played with the spoons. "Can't really argue with that. At least you got to hang out in an ice cream shop, though."

"Except it wasn't always an ice cream shop. That changed when you got here."

"Oh," I said, then paused. "What was it before?"

The priest blushed.

"Never mind," I blurted. "I don't think I want to know." Oh gracious, I'd had dirty thoughts in front of a priest. Poor man. "So what do you guys do in here?" I did my best not to look over at the crew glowering at me from the counter.

"We wait," the priest said calmly. "Nothing we can do until you decide to free us."

"And we're hungry," bellowed the pizza boy.

I winced. "See, here's the thing. I don't exactly know how to free you."

The priest leaned forward. "I gathered as much," he whispered. "I would imagine we are in even more dire straits, considering the fact that you are now trapped in here with us."

He had a point. I frowned. "I don't know how I got in here. Succubi don't sleep."

"This isn't a dream. We're somewhere else. I think perhaps we are in your subconscious."

"Well, how did *I* get stuck in here?" My powers had never worked on myself before. I ruled out the thought of knocking myself out—because if I had, I was in really deep doodoo, since I didn't know how to get back.

I thought back to the hand that had touched my arm just before I'd appeared here, and my hand went to the *gris-gris* around my neck.

I'd been warded against everything that wished me harm . . . everything except succubi. *"I can't ward it against myself,"* Delilah had said before handing it to me.

That little double-crossing bitch. "I am *so* going to kick her ass when I get out of here."

But why wait until I was alone to knock me out? She'd had plenty of opportunities to knock me out before, and she'd never done it. Something wasn't adding up. Remy? I dismissed the thought as soon as it occurred. Remy was still trapped in my closet.

"So." I drummed my fingers on the table and looked around. "Since we're going to be here for a while, what do you guys do for fun?"

"Bingo," said the priest.

Riiight.

Several hours later, I scowled at my card. "I need two numbers for a blackout and you won't call them!"

"They're random numbers, my dear," the priest said in

his effortlessly calm voice, and pulled another Bingo ball out of the machine set up at the front of the ice cream parlor. "G-48 is the next number."

I swore at my card and peered over my shoulder at the pizza boy's. Damn, he only needed one more number.

"Bingo!" cried George, getting up from the table and waving his ink-smeared card in the air. "I win!"

"It's my brain," I said sulkily. "I should get to win."

"If it was your brain, every single number he called out would be 69," the chucklehead cop next to me said.

Before I could come up with a wickedly witty retort, the ice cream parlor swam before my eyes and went dark.

"Wakey wakey," a low, smooth voice said, and a hard fingertip tapped against my forehead.

I jerked awake, my eyes fluttering open. My legs hurt, my neck was killing me, and I had drool tracks at the sides of my mouth. I tried to focus my bleary eyes on the hand that tapped me on the forehead again, then moved away.

As consciousness returned, I lifted my hand to wipe my mouth and discovered something disturbing. My hands were cuffed together with zip-ties, the plastic bands cutting into my skin. An experimental shift of my feet revealed an identical situation, and there was a tight band around my knees that hurt as well. Some weird silver manacle around my ankle burned hot against my skin.

Okay, so someone had me tied up. No reason to panic just yet. My eyes flicked over my surroundings: I was crammed into the backseat of a car, my long legs folded up so I'd fit into the vehicle. My head was tilted in an awkward angle against the door, which explained the pain in my neck. From this angle, I couldn't see my captor. I tried to straighten up, but every muscle in my body protested and I gave up. "What is going on?"

A masculine chuckle rolled from the front seat, one that I recognized and made my blood cold. Luc.

"I'm surprised you haven't already figured it out," he said, his voice completely unruffled. "Perhaps I've put too much stock in your intelligence. You did say you were an archaeologist, correct?"

"I never told you that," I said, forcing myself upright. Oh God, the pain that shot through my legs was intense. A flurry of pinpricks cascaded through my feet and hands, signifying that my circulation was cut off. "Gee, you think you could have tied these things a little tighter? My hands haven't quite fallen off just yet."

"There's my girl," he said, and I caught a hint of a smile in his voice. "Covering your fear with your stunning wit. It's a good thing, *ma belle*. You should be afraid of me."

Oh, I was definitely afraid. And the possessive way he called me *ma belle* made me think he had some sinister plan in mind. I stared out the window at the highway that sped past. More trees, and the sun was edging into the horizon. Sunrise soon. That meant we'd been driving all night. "Where are we?"

"It would be rather foolish of me to tell you, wouldn't

it?" He didn't sound a bit concerned. "Suffice it to say that we are a nice, healthy distance from New Orleans. By the time they find you, it will be too late."

I sure didn't like the sound of that. "By the time who finds me?"

"Why, the queen and her little dog that keeps panting after you."

I guessed that the "panting dog" was Zane, but the queen? The vampire queen? Fear shot through me again—a sensation that was happening all too frequently for my taste. "Queen Nitocris? What does she want with me?"

"Good question." Luc pushed an item on the dashboard—his BlackBerry, tucked into a leather holder. "Dial Zane," he said as the screen lit up.

"Luc!" Zane's voice immediately roared into the phone. "You goddamn bastard, what did you do with her? Is she all right?"

I slid forward on my seat, my heart leaping at the frightened tone of his voice. "Zane, I'm here!" I yelled.

"Princess! Are you okay, sweetheart? I'm coming for you."

"Let me talk to her," Noah said from a distance, and I heard the two men begin to argue.

Relief flowed over me, and I nearly cried with joy. They were coming to get me.

"I hate to interrupt the sausage party over there," Luc said. "But Jackie has a question, and I thought perhaps Zane might be able to answer it for her."

A pause. "What is it?"

What was Luc trying to do here?

My captor sighed. "Darling Jackie here was just curious as to why the queen wanted her."

Silence fell. For a long moment, nothing was said.

A smile curved Luc's mouth as he switched lanes. "Sounds like we've been disconnected, Jackie. Isn't that a shame—"

"I'm here," said Zane. Low. Angry.

Guilty.

"Zane," I said, a knot forming in my throat. "Why does the queen want me?"

Another round of silence. Then, slowly, "She wants another succubus under her control. Like Luc. But that was all before. It's different now."

"What do you mean?" I had to blink back sudden tears. He'd known about this all along?

"It's not what you think, Jackie. It's all changed—"

Luc reached over and flipped the BlackBerry off before Zane could finish. "I'm low on minutes, so you'll have to forgive me if we finish this conversation some other time, *ma belle*."

I stared at the back of Luc's head. What had changed? What was going on? "What did he mean, 'another succubus like you'?"

"Come, *ma belle*, it should be obvious. You have not figured it out yet? That's rather sad, *non*?"

I shifted my hands in the ties, trying to get a little more room so my fingers would stop aching. They looked purple in the early light. If Luc was a succubus, that would explain why he followed me at all times of the night and day. It also would explain how he'd been able to knock me out by forcing me back into my own head.

"But I thought all Sucks were girls," I blurted out.

"I am an incubus," Luc said without bothering to glance back to see my reaction. "The male version of your kind. Very rare." He seemed proud of it.

There was something not adding up. "But I thought . . . Sucks are made by sleeping with an angel and being drained by a vampire in the same night. And all of them are male, so . . . Oh." I looked back at him. "You're gay? There are gay vampires out there?" Gay angels, too?

He chuckled. "Nothing is as simple or cut-and-dried as the human categories for it. I simply taste all, love all."

I remembered the inherently wrong taste of his kiss. "No wonder kissing you tasted like I was kissing my brother." And he'd been tasting and loving all over town. Ugh.

"Have you had sex with your brother often?" He glanced in the rearview mirror, eyebrows raised.

"I don't have a brother, and it's just an expression, jackass," I fired back, then gave my hands a vicious twist. "And these hurt."

"If you were not in the bad habit of running away, I would not need to tie you up."

"So what are you going to do with me?" I sounded defeated, even to myself.

Luc's smile in the rearview mirror was chilling. "Oh, what *aren't* I going to do with you, *ma belle*?"

We were still in the South. I'd guessed that by the small towns amid the trees, the run-down gas station we were currently parked at, and the overabundance of Whataburgers along the highway. Luc whistled as he pumped gas, not a care in the world. The sun was hot overhead and with no A/C blowing, the backseat was almost unbearable.

At least I didn't have the Itch. Yet that disturbed me—after living so long with it constantly preying on my mind, the absence was frightening. Did it mean that Luc had taken advantage of me while I slept?

Eeww.

I shifted my hands and feet again. No luck. The zip-ties were just as tight as before, and now my skin was blistered and raw around it, which made any efforts hurt even more. I eyed Luc from the window as he casually leaned against the car, his hand on the gas-pump handle. Now would be the perfect time to escape . . . if it weren't for my knees and feet tied together. He'd also removed the back door handles, so I couldn't even let myself out, even though I wouldn't get far.

And I had to pee.

I glanced around the gas station. We were off the

main highway, and no one was here—maybe due to the run-down nature of the gas station, and the nice, shiny Shell station just down the street. Or maybe it was the fact that they were charging a quarter more a gallon than Shell.

Maybe my questionable luck had finally run out.

Luc slid back into the front seat and grinned at me. "Ready to go?"

"I need to go to the bathroom." I held up my hands. "And these still hurt."

"You will just have to wait, *ma fille*. We are almost home." The way he said *home* made me panic a little. I had a feeling that if I saw "home," I'd never come out again.

As he leaned forward to start the car again, I had an idea. I could stop him the same way that he'd shut me down. Reaching forward with my tied hands, I planted them against his ear. "Sleep, you bastard."

He merely sneered at me and batted my hands away. "I am much older, and much, much stronger than you. Your powers will not work on me."

Uh oh. I gave him a bright smile, trying to defuse the situation. "Well, this is awkward." I sighed. "How about we settle for a big 'Up yours'?"

He reached backward and tapped my forehead, an irritated look on his face.

The world went black one more time. Inside, I felt something shift loose, a rather disgusting, slimy feeling that I hoped I'd never have to experience again.

And then I appeared back in the ice cream parlor.

"Oh good," said the priest with a smile. "We're about to play Double Bingo. You're just in time."

Six rounds of bingo later (none of which I won), Luc tapped my forehead again, drawing me back awake.

I had a throbbing headache, so intense that I shut my eyes again. "Ow."

"Behave and I won't do it again," Luc said in that smooth voice. The acoustics had changed, and I cracked my eyes open to stare at my new surroundings.

I sat in a wooden chair, the back carved into a wagon-wheel shape that jabbed spokes into my back. A round dining room table in front of me matched the chairs, and a cold wood floor was under my feet. The room was dark, an old standing lamp in the corner throwing off yellow light, and red-and-white checked curtains covered the windows. No sunlight shone through them, so I'd been asleep for quite some time. A leather couch sat against the far wall, and the entire thing screamed country home.

"A log cabin?" I said in surprise. "Are you kidding me?" I shifted my feet, and noticed that my hands and legs weren't tied anymore.

Glory, hallelujah!

Relief was short-lived, however, when I realized that my left ankle was still cuffed with the silver manacle . . . decorated with a chain that attached to the wall nearby.

Chained like a dog.

Luc paced near the couch, crossing the small room in frenetic strides. His arms were folded over his chest, his figure lean, his cheekbones as beautiful as any woman's. His light gray eyes flicked to me, then he went back to pacing.

"Your eyes," I blurted out, realizing. "They were gold." Now their pale, smoky color perfectly matched mine, a clear sign that he was a succubus. Incubus. Whatever.

"Contacts," he said. "Would you have trusted me if you had known I was one of you?"

Well, he had a point there. Which brought me to another question. "Speaking of which—why aren't I Itching?" Because I felt as calm as the day I was born, which wasn't natural at all. "Is my curse gone?"

"No." Luc approached me, a smug smile curving his face. "Would you like to see?"

That little smirk seemed a bit ominous, but I did want to see, so I nodded.

He knelt before me, then skimmed his hand down my leg and rested on the ankle cuff.

The cuff didn't have a key. It didn't have anything at all holding me there except a ridiculously small clasp, and I wanted to laugh aloud. I could escape at any time.

Then he undid the clasp and the cuff fell away from my ankle.

The Itch rushed through me like an inferno, sending my nerve endings tingling with awareness and making my skin crawl. Hard, hot *need* flared through me, so strong it was painful, and the world tilted. The scent of Luc standing so close to me became unbearable.

I grabbed his face and pulled it to mine. My mouth opened under his, my tongue sweeping into his mouth with voracious hunger even as my hands reached for his cock. It was taking much too long to get the relief I badly needed. A shudder wracked my body as I struggled to free the hardness in his pants, and I placed my fingertips against the back of his neck.

His hands touched my hair, and a great double-handful fell out. I broke free, realizing that the shudders weren't just about sex and need. My body was shutting down, decaying from within. I held my hand out and watched my fingertips lose their plump fullness, drying like small prunes.

With a whimper, I bent down and snapped the clasp back around my ankle.

Immediately, the cool rush of magic swept over me again. My skin fleshed out once more, and that awful, gnawing hunger disappeared.

I stared at Luc with horror. "What have you done to me?"

"Nothing new, I'm afraid," he said, his eyes flickering to bright blue as they stared down at me intently. "Your curse is so far advanced now that the magic in that link is the only thing that is keeping you from dying within minutes." He gestured at the door of the cabin, a thin smile curving his lean face. "But you are welcome to leave at any time, of course."

"I can't leave," I said, picking up the hank of my hair on the floor with horror. "I don't want to die."

"Then it seems like you're my guest," he said, kneeling down to eye level with me, his eyes bright. "I have so much fun planned for you, *ma belle*."

I stared at him uneasily, wondering how I'd managed to miss the fact that he was batshit-crazy.

From across the room, his BlackBerry rang again. The smile on his face widened and he stood, going to answer it.

"You have her, warlock?" I could hear the queen's evil voice through the room. It slid in like oil, sonorous and awful, and I shuddered.

He was a warlock *and* an incubus? Wasn't I just the luckiest?

"She's with me," Luc said calmly, watching my reaction.

"You were to bring her to *me*." Her words drew down in a low hiss, and I thought of those terrible fangs and evil eyes.

"I know," he said, his eyes on me. "But I have need of her for a bit longer."

Oh, great.

"The prince is most displeased," the queen said, her cold voice sending a chill through me. "There has been a change. Bring the slut to me and I will give her to him."

I was going to be given to some vampire prince? What was going on?

Luc's smile faded, and his shoulders went stiff. "My queen, that was not part of the deal."

"The deal has changed—"

Luc clicked the phone off and tossed it onto the table. He ignored it when it started to ring again.

"What do you want with me?" Beyond the obvious, of course. Luc was beautiful. He wouldn't have any trouble finding someone to have sex with, so there was no need for any crazy schemes to lock me up.

He smiled, such a pretty, white smile. "It must be nice to have two masters so desperately in love with you. I wouldn't know how that is. Mine sold me to the queen's service centuries ago." His mouth hardened. "Which is why I need you. Your blood—the blood of a dying creature born from Serim and vampire—for a spell. When I spill your last drops of blood across my altar, it will free me from my obligations to my masters once and for all." He glanced back at his phone. "And since she is trying to round them up right now to get me under control, I'd say we have about a day before they find us."

CHAPTER TWENTY-ONE

I tinkered with the chain as I sat with my back against the wall. The links were soft and smooth. Probably wouldn't hold up against a good pair of pliers. Too bad there weren't any near me. I squinted at the window, trying to judge the time. Still daylight. Was Noah worried about me? Frantic looking for me? Or was he busy drowning his sorrows in Delilah's arms? I scowled at myself for even thinking it.

Then I pondered the queen's words, about how the deal had changed. Zane had mentioned the same thing. Did he have something to do with it? A small bit of hope burned inside me—maybe he'd changed his ways, after all.

Not that I'd live to find out.

"You seem unhappy," Luc commented as he re-arranged the furniture on the far side of the room. He'd cleared away a large portion of the living room and was creating a shrine of sorts—I could guess what it was for. "Problem?"

He was asking me if I was unhappy? Like we were best friends forever? "You mean other than sitting here, chained to a wall because if I leave, I'll turn into a dried-up mummy within minutes? Yet if I stay, I become a human sacrifice? That kind of unhappy?"

Luc shrugged and put a small stool near the altar. "It's nothing personal, Jackie. I'd give you a good, hard fuck before the send-off, but I need you starving." His eyes gleamed even bluer at the thought.

I shivered. "Don't touch me, you sick freak."

He smiled and disappeared out the front door of the cabin, whistling again.

I was so screwed.

I had to figure out something and fast, because there was no way that I was going down without a fight. I tugged at the chain binding me to the wall, wishing for the millionth time that I'd been given supernatural strength instead of a supernatural libido.

The whistling returned, and Luc reentered the cabin with a pair of sticks in his hand, a small knife in the other. I immediately froze, but all he did was sit on the stool and began to whittle the sticks.

"So," I said, trying to focus my thoughts. "Did you kill Drake?"

"I did," he agreed, almost cheerfully.

"Why?"

Luc slid the knife over the stick, peeling off the bark and revealing the pale flesh of wood underneath. He shrugged. "Had to be done. I'd met him before, a long time ago when he was much younger and less disgusting." He smiled as he examined the wood. "It's flattering, I suppose, to think that a drunken one-night stand made that much of an impression on the man. But when he saw me coming out of your hotel room, he knew something was up and I didn't want him exposing me. So I killed him."

"You ripped out his throat like an animal."

Luc didn't react. "I was angry. I used my teeth and fingernails so they'd think it was one of the vampires." He smiled. "A warning, of sorts."

The image made me gag. To think I'd put my mouth on his. I swallowed hard. "So it's been you all along?"

"Me all along," he agreed.

"Why wait until now to grab me?"

Luc smiled. "I'd have to wait too long for you to starve to death." He admired one of the sticks, then winked at me. "You're right where I want you now. And I love the thrill of the chase."

Just like a serial killer. "So *you* laid the original curse?"

"I did," he said. "Brilliant, is it not?"

"Why a curse?" And how did it get to me? *Come on, tell me all your dirty secrets.* If I knew enough, maybe I could figure out a way to reverse it.

"Why not?" He looked up at me, smoothing his thumbs over the wood. "Are you pumping me for information, *ma belle*?"

"Why not?" I retorted back. "Or do you think I'm going to manage to somehow free myself in a few hours and foil your dastardly plans?"

A slow smile tugged at his mouth. "No, not really."

That made two of us.

I sighed. "Since I'm going to die doing you a favor, you could at least do me one and tell me what's going on."

"Fair enough," he said, smiling.

Like we were friends. I clenched my hands in longing, wanting to put my fist through his mouth and break all those pretty white teeth.

"I was born Romani many hundred years ago," he began. "My people were nomadic and poor, but even back then, I was not like them. I liked the things that Romani men did not crave. A beautiful house, many riches." He looked back at me with those pale eyes. "Power."

So he was born a gypsy. "The curse on me is a gypsy curse?" No wonder Delilah hadn't been able to figure it out.

A hint of pride crossed his face. "My ancestors were well versed in Romani magic, and after I was changed over, I had many hundreds of years to improve the practice."

"Lucky you," My mind was racing. If I could get free of him, maybe I could find another gypsy warlock to remove the curse.

Provided I lived long enough. "So why did the queen ask you to put a gypsy curse on me?" It didn't add up.

"Romani magic," he corrected with a bit of a sneer. "Do not correct me."

"Sorry," I said, pretending to be chastised. "Please continue." Eat shit and die, but please continue.

Luc smiled, returning to the sticks he carved. "The queen hates you," he said mildly.

Like that was a news flash? I straightened my legs in front of me and flexed. Sitting on the floor was killing my butt, but it beat playing Bingo in my head with a bunch of weird guys. "The queen hates all succubi."

He chuckled. "No. I mean she *really* hates you. Because of Zane."

Goose bumps prickled my skin. To earn the vampire queen's undying enmity was not high on my list of to-do accomplishments. "Super. She and Zane are very close, I take it? He's her favorite lackey?"

Luc looked at me in surprise. "You don't know? He's the prince."

The world spun, and it was suddenly hard to breathe. "What?"

"Her chosen successor," Luc clarified, amused by my ignorance. "Didn't you know?"

"Someone neglected to tell me that small detail," I said, gritting my teeth. "He told me he'd fallen from Heaven, like the others."

"Oh, he did," Luc said. "They all fell from Heaven. But the vampire clan has a specific hierarchy. Queen Nitocris is considered the head of the vampire clan, and her chosen successor is the prince. Zane." He whittled rapidly. "The fact that the prince chose you over her kingdom does not sit well with her."

"But she cast him out," I said.

Luc didn't look up. "She is always casting them out for one reason or another. They always come crawling back to her, desperate for her approval and love. The vampire clan have been that way for centuries. Eons. Always they misbehave and are embraced back into the fold when they atone. The queen is their reason for living, the reason for their being." He eyed me slyly. "At least, for most of them. And she is not fond of competition."

I don't know if his words made me feel worse, or better. Better, because I knew how much Zane cared for me. Worse, because I knew I'd never win against Queen Nitocris. Hot sex and a Master-Suck bond versus millennia of adoration and a kingdom to inherit? "Ha. So she wants to get rid of me to get Zane back into the fold?"

He nodded, brushing wood shavings off of his jeans. "There are only two ways to kill a succubus, after all. Kill both of her masters, or starve her out."

And the queen didn't want to harm Zane, she just wanted him back under her control. "So she went for starvation."

"I have worked for the queen many times before," Luc said, rising and heading over to the altar. "Romani magic is very flexible. A slight twist of the magic here or there, and you can make a curse do anything you like. In this case, I simply sped up your natural metabolism."

"Like you did to Victoria?"

He looked amused by my accusation. "Remy told you about that, did she?"

"You cold bastard. How could you do that to her? She was a succubus, too. You should be working with me, not trying to destroy me."

He laid the wooden cross that he'd created on the altar,

and strode back to where I hunched in the corner. He grabbed me by the arm and hauled me to my feet, anger blazing in his eyes. "Work together? Stick together?" He laughed in my face, his breath sweet, his voice harsh. "You will soon learn, my sweet, that in this pathetic After-life, no one looks out for a succubus but themselves. You and I were created to be a pawn for the important ones, a plaything for immortals. Never think for a moment that they don't use that to their full advantage."

I shied away, trying to pry his hand off my arm. "Okay, okay."

His lip curled in a sneer. "You think you are so clever, with your masters wrapped around your pretty little fin-ger." His eyes blazed blue fury into mine. "Do you never stop to wonder why they are so fascinated with you? Why they are obsessed with possessing you and stealing you away from the other?"

"All those Kegel exercises?"

Luc backhanded me. Pain flashed through my head, a reminder that I needed to learn to shut my mouth.

"You are a stupid girl. Die an ignorant fool, then. It makes no difference to me." He thrust me away from him and strode back to his altar.

I slid back down against the wall, disturbed. He care-fully hung the cross upside-down on the wall, then returned to the altar, whittling as if nothing bothered him.

It made my flesh crawl.

My thoughts turned back to what he'd said. What had Zane done to get back in the queen's good graces? Had he deliberately let Luc cast a curse on him, knowing he'd pass it to me? He'd said that he didn't do it, but I didn't know what to think.

But the most disturbing question was, What had Luc meant about bitter rivals? About my masters both being obsessed with me for an unknown reason. Frustrated, I shifted position, making the chain tighten. Unable to stretch my leg out all the way, I jerked on it in irritation.

The bolt in the wall moved a little.

I froze, wondering if I had imagined it. I glanced over at Luc, who stood in front of the altar, carefully painting symbols on the wood and humming to himself. I slid closer to the bolt and examined where it was screwed into the wall.

Whoever had put a bolt in the wall of a log cabin was a real dumb ass, I thought as I gave it another experimental tug. The wood was soft and probably rotten in the middle. When I tugged, I felt the wood give a little, but not enough to make a noticeable difference. Still, if I had a few hours to play with it, maybe I could work it out of the wall.

No one was coming to save me. Not Zane, not Remy, not even Noah. Not Delilah and her voodoo magic, or the *gris-gris* that hung around my neck. No matter how much I depended on the others, it was all up to me this time.

Not good.

CHAPTER TWENTY-TWO

Hours passed. My butt grew numb from sitting on the hard floor, and I shifted positions repeatedly, careful not to make a lot of noise with the chain and even more careful to work at the bolt in the wall when Luc wasn't paying attention. My constant efforts were slowly stripping the wood around the bolts, and with enough time, I'd be able to rip the whole thing from the wall.

Luc was busy with his own plans as the sun slid across the sky and beyond the horizon. He finished his altar, decorated it with candles, then fixed himself an enormous meal—not offering any to me. His BlackBerry continued to ring constantly, but he didn't answer it. "I know it's my master," he said with a reproving smile. "As if I'm foolish enough to answer."

His eyes grew an even darker blue as the hours passed. He eyed me repeatedly, his hand sliding to the bulge in his crotch, but every time, he forced himself to turn away and headed into the shower. The Itch was bothering him, but the need to be free of his master was even greater, so he deprived himself.

That suited me just fine. I didn't want to have sex with the creep.

As Luc appeared naked from the shower this time, toweling his long hair, his half-erect dick jerked at the sight of me.

I turned away, disgusted that he was so horny while I was sitting here captive. "Can you cover your junk up, please?"

He threw his towel at me, and I caught it and shoved it against my side, glaring at him as he sauntered toward the bedroom.

"So what does all of this have to do with you?" I called after him. Maybe he would be in a talkative mood again, and I could squeeze more information out of him.

At first I thought Luc didn't hear me—he was quiet for so long.

Then he returned back into the living room, his wet hair slicked back into a ponytail, a white T-shirt over his chest and boxers over his naked bits. "What do you mean, what does it have to do with me?"

"Why does the queen have you do her dirty work?"

Luc sauntered past me into the kitchen, paying no more attention to me than if I were a dog lying on the carpet at his feet. "I've proved myself valuable to her many a time. There's no need for me to explain otherwise."

"Yeah, well, she's not going to be too happy with you now," I pointed out. "She probably wanted to kill me herself." When he looked back at me, I knew I'd hit a sore spot. "And just think how pissed she'll be when she finds out that you used me to perform some selfish little magic trick to further extricate yourself from her grasp."

"She does not want to kill you," Luc said, his voice mild. "I do."

As if I'd forget a minor detail like that? "She's still going to be furious. You think she's mad at me? Wait until you double-cross her."

The blue eyes narrowed at me, and he jerked out the silverware drawer, rummaging through its contents. "You don't know what you're talking about."

Actually, I was on to something here. "She's a control freak. She wants everything under her control. I've met her. I know. If she can't control you, she wants you dead. You're of no use to her, so when you show up, all footloose and fancy-free, what do you think she's going to do? Throw you a party for being clever enough to free yourself? Or put you under the same manhunt that she put me under?"

"Do you think I care what she wants?" Luc sneered. "Do you think I like answering to her and her lackeys at all hours? Forced to do their bidding because of my ties to my master? That's what this is about—what *all* of this is about." He slammed a large knife on the counter, and I jumped. "No more demands." He slammed the knife drawer shut. "No more doing her bidding." He picked up the knife. "Just freedom. A Romani craves freedom above all else." He headed toward me, knife in hand.

"You probably make the Romani sick," I said, standing up against the wall. "A pretty little lapdog to the queen.

Yes, master. No, master. Whatever you say, master." I forced a smirk to my face as I watched his fingers tighten on the knife.

In a moment he was at my side, grabbing my upper arm and shoving the knife against my throat. "I grow weary of your mouth."

I stilled, frightened. Even though I'd survive a throat-cutting, I had no desire to experience the sensation of choking on my own blood until the cut healed. Provided I made it out alive, of course.

"Take off the cuff," he said to me, his eyes murderous.

"No," I said, swallowing hard when the knife moved closer. "Take it off yourself."

His body shifted against mine, and I felt the poke of his erection against my pelvis. His blue eyes searched my face, his breathing coming faster. "Remember how you moaned and squirmed in my lap in the car? You liked it when I touched you." The knife slid down my skin, the cool blade caressing my neck. "I'd like to see that again before I kill you. I'd like to stick my cock inside you and make you scream for hours." His eyes focused on my mouth and he slid the blade upward, lightly touching my lower lip. "After all, I can kill you in a few hours as easily as now."

I held back my shudder. If he took the cuff off, it wouldn't be rape. I'd be so hot for his loathsome self that I'd do anything I could to get him inside me. I hated the thought of it.

"You'd let me live for another day?" I said, my voice breathless as my hand trailed down his front, trying to make it seem like I'd do anything to buy myself another day.

"Maybe," Luc said, his eyes intent on my face as my hand slid into the waistband of his boxers.

I put my hand on his cock, stroked the length of it suggestively, and bit my lip in the most seductive way I knew possible. "You want to fuck me?" I whispered against his face, arching my neck so the knife seemed more like foreplay than a threat.

His blue eyes blazed into mine, all the answer I needed. He wanted to finish what we'd started in the car just a few days ago. "You want to buy yourself a few hours, *ma belle*?"

"Hell, no," I breathed, wrapping my hand around his dick and twisting viciously, my fingers digging into the skin.

He screamed and dropped to the floor, his hands covering his balls. I couldn't resist kicking him in the nuts twice, as hard as I could. Most of the force was probably stopped by his cupped hands, but I didn't care. "I hope that fucking hurts, you asshole!"

Luc groaned, twisting in agony, and I grabbed the knife. I stuck it between my teeth pirate-like, wrapped both hands around the chain, and pulled as hard as I could.

It didn't budge.

"Please," I groaned, jerking the chain again. It had seemed so loose before. My hands were slippery with nervous sweat, and I swiftly wiped them down. Luc

grabbed my ankle at that moment, and fear fueled my next tug.

The bolt came free, along with a good chunk of the wall.

"Little bitch," Luc said, still curled around his private parts, his hand tightening around my ankle. "You're going to pay for that."

Panic threaded through me and I quickly wrapped the chain around my hand twice, then smashed my fist into his face. Terror and the help of the chain allowed me to strike a solid blow. He flinched backward, releasing my ankle.

I ran to the kitchen, looking for his phone and car keys. I wouldn't get very far on foot; I'd watched enough horror movies to know that.

The counters were bare of Luc's possessions; no sign of car keys anywhere. Frantic, I turned around, the knife clutched in my hand.

Luc hovered at the other end of the kitchen, his face bloody where I'd clocked him in the nose. He still hunched over as if he were unable to stand upright, but gave me a deadly look. He blocked the only way out of the kitchen, standing between me and freedom.

"You idiot," he said, advancing toward me. "It's going to give me great pleasure to wring your neck."

I backed into the corner against the stove. Frenzied, my eyes searched the small kitchen for anything that would help me. Nothing was in reach except the sugar bowl, and it was useless.

Or was it?

An idea flashed through my mind, and I acted before I had time to think about it.

"Mae, I invite you," I cried, then turned the sugar dish over just as Luc grabbed my arm.

A flash of crimson and sulfur filled the small kitchen, and we were both rocked backward by the force of her entry into the house.

"Well, well, well," Mae said, looming over the two of us sprawled on the tile floor. Beside me Luc panted furiously, his breath shortened with fear. Gone was the genteel businesswoman outfit she normally donned; this time she was a full demon: cloven hooves, razor-sharp teeth, and burning eyes. "To what do I owe this honor, you nasty little slut?"

I scrambled to the corner of the kitchen. "I brought you a present," I panted, gesturing at Luc. "I'll trade him in exchange for my escape."

Her red eyes gleamed in delight as she focused on Luc, who cringed. Then her gaze swung back to me. "And why shouldn't I take you first? You betrayed me."

The *gris-gris* grew hot around my neck as she approached. "Because you can't," I said, hoping that Delilah's magic was still effective.

If not, I was screwed.

The demon eyed me for a moment, pondering what I said. Then she smiled slowly, revealing too many teeth. "You're a clever one. Very well." Her reddish black hand wrapped around Luc's throat and she hauled him into the air. "This one will make a tasty surprise. You have my thanks."

As she lifted him into the air, I crawled on hands and knees under their legs, escaping the kitchen. Behind me, Luc choked an unintelligible string of syllables, and the demon tsked at him. "No spells, my sweet." He made a choking noise and grew silent, and I pictured her clawed hand squeezing his throat shut.

The chain slapped against my leg and I froze in the hallway, reminded of my curse. "Wait," I said, turning. "Before you do . . . whatever . . . with him, I need my curse removed."

Mae stroked Luc's dark hair with clawed fingers, and gave me a dismissive look. "The deal was his freedom for yours, precious. Now run away before I change my mind."

I clutched the *gris-gris* around my neck and hesitated. I was dead if I didn't get rid of this curse, and Luc was the only one that could do it. "What if I made you another deal?"

The red eyes narrowed. "I'm listening."

God, this was the stupidest idea ever. "If you can force him to remove my curse, I'll . . ." I paused, thinking. "I'll owe you another favor, to be called in at a future date."

"Done," said Mae quickly.

"Not so fast," I said, panicking. "I want a few conditions on the favor."

She gave me an exasperated look and pulled Luc closer as he writhed to get free. "You silly humans and your conditions. Very well. Name them."

I thought hard for a moment. "You can give me three tasks, and I get to pick the one I want to do. And nothing that would compromise my values . . . I don't want to kill anyone, or anything like that. Nothing that would cause me to tilt my soul's balance in one direction or another." God, would she agree to all that?

She eyed me for a moment. "I should say no, but I'm intrigued. You do realize I'm going to do my best to find a way around your conditions?"

I sighed. "I know."

Mae smiled. "Then we have a deal." She grabbed Luc by the jaw and forced his mouth open slightly. "Come now, my pet. Remove the curse from her, and I'll be gentle with you."

His eyes were wild as they flicked back and forth between Mae and me. His throat worked for a moment, and I heard two syllables rasp from his throat.

"Fuck you."

"Tut tut," Mae said sweetly. She slid a hot claw down his chest, leaving a smoking line after it. Luc gurgled in pain. "That's not nice, sweetie. Do you know what the punishment is for those who aren't nice?" Her smoking hand slid down into his shorts, and a burst of smoke puffed from within the shorts. His scream was cut off by her hand again. "Now. Remove the curse or things will get ugly."

I felt sick to my stomach. No one deserved to be treated like that. I had to remind myself that it was him or me, and that he'd planned on killing me.

When he screamed, though, it didn't make things any easier.

A nonsense string of syllables erupted from Luc's throat in a rush, and his hand moved in a feeble gesture. He shouted a few more words, then grew still, closing his eyes. Mae looked satisfied, and turned back to me.

"There you go, my pet."

I didn't feel any different. Was this a trick? I reached down and undid the clasp on my ankle . . . and nothing happened.

I laughed with relief. "It's gone!"

"A deal's a deal," Mae said sweetly. "We'll be seeing each other again."

I took one last look at Luc, then ran out the front door of the small cabin.

His screams echoed in the distance as I ran away, tears streaming down my face.

CHAPTER TWENTY-THREE

I ran until I reached the road—I didn't know or care how many miles it was. I just ran, and when I my breath caught in my throat and demanded that I stop, I forced myself to continue walking. Anything to get away.

The main road was empty, and after a few more miles I hit a suburban area. Neat houses lined up in rows in the twilight, so innocent and sweet.

I felt dirty as I approached the first one, disheveled, my clothing wrinkled and spotted with blood. An old woman answered the door, and I did my best to seem as meek and terrified. It wasn't hard; big tears rolled down my face. "Can I use your phone?"

"Of course, dear," the woman said, a look of concern on her face as she ushered me inside. "Come right in."

I made a few quick calls. One to Noah's BlackBerry, but I just got voicemail since he was out cold for the night. I left a message there, and on the Gideon Enterprises voicemail, then I dialed the last number.

"Hello? Jackie?" Zane picked up on the first ring.

I hesitated. Either I could trust him, or I couldn't. Luc

322 • JILL MYLES

had said Zane wanted me back. But was that so he could turn me in to the queen? I was suddenly tired of running. "Can you come get me?" I said dully.

I gave him the address—somewhere in Mississippi again—and he promised to be there very soon. So I sat down on the afghan-covered sofa, drank some coffee with the woman, and waited.

True to his word, the doorbell rang sometime after midnight. "I bet that's your young man," the old woman, Maribel, said sweetly.

I smiled at her and stood. "Thank you so much." I glanced at the door, then back at her. "May I have one more cup of coffee before I go?"

"Of course, dear." She patted my hand. "I'll go get it. You just wait right there."

As soon as she disappeared into the kitchen, I ran for the front door. I didn't want Zane and his goons to see poor sweet Maribel, in case they needed a midnight snack. I didn't want anyone else getting hurt because of me.

When I opened the door, though, Zane was alone. Relief flitted across his face. "Jackie, you're all right."

I slipped my hand into his, expecting him to tug me down the sidewalk and into the shadows. What I hadn't expected was for him to envelop me in his arms, kissing my hair, stroking my face, softly whispering "It's all right" against my face. I felt the flutter of his wings surround me in their dark warmth, and I wrapped my hands around his waist, loving his body against mine.

"You came alone," I said softly.

"I did." Zane pressed another kiss to my forehead. "I told the others I had a few things to take care of before I returned. And I wanted to see you and . . . explain."

The porch light flicked on behind us, and Zane grabbed me by the waist and lifted us into the air with the ease of one who lived to fly. I wrapped my arms around his neck to anchor myself, and his hands slid to my ass. "Wrap your legs around me, Princess. We've got a long flight back to New Orleans."

I did so, huddling my face against his neck, trying to bury myself against his warm skin. The wind ripped at us, but I wasn't going to stop it from letting us talk. "Why did you curse me, Zane?"

A ragged breath escaped him. "I didn't know about it, Princess. The queen had Luc lay the curse on me while I was in daylight hibernation. I didn't find out about it until you told me at the rest stop, and I suspected the worst. It's just like her to target someone that I care about."

I believed him, and nodded against his throat.

"When I found out about your curse, I knew Queen Nitocris had a hand in it. So I left you behind—I thought for sure that you'd be safe with Remy—and I confronted the queen." He was silent for a long moment, the only sound between us the thumping of his heart against mine, the rasping of our breath in the chill night air, and the steady flap of his wings as we rose and dipped through the air currents. "She admitted everything. She's proud of the fact that she was able to curse you. It was to get back at me."

"Luc said she wanted another succubus under her control." I shuddered, thinking of an eternity in which I was forced to do the queen's bidding. Living under her rule, her whims, her desires. It would be Hell on earth.

"I think she did, originally. But when I confronted her, she changed her mind. It was the perfect time to make a deal. If I would come back to the fold and be her loyal prince once more, she'd exchange my freedom for yours. I agreed."

He'd done that . . . for me?

A desperate note entered his voice, made ragged by the wind. "I'm not back with the queen by choice, Jackie. She's tried to woo me back for many months, and I've been able to withstand her tantrums. I wanted to be free to enjoy our life together, but when it came down to choosing between you and freedom, I chose you." His mouth nudged against my temple, and he pressed another kiss there.

Tears spilled from my eyes. "I apologize for doubting you."

He laughed, a short, bitter sound. "You had every right to. I would have been angry at me if I were in your shoes. Once I'd spoken with the queen, I knew Luc was on your trail, but he was very evasive. Every time I'd call him to tell him the plans had changed, he'd hang up on me or delete the text messages unread."

I thought back to my hazy, drugged-out evening in the hotel. Luc's phone had kept vibrating with incoming calls. We'd almost had sex, but he'd pulled back because of the calls. My eyes widened as I realized it was Zane who'd been desperately trying to get hold of Luc and get him to leave me alone. "So you've been looking out for me? And you didn't tell me?"

His mouth quirked to one side. "I couldn't tell you the truth until she'd kept her part of the bargain and released you from Luc's little scheme."

Which reminded me. "I, uh, did a bad thing to Luc."

"Nothing that he didn't deserve, I'm sure."

"I sold him to a demon in exchange for my own freedom," I confessed.

He laughed, the rumbles vibrating in his chest. "The queen will love that. I imagine she'll leave him in the demon's clutches for a bit before she ransoms him, just to teach him a lesson."

I perked up a little. "Do you think she'll free him?" I hated the thought of even Luc stuck in Mae's hands for all eternity.

"Luc's her favorite double agent," Zane said. "She might punish him for a time, but she'll bring him back to the fold eventually."

I snuggled back against his chest. "He deserves punishment, that's for sure."

"I couldn't agree more," Zane whispered in my ear. "And if he touches you again, I'll kill him with my bare hands."

Even though it was just an expression, it warmed my heart, and I let the rhythmic sound of his wings relax me.

Zane landed on Delilah's roof about an hour or two before dawn. The house was quiet, and I unwrapped my legs from his body slowly, reluctant to leave him. "Are you coming in?"

"No." Zane shook his head. "By now, she's got the entire place warded to Hell and back. I can feel them on my skin." A hint of a sad smile tugged at his full mouth. "And I need to get back to . . . the others. They'll be looking for me."

My breath hitched in my throat. "When will I see you again?"

"I don't know." He touched my cheek, then leaned in to give me a kiss. "I'd say that I could sneak away to see you, except that the queen will be having me watched, and I want to keep her away from you." He stroked my hair, then softly said, "I think it's a good idea if we don't see each other for a while."

He was sacrificing himself for me, to keep me safe. My eyes burned with tears. "It's not fair."

He wiped my cheek with his thumb gently. "It's never fair in love and war, Jackie."

I laughed through my tears. "Is that what this is? Love and war?"

"I know it's love," he said quietly.

My heart stilled at the soft admission. It was love that motivated him? Not just a master's affection for his own creation?

"Here," he said, pulling something out of his pocket. "I want you to have this."

He held out something shiny on a chain. I took it from his hands, tracing the tiny links and the pendant that dangled from it. It felt like some sort of metal acorn.

"Part of my deal with the queen," he said, his voice wry. "I asked her for a charm to remove your curse. There was no such thing, but she did have another of her warlocks make a charm to suppress magic. I figured you could use it until I found you a cure."

Interesting. I wondered what the charm had cost him in favors, and shuddered. I didn't want to know. "Thank you, Zane. This could have come in handy a few days ago."

"That's why I was bringing it to New Orleans," he said, his hands tracing along my face, my neck, trying to memorize me with his touch. "But since you don't need it any longer, give it to Remy. It should help her keep Joachim under control."

My breath sucked in and relief rushed through me. I could save Remy after all. "Zane, I don't know what to say." Gratitude and sadness clogged my throat. "Thank you."

"I'd settle for a kiss before I leave." A hint of the old, devilish Zane had returned.

That I could most definitely do. I tilted my face up to

his and slid my hands inside his shirt, the chain wrapped around one hand. I wanted to give him more than just a kiss good-bye.

There wasn't much time, and far too many clothes. We sat on the roof, shedding our clothes with haste and reaching for each other with eager hands. I clung to his hot, hard form, my pale white skin brushing against cool black wing. The meeting of our bodies was not gentle; nothing tender in the desperate kisses that fueled us or the way he jerked my leg around his waist and slid his cock into me as I lifted my hips to meet his thrust. This was Zane, this was love, and I was going to be miserable without him.

My ankle slid over his shoulder, my toes tickling against the thick fall of wing-feathers. The mix of textures was sensory overload—his hard fingers wrapped around my ankle as he thrust deep, over and over again, the roof tiles abrading my back as I moaned with pleasure. Within moments I found my release, muscles tensing and body locking as I shuddered, my teeth digging into his shoulder to buy my silence. He came a moment later, wings spreading and arching into the night sky, blotting out the moon with their span.

The whole process had taken only moments.

After we pulled apart, I couldn't stop kissing his face as he buttoned his shirt and helped me dress.

"Say you'll send me notes. Or call me. Email. Twitter. Something. Anything." I didn't want to think of him leaving me forever.

Forever was so very long when you're immortal.

Zane gave me a crooked half smile. "I'll see what I can do, Princess." Which was guy code for "Don't call me, I'll call you."

I understood—he wouldn't contact me for my own safety. I nodded, unable to speak for the knot in my throat. I clutched the acorn charm tight in my hand as Zane picked me up in his arms and fluttered slowly to the ground, dropping me in Delilah's yard with the gentlest of care.

He brushed his hand tenderly along my cheek, then stroked my jaw with his thumb. "A few weeks ago, the thought of you with Noah was eating me up inside. But I want you to promise me that you'll stay with him, since I cannot be here for you. He'll keep you safe."

I didn't have the words to answer him, so I nodded.

Zane touched my cheek one last time and then was aloft again.

I wanted to say so much before he left me, to explain that I was sorry for everything that I'd misunderstood. But I just waved sadly, then went back into the house.

I would not cry. I *would* not cry, I repeated, even as I felt tears sliding down my cheeks.

A sad smile touched my face. I'd managed to get the curse removed without anyone else's help. Sort of. And even though I had to make a deal with a devil to do so, I was pretty proud of myself. At the start of this trip I'd been completely dependent on both Remy and Zane, and now I needed no one in my life. If they were there, it was because I'd chosen them to be there.

Zane had made his own choice, and I could respect that. The ache in my heart was heavy, but I'd bear it because I had to.

And I refused to think that this would be the last time I'd see Zane ever again.

Delilah came running out of the kitchen, a knife and a jar of powder in her hands as I came through the front door. "Oh. It's you."

"Nice to see you, too," I said, wiping my wet face.

"What happened?"

I didn't feel like explaining it. "Too much. I'll tell you some other time."

"All right." She cocked her head, regarding me, her dainty face perfect. "Did you get those vampires to leave?"

"They're gone. They won't be back."

"Good." She gestured at her sitting room. "The priest is still in there. Noah's upstairs in hibernation." Delilah eyed me. "Your curse?"

"Gone," I said, a wealth of emotion in that small word. "And so is the creep that put it on me."

"Nice job," she said, and then left.

I stood in the hallway a moment longer, surprised at her casual dismissal. Didn't she care about what I'd gone through?

I guess when you'd lived for seven hundred years as a succubus, you learned to care only about yourself. I didn't want to become like that. Not now, not a hundred years from now.

Though I longed to go crawl into bed next to Noah and forget about everything that had happened, I found myself drawn to the sitting room instead. The priest was laid out on one of Delilah's plush velvet sofas, his arms propped on his chest as if he were dead.

I reached out and brushed my fingertips across his forehead. Could I bring him back, now that my powers were under control?

Concentrating, I closed my eyes and thought back to the minds inside my own, separating them apart, willing the priest back into his body.

He coughed, and I opened my eyes.

"I'm back," the priest said, and smiled at me.

"I'm glad," I said, feeling a much better.

After the priest left, I got into bed next to Noah, watching him sleep. Having him beside me helped ease the pain of Zane's loss. Noah was beautiful in the moonlight, and I could see the beauty of Heaven in his face.

What must it be like, to be cursed to spend an eternity in an existence like his? I hadn't chosen to be a succubi, but I could think of worse things. Like being cast out from Heaven . . . or forced to spend an eternity catering to an evil vampire queen's wishes. I stroked the blond locks of hair off Noah's forehead, my mind awash with melancholy thoughts. And even though I knew Zane wasn't coming back, I couldn't help looking out the window, hoping for a flash of black wing.

Noah stirred awake a short time later, blinking at me twice before crushing me to him in a giant bear hug. "Jackie! Thank God. You scared the life out of me."

I let him cuddle me close, enjoying the warmth. "I'm okay," I said softly.

He ran his hands over me, checking my body with worried eyes and fingers, and kissing every inch of my skin that he could. "Your curse?"

"Gone," I said. "It was a long night, though, and I'm tired. Can we talk about it later?"

"Of course. Whatever you want."

"Just hold me right now," I said, laying my cheek against his chest and breathing in his wonderful scent. "I'd like to spend a day in bed with nothing to bother us. No vampires, no monsters, no demons, no voodoo. Just a day in bed with TV and food."

"We can do that," Noah said, stroking my hair. "We'll talk about the rest when you're ready."

I nodded. Now was the perfect time to ask about Delilah's concerns. "Noah . . . are you in trouble with the other Serim? For making me? Dee said it's forbidden to create a new succubus."

He cleared his throat. "Ah, yes and no."

I didn't like that answer. "How about you go into a bit more detail?"

"Yes, it's illegal, and no, I'm not in trouble. I paid a fine and reported the misdeed to the council. You're safe with me." He rubbed my arm, as if realizing how upset that would make me. "Just trust me, Jackie. It's all taken care of."

Misdeed? How depressing, to be considered an unfortunate accident. "Speaking of misdeeds," I said, changing topics. "The priest is back in his body."

Relief washed over his face. "You figured out how to put him back? That's wonderful."

"I need to go see the others, too, and put them back in their bodies." I wasn't asking for permission before doing what I wanted this time.

"We can do that," he agreed.

That was why Noah was so wonderful—supporting me, no matter what. I gave him a soft smile. "I saw Delilah downstairs. She looked good." Like she'd never been in a knock-down fight with a vampire or possessed by a demon. "How is Remy?"

"Delilah's always fine; she heals fast. As for Remy, Dee tried but she still can't make contact with her. She might be lost for good." Sadness seeped through his voice. "My poor friend."

"Zane gave me something that might help. It's a magic charm that nullifies the magic of the wearer. He was going to give it to me for my curse and I don't need it now."

Noah nodded slowly. "Perhaps he was looking out for you in the only way he knew how."

I swallowed hard at the knot in my throat. "Let's see if it works on Remy, shall we?"

We got up from the bed, heading to the end of the hall where my old bedroom—and Remy's closet—lay. I flicked on the light switch as we entered the room and in the corner, still trapped in by the thick line of rice powder, Remy hissed at me. Her eyes glowed a deep, angry red.

"Do you want me to put the charm on her?" Noah said, extending his hand. "She might be dangerous."

"No, I can do it," I stepped forward, letting the necklace swing from my fingers. This was my doing, and I'd be the one to fix it. I approached the closet with cautious steps, crouching just before the line of rice powder but not crossing it.

Remy looked exhausted, despite the unholy fire that lit her from within. Deep shadows ringed her eyes, her lovely olive skin was spattered with dried blood and Lord only knew what else, and tangled hair slid all over her face. She looked like a wild creature, and she even hissed at me again when I approached.

"A present for you," I said, holding the dangling necklace in the air so she could see it. As I took a good look at it in the light for the first time, my jaw dropped.

The hard charm that I'd mistaken for an acorn? A big, marble-sized diamond. It seemed to have a life of its own, dancing and glittering so brightly that it seemed to be glowing in the sun rather than just the lighting of the bedroom.

A low, barking laugh erupted from Remy's throat. "Do you think I'm stupid enough to reach for that, foolish succubus?"

I admired the necklace for a moment longer. "Not really."

Before Joachim could ponder my response, I crossed the rice powder line and tackled Remy, pressing my elbow to her throat. Either I'd caught her by surprise or her body was weakening from lack of sex, because I had the upper hand.

She screamed and thrashed under me, her hands reaching for my face like claws to scratch my eyes out. I pushed down harder on her throat and her breath turned to faint gurgles as her hands frantically scratched at my skin.

I held the necklace high out of her reach.

How was I going to get it over her head?

Noah appeared by my side, crowding into the closet next to us. With one strong hand, he held down one of Remy's arms and drove the other wildly thrashing one down. "Do it before she hurts herself," he said between gritted teeth.

Rushing to unclasp the necklace, I sat atop her stomach, straddling her body. Even though her physical form was weak, malevolence emitted from her, and I could feel the unnatural fury building. Joachim was readying to attack.

I leaned in to put the necklace around her neck, fumbling to clasp it behind the snarled mass of her hair.

Remy sank her teeth into my arm and began to snarl.

I swore, but she only dug in deeper, her red eyes flaring. It hurt like a bitch, but I wasn't about to let Joachim win this one. I concentrated on hooking the tiny clasp.

As soon as I released the necklace, the thrashing of her body stopped. She quit shaking my arm like a ravenous pit bull, and her growling died away. I remained seated atop her, warily scanning her face.

After a moment, she opened her eyes and stared up at me with mild blue gray eyes. Her mouth slid off my arm. "I suppose there's a logical reason why I'm chewing on your forearm?" she asked in an exhausted voice.

"Stuckey's was out of pecan logs," I said, sliding off of her. My heart pounded with relief as she sat up, slowly testing her limbs.

"What happened to me?" She touched her face and hair, giving me and Noah a puzzled look. "Why am I so disgusting?"

"Joachim." I pointed at the diamond around her throat. "Keep that thing around your neck at all times, and you'll keep him away." I watched her anxiously. "How do you feel?"

"Like I need a vacation," she said, pushing her hair off her face.

That sounded like the Remy I knew. I reached forward and hugged her close. "Vacation sounds wonderful." I was getting weepy again.

"How about a road trip?" Noah asked innocently.

We both glared at him.

He chuckled. "I can think of the perfect place to get away from it all. Tropical beaches, exotic temples, just you and a few dozen archaeologists, and a certain investor."

The dig.

"It sounds horrible to me," Remy said, her head resting on my shoulder. "I was thinking of something more along the lines of a spa."

I'd completely forgotten about the big archaeological trip. "What about Dr. Morgan? I haven't talked to him in days—he'll think I've fallen off the planet."

Noah shook his head. "I told him that you weren't going to miss the dig. You have your heart set on going, so I told him there was no way I was going to pull funding." He glanced at Remy. "I can ask if there's a spa, though."

I smiled. "That's wonderful, Noah. I thought for sure Morgan would have fired me by now."

"And piss off his biggest financial patron? Not a chance." Noah got to his feet in one fluid motion. He extended a hand toward Remy and she stood, wobbly and slow. "They leave next week, if you're still interested in going."

Remy shuffled to the door. "You guys figure out the trip stuff. I need food."

Part of me wanted to follow her to assure myself that she was all right, but I put my faith in the necklace—and in Zane. I turned to Noah. "So how can you go with me on the dig?"

"The miracle of modern technology," Noah said. "One

can run a financial business even from the wilds of Panama."

"Actually, it's the Yucatán." I said, dusting off the rice powder covering the undershirt he'd been sleeping in. "You sure don't know much about the Mayans, for someone who's putting down a small fortune to get them dug up."

Noah smiled and wiped a bit of rice powder from my face. "That's okay. I'm just hoping to get laid. Tell me, is it working?"

"Archaeology in exchange for sex?" I gave him a playful look. "You drive a hard bargain." I felt a bit guilty at the surge of happiness. My curse was gone, Noah and I were back together, and Remy was all right. I didn't have Zane, but hopefully that ache would dull with a distraction and time.

And I had nothing but time. I could wait.

Noah arched an eyebrow. "That sounds like a deal to me."

I slid my hand under his ribbed cotton shirt and said lightly, "As you told me, everyone makes deals in the Afterlife. And I intend to hold you to mine."

And I did.

Turn the page

for a special look

at the next deliciously sexy novel in

The Succubus Diaries series

by Jill Myles

Coming soon from Pocket Books

At Fred's subtle touch, my breath caught in my throat. A small moan of delight escaped me, and I clutched at the sleeve of the man I clung to. "Do it again," I whispered.

He moved his fingers over the spot once more, his breath coming hard with excitement. I had to bite my lip to keep from crying out with sheer pleasure.

"What do you think?" He moved in and murmured huskily in my ear.

Oh God, I was in danger of losing control if he didn't stop.

"Jackie?"

"Classic Puuc," I said.

"Do you think so?" He touched the monitor again and zoomed in on the area in question.

Archaeology was better than the best orgasm. My fingers spasmed against his sleeve in excitement. "Oh my God! Stop! Stop right there! Look!"

Fred turned the monitor to me.

I stared at the blocky red shape on the screen of the radar equipment with something akin to utter delight. "Definite classic Puuc. Look," I said, pointing at the edge of the red blob with my fingernail. "Thick, heavy veneer stone with a clean edge. These lighter spots around the side suggest doorways cut into the rock. I bet if we dug it up, we'd find a stone relief to rival that of Chichén Itza." I leaned over the monitor with excitement, my heart slamming in my chest. "Can we pan out to the rest of the jungle?"

Too late, I realized it was a bad idea to lean over the table. Fred leaned over me, plastering his groin against my backside. My co-archaeologist was the possessor of one raging boner.

Ugh. Not again.

"Jackie," he murmured in my ear. "Forget about the dig for a moment. I need to talk to you."

I clamped my thighs together tightly, trying to rid myself of the unwanted feelings of pleasure. Yuck. Despite the fact that I didn't want Fred in the slightest, my stupid cursed body reacted to his touch. I shoved my elbow backward, hard. "You need to get off of me."

"We're finally alone." Fred said. "I wanted to tell you how I feel." His young face was alight with desire, his dirty brown ponytail damp with sweat. "No one's around."

I glanced around and sure enough, the local Mayan workers that we hired to help out around the dig were nowhere to be seen. None of the university team was around, either. That was odd. All the guys at the site were normally so taken with my looks that I couldn't shake them, no matter what I did. I had an adoring admirer or two following me at all times, even to the port-a-potty.

It really sucked to be supernaturally beautiful.

Fred moved forward to me again and caught my hands. "I've been holding back for months, waiting for the right moment." He pressed a fervent kiss to my hand, despite my efforts to yank it out of his grasp. "You're so beautiful, Jackie."

Sigh.

Of course I was beautiful. I was a succubus. We were cursed to have our faces and bodies remolded into that of a man's ideal fantasy. To think I'd once complained about how mousy my old looks were. I never realized how damned inconvenient it would be to be gorgeous.

"I've never met anyone like you." He continued to kiss my knuckles, pressing moist lips against them.

"Fred," I began. "You do realize that Noah's going to kick your ass if he sees this?" It was a bluff of course. Noah—my beautiful Serim boyfriend—might glare sternly at Fred or throw some money around to make sure that Fred was removed from camp, but I doubted he'd actually get physical with the guy.

My suitor shook his head. "He's busy right now. And this might be my only chance to show you how I feel."

I struggled again to break his grip. Why, oh why weren't succubi gifted with super strength? I couldn't think of anyone who needed it more than a hot immortal girl. Men were compelled to fall in love with my new face, and I'd have happily traded it away for the ability to punch the hell out of Fred at the moment.

So I used the only other weapon I had available. I pretended to faint, my limbs going limp in his arms.

As expected, Fred released my hands to catch me as I went down, and I slapped my open palm against his forehead.

It worked; he went down like a light.

I didn't hit him hard, of course. But his mind shut off with the touch of my hand to his forehead, and he went down for the count.

There was one perk to being a succubus, at least. I could

shut down his mind and put him into a deep, dreamless sleep and then pick through his memories. Not the most handy skill, depending on the situation, and I tried not to use it much since it tended to backfire in rather spectacular ways. But desperate times called for desperate moves.

I didn't let him stay unconscious long. Kneeling beside his prostrate body, I touched his forehead to wake him up again, and patted his hand as if I were worried about him. "Fred? Fred? Are you all right?"

His eyes fluttered open slowly, and focused on me. "What . . . what happened?"

I put on a concerned expression and squeezed his hand. "You were leaning in to kiss me, and you passed out," I lied.

Fred sat up, cradling his head in his free hand. "I did?"

"You did." I helped him to his feet, then dusted off his shirt. "Fred, I'm not sure but . . . I think you should go see a doctor." Step one—lay the trap.

He gave me a concerned look. "What do you mean?"

I forced my eyes wide. "Well, you *do* know that if you pass out when you get an erection, that's an early warning sign of extremely high blood pressure. And you're far too young to have that sort of thing happen to you."

Brushing the sweaty hair off his forehead, Fred stared blankly. "I've never done that before." His hand went to his wrist, as if checking his pulse.

"Of course not," I said sweetly, taking him by the elbow and pointing him toward my jeep. "I'm sure it's nothing to be worried about." Step two, play to the ego. "You're a healthy, strong man. It's probably nothing. But just to be safe, don't you think you should head into Mérida and get yourself checked out?"

"But . . . the survey equipment . . . the dig . . ."

"There's nothing that can't wait until the crew returns later tonight." I pulled my keys out of my pocket and placed them into his hand. "Why don't you take my jeep, go to town, spend the night in air conditioning, get checked out by the doctor, and come back in a few days? I'll explain everything to Mr. Gideon."

"Everything?" Fred swallowed hard.

I took pity on him. "Almost everything." I shook my finger at him. "And as long as the rest never happens again, it'll remain our secret."

Sorta.

In a daze, Fred climbed into the jeep and started the engine. I tried not to smile too cheerfully as he left, waving as the jeep disappeared down the dirt road into the thick undergrowth of jungle. My problem neatly disposed of, I raced back to the GPR equipment to get another glimpse of those red blobs. To think that we had found another set of outlying buildings! We could expand on the dig, perhaps get another grant from the university!

But Fred's fall had jostled the computer, and the screen was dark. I tapped the monitor twice before glancing down and seeing the plug hanging out of the socket. I sighed in disgust. Without someone to help me move the bulky surface antenna, I couldn't do any further radar scans until the crew returned from Mérida.

Annoyed, I packed up the equipment I could and then picked through the clearing of the campsite. We'd decided to set up in the least thickly forested portion of Yuxmal's ancient grounds, and workers had cleared even more area so we could set up the tent city that had been our home for the past few months.

The tent I shared with Noah was at the edge of camp,

near the base of a massive stone pyramid—the discovery that had started the dig. As I approached my tent, I could hear the generator humming, and the sound of rotating fans buzzing. I paused outside—the door-flap was down, which seemed like a bad idea, given the heat and humidity. Inside, I heard a muffled curse.

Noah was here, at least. I ran my long fingernails along the weatherproofed canvas. "Knock knock."

"Don't come in," Noah barked.

I frowned and ignored that, lifting the flap. "What do you mean, don't come in?"

My jaw dropped at the sight before me. Noah stood in the tent, clad in nothing but boxer shorts, dripping sweat. His blonde hair was plastered to his skull, and beads trailed down his flat, golden abs. A large table filled the middle of the tent, covered with a paper tablecloth that fluttered in the wake of the rotating fans set at each corner of the tent. Two place settings decorated the table, along with a large covered dish. A row of pale candles was lined up in front of Noah, a box of matches in his hand. "What is all this?"

"A surprise. Or it was." His eyes were bright blue in his golden face, almost as brilliant as the scowl on his face.

I let the flap slide shut behind me, and fanned my hand at my face. In the heat, with the humidity, no amount of rotating fans could make the tent feel like less of a sauna. It seemed awfully odd to have an elegant dinner set up in the tent, but that looked like that was Noah's plan. I was torn between thinking he was sweet, or thinking he was mad. "Where did everyone at camp go?"

"They went to town. Paid vacation day," he said, irritable as he pulled another match out of the box. "Fred was supposed to keep you busy for another hour."

I snorted and moved to the far end of the table, where a chair was set out. "If by 'keep me busy' you mean declare love for me and try to molest me, I'd say he finished early."

Noah ran the match along the side of the box, and a small flame flared to life. He leaned toward the closest candle, and it abruptly sputtered as the breeze from the fan blew the match out. He swore again and pulled out another match.

Well, now. Noah seemed a little crankier than usual, but I blamed it on the blue in his eyes. The closer we got to the full moon, the more moody he became as the curse came over him and the need for sex arose.

Of course, the sight of those blue eyes and that delicious, bare, sweaty chest gave me another idea, a rather naughty one. I moved to his side, my finger tracing one runnel of sweat down his chest. I dipped my finger in the damp bead and met his eyes, then tasted the droplet, a blatant suggestion if there ever was one.

"Not now, Jackie," he said, irritable.

With a sigh, I dropped my hands and went back to the far side of the table and sat down so I wouldn't be tempted to touch him again. Another symptom of the full moon curse— Noah was completely and utterly uninterested in sex until the day of the full moon itself (upon which we'd stay in the tent the entire day and have sex until he passed out).

I gave him a bright smile. "So when are you due . . . so we can get back to normal and I can get laid?"

He pulled out another match, glaring at it with all the hate in the world. "The moon rises in two days."

Well, thank God for that. I did a little fast math in my head. We'd had sex yesterday morning and I would be due tomorrow morning. If I had to wait another day after that . . . well, it'd be miserable as hell, but I wouldn't die from it. An overdue succubus was an exceedingly horny one, so I'd just have to avoid the other men in the camp for the day or I'd have the men trailing me like I was the Pied Piper of Hamlin.

"That day can't get here soon enough," I murmured. Just the thought of not having sex for another two days made me crave it, and I crossed my legs.

Noah looked over at me, a hint of a frown marring the line of his eyebrows.

The scent of sulfur grew strong in the small tent. "Don't worry about the candles," I said. "They're giving me a head-ache."

His jaw was set in a stubborn line that I recognized about once a month. "Fine." He put down the matches and placed the candles back in an orderly row along the table. "What were you saying about Fred?"

I glanced at the covered tray, my mouth watering as I wondered what was underneath. Was it someone's birthday? My taste buds gave a little thrill at the thought of birthday cake. Maybe chocolate, to take the edge off my desire. Noah knew that I loved to eat. "Fred confessed undying love for me," I said, distracted by the tray and my rumbling stomach. It had been a few hours since breakfast, and lunch sounded rather tasty at the moment. "Though I promised him that I wouldn't say anything to Mr. Gideon." I gave Noah a pointed look. "Consider yourself out of the know, Mr. Gideon. And don't worry. I used my Suck powers to draw him off and convinced him to visit town."

Noah gave a little shake of his head. "Jackie, we've had this conversation before. You need to be careful around the men at camp."

My jaw dropped.

Careful?

Steamed, I grabbed my steak knife off the table. With my other hand, I took off my dirty baseball cap and shook down one of my long, bright red braids. I held the braid out from my head at a straight angle and in fast, jerky motions, I hacked the entire thing off, tossing it down on the table.

Noah rolled his eyes at my dramatic show.

Still furious, I shoved a finger in my mouth and bit down on the nail, sawing it down to the quick with my teeth. I spit the brittle crescent out on the table.

He gave me a faintly exasperated look. "Jackie—"

"Watch," I said, crossing my arms over my chest.

Sure enough, less then a minute later, I felt the hair follicles on my scalp slither, and the familiar tingling that told me my hair was growing back. I grabbed a handful of the sheared ends and watched in disgust as they grew, my hair pouring down my shoulder and over my shirt, becoming long, flame-red curls. I extended my hand to him—my fingernail had already grown back to the long, unpractical length.

"Do you see this?" I jerked at my T-shirt. "I'm wearing a Led Zeppelin tee and cargo shorts and a baseball cap. Not exactly seductress material."

"Zane's shirt, I noticed."

Grr. He was missing the point entirely. "What I'm *trying* to tell you," I said, "is that no matter what I do, I can't disguise how I look. I've shaved my head. I've worn thick glasses. I've done everything short of a ski mask, and it's no use. I could go out in a trash-bag and someone would still hit on me."

"Jackie—"

"You know," I carried on, angrily re-braiding my "new"

hair. He was going to sit and listen to my complaints, darn it. "I thought going on this dig would be good for my career. I could finally set myself up as a serious archaeologist. But it's like I'm the Hooters girl at the church social! The men leer at me constantly. Someone tries to cop a feel if I bend over. All the women on the team hate me because they think I'm blowing you just to get you to sponsor the dig."

"You *are* blowing me," he interrupted, a hint of a smile playing on his face.

"Not to further my career," I bellowed. "Remember that whole have to have sex every two days thing? Hello? Succubus?"

He gave me a patient look. "I wouldn't be out in the jungles of Yucatan spending a small fortune on radar equipment if it weren't for you. So they do have a point."

My eyes narrowed. "You are *so* not helping your case right now, buddy."

Noah chuckled, showing me a glimpse of the good-natured, strong protector that I normally adored. He moved to my end of the table and pulled me up into his arms. "Poor Jackie. I'm sorry this isn't turning out like you want." His warm hand stroked down my back.

My bad mood was rapidly dwindling, now that I was pressed against his hard, sweaty body, and I slid my hands up and down his bare, damp skin. He felt good against me. *Really* good. It reminded me that I was due for the Itch in a short time, so I reluctantly pulled away. "Unless you want to make out on the floor, maybe we shouldn't touch."

I wanted him to protest, to kiss me senseless and prove me wrong, but he said, "You're right," and released me. Spoil-sport.

I sighed. I hated the days up to the full moon.

"I brought you a few presents from town," he said, moving back to the other end of the table.

Sitting back down, I clapped my hands in delight. "Edible things?" In this part of Mexico you could get a lot of standard stuff from the big Wal-Mart in Mérida or the local *tedejon*, but I missed the small luxuries like Pringles and my Aveda shampoo. Noah was constantly bringing me boxes of treats as a result. Last week it was foil-wrapped Ding Dongs, which I tore through in about five minutes.

Succubi weren't known for their self-control when it came to food.

Noah smiled at my delighted expression. "Part of your present is edible, yes." He disappeared under the paper tablecloth and reappeared a moment later with a large cardboard box. The word "Pop Tarts" was printed across the side of the box.

I squealed. "Oh my God! Pop Tarts! A whole case!"

"I had them special ordered for you in Mérida. They're chocolate." At my second squeal of delight, he chuckled. "Try not to eat them all in one day."

I eyed the box with hungry, avid eyes. "They might last two days." Maybe three, if I paced myself.

A radar discovery and Pop Tarts. This day just got better and better.

Noah seemed pleased by my reaction, his eyes so blue they glowed in his tanned face. "I never thought I'd see a woman get so turned on over a package." His voice had dropped to a huskier octave, showing that he wasn't quite immune to my charms just yet.

Encouraged, I leaned over the table, my voice turning into a purr. "Show me your package, and I'll show you an even more turned-on woman."

His eyes flashed and I recognized the interest there, fighting the lethargy that always set over him before the full moon. "Your other present first," he murmured.

"Whatever floats your boat," I breathed, clamping my thighs together so they'd stop quivering with excitement.

Hot diggity, I *was* going to get laid today, after all.

He leaned over the table, placing his hand on the dome of the silver platter. I was a little excited to see what was under the mysterious covering. This was why he'd sent everyone away from camp to be alone with me, the reason behind the big table and production. "If that's a milkshake under there, they're going to have to pry me off of you with a crowbar," I said, my eyes glued to the tray.

He lifted the lid.

No mountains of cheeseburgers. No milkshakes. No decadent cascades of chocolate, french fries, or a fat, fluffy cheesecake.

A tiny box with a bow lay in the center of the plate. It looked like . . . a ring box.

"Shit," I blurted.

"That's not exactly the reaction I wanted to hear," he teased, but there was an uncomfortable tone to his voice that spoke volumes.

I stared at the small box, unable to move my hand toward it. I knew—I just *knew*—what it contained. And the dreadful knot forming in the pit of my stomach told me that I didn't want it.

"Jackie?"

Steeling my nerves, I forced myself to reach for the box. I owed Noah that much, right? My fingers were trembling (not in a good way) as I flicked the box open. And stared at the ring inside.

A simple band of platinum clung to the biggest damn diamond I had ever laid eyes on. The size of it blew me away. I pulled it out of the box to make sure that I wasn't seeing things. It was the size of a large button and stood up from the setting like one of those candy lollipop rings. The inside of the band read "Tiffany & Co." It even felt heavy. "Jeezus, Noah."

"It's four carats. I figured if everyone was going to stare at you all the time, they might as well have something else to fixate on."

He wasn't kidding. "It's . . . enormous."

Noah chuckled. "A guy loves to hear his woman say that."

His woman? Oh God. Anxiety and stress came crashing down around me, and I carefully put the ring back in the box. I loved Noah. Had great affection for him. Loved spending time with him. We got along very well, and he was pleasant to live with.

So why did the thought of marrying him scare the holy heck out of me? Was it because eternity was such a very, very long time to be married to someone?

Especially when you still missed your ex-boyfriend?

"Well?" he said as I held the box in my hands.

I hesitated. There was no good way to put this, really. "Noah, I don't know. It's just such a big step."

"Jackie, we've been living together for six months, most of that in this jungle. We work very well together. I love you and you love me. Despite the fact that we're both compelled to have sex on a regular basis, we've both been monogamous for the past six months. I've been monogamous since I met you." His head tilted slightly and he continued to study me with those intense blue eyes. "Why not take this a step further and commit to each other? Show our commitment to everyone? If we're married, I can protect you."

"From what?" I had to ask.

"Everything."

Even that blanket statement didn't make me leap to put the gigantic rock on my finger. I flipped the small box back and forth in my hands.

"Noah," I started. I needed to express myself to him . . . but how to do so without hurting his feelings? I wasn't much for articulating these sorts of things. "You're four thousand years old. I'm barely pushing twenty-seven."

"I'm prepared to spend the next four thousand with you." He made it sound like a challenge.

"What if circumstances forced me to cheat on you?" I still recalled with vivid discomfort my trip to New Orleans, and my run-in with an incubus named Luc. Cursed to want sex within hours, stranded from my two guys, I'd had no choice but to fuck around with Luc, and our brief rendezvous had had dire consequences.

His jaw flexed. "We'd work through that. I wouldn't hold it against you."

"I know you won't," I agreed. "It's just that . . . *I'd* hold it against me." I placed the ring box on the table and nudged it away. "Maybe I'm still thinking too traditionally, despite being a succubus, but . . . to me, marriage means commitment. Forever commitment." The kind that I'd always wanted when I was human, but scared the hell out of me now. "Commitment to me means that I'd never desire another. And I don't think I could make that commitment in good faith."

I expected him to make an excuse for my nature, to assure me that it would be all right. Noah was always so supportive.

But his jaw clenched. He stood up, glared down at me for a moment, and then turned away, moving to the back of the tent. There he began to dress, pulling a white shirt over his head.

I frowned at his back. "What are you doing?"

He glanced over his and gave a small, hard laugh. "You know, Jackie, with everything that we've gone through over the past six months, I thought we could at least be honest with each other."

"I am being honest with you," I said, bewildered.

Noah shoved his shirt into his pants, then crammed his wallet into his pocket. "No, you're not. You tell me that it's about cheating with Luc, when we both know it's about Zane."

My mouth went dry. "No, it's not."

"Oh, come on." His voice took on a cold, hard edge that I'd never heard before. "You can stand there in his shirt and tell me that with a straight face? You even smell like him."

I flushed in embarrassment. Like any other lonely ex-girlfriend, I occasionally sprayed my boyfriend's shirt with his cologne—Lagerfeld. I hadn't realized that my current boyfriend was quite that observant and had noticed.

Guess that made me a bit of a jackass.

"Just tell me, Jackie," Noah said, approaching me. He took my hand in his and clasped it against his chest. "Tell me honestly that the reason you're saying 'no' isn't because of Zane, and I'll let the whole thing drop."

My throat closed, and I stared up into his beautiful, hurt blue eyes. I wanted to reassure him, to go back to the easy companionship we had before. But that was gone. He wanted more, and I wasn't sure I could give him more. Even though Zane had been gone six months now, I still thought of him every time the sun went down and I was left alone.

I missed him dreadfully.

"I can't tell you that." I pulled my hand out of his. "I'm sorry, Noah. I wasn't trying to hurt you."

He leaned in and kissed my mouth softly, his eyes sad. "I know." He released me, lifted the tent flap and walked away.

I followed after him. "Where are you going?"

"To town. I need to clear my head." He didn't look back at me.

I glanced up at the sky. "It'll be dark in a few hours." Every twelve hours, the Serim were cursed to pass out into a deep hibernation, from which they couldn't be wakened. Serim took the daytime hours, and vampires ruled the night, with a little bit of overlap between worlds. "Don't stay out too late."

Noah glanced back at me, a wealth of pain in his eyes. "Don't expect me back tonight."

He'd rather spend his vulnerable nighttime hours alone or with strangers than with me. That stung more than anything else as I watched him go.